A Daughter of Francis Martin

by Virginia Chute

Preface by William David Barry

Cover art: REVERIE by Thomas Couture with permission from Norton Simon Art
Foundation, from the Estate of Jennifer Jones Simon

Map on p. ix & x Used with permission.
Map FF-319 from the
Collection of Maine Historical Society

Library of Congress Control Number: 2013939144

Chute, Virginia
A Daughter of Francis Martin/Virginia Chute
Editor: Robert M. Chute
p. 214
1. Fiction-Historical-General 2. Fiction-Colonial America
I. Title.

Soft cover: 978-1-934949-69-6
Smashwords: 978-1-934949-70-2
Kindle: 978-1-934949-75-7

Published by:
𝒮𝒲ℬ
Just Write Books

Topsham, ME
www.jstwrite.com

Printed in the United States of America

*This book is dedicated to
the unfinished work
that each of us must leave.*

Adultery which is the defiling of the marriage bed, to be punished with death. Defiling of a woman espoused, is a kind of Adultery, and punishable by death, of both parties; but if a woman be forced, by death of the man only. Whordom of a maiden in her father's house, kept secret till after her marriage with another to be punished with death.

From *AN ABSTRACT Of the Lavves of New England* London, *1644* (Rev. John Cotton of Boston)

Preface

Novelist Virginia Chute sets her readers within the 17th Century English settlements of Casco Bay (Falmouth), Province of Maine, and the wharves and lanes of Plymouth, England, as gracefully and convincingly as any writer that I am aware of. The keys to the success of her Atlantic-world saga, *A Daughter of Francis Martin,* are manifold, including: clear, sustained prose; a poignant story, well told; a sure feel for the topography, through which her multi-dimensional historical characters pass; a keen but never showy knowledge of society, religion, trade" politics and sexual convention in the 1640s, and most especially an intuitive understanding of individual human beings. Here it is understood that one can be wearing a shepherd's cloak, a Monmouth cap or Bo-sox cap and experience events as old and gory as those drawn from Genesis or as fresh as a sexual outrage sliced from today's headlines or reported with studied emotion on television news.

In this fine volume, Chute follows and considers, with measured care, the life and betrayals of Mary Martin (c. 1625-1647), a young Casco Bay pioneer who came over with her father and sister. Previously Mary was known to historians and genealogists only through court records, provincial deeds and occasional asides from the praying, braying elders including Governor John Winthrop and Cotton Mather. Such men never knew her as a human being but as an object lesson in a lethal religion and legal morality play. Therefore Mary has survived as a shadowy footnote to an obscure colony, soon to be deserted itself and as a somewhat sinister name in a family line marked "no issue."

That Chute breathes vigorous new life into the foot-noted Mary, and gives the young woman plausible, almost inevitable intellectual and fleshy dimension is truly remarkable and in doing so she brings the entire pre-1672 Casco Bay community into the colorful focus it deserves. It can be argued that from a professional historical point, she has it about right, as only one, armed with the facts and a sublime imagination, could. Consider how little anyone knows about this shore in the 1600s. Consider too, what scant knowledge we have concerning William Shakespeare (1554-1616), the man and the vast debt our culture and literature owed his plays. Then note that the inhabitants of Falmouth, including the much honored "founding father" George Cleeve (c. 1586-1666) was a partial contemporary of the Bard.

In the 1670s war broke out with the Abenaki. In short order every English building was burned, every woman, child or man killed, made captive or a refugee in Massachusetts. Only a few documents remained and the next generation did not reclaim homesteads until after 1711. This is eloquently echoed in Edwin's A. Churchill's dissertation "Too Great the Challenge: The Birth and Death of Falmouth, Maine, 1624 -1676" (Orono,1979) or with more brevity in Emerson W. Baker's, readable essay "Formerly Machegonne, Dartmouth, York, Stogummor, Casco, and Falmouth: (*Creating Portland*, edited by Joseph A. Conforti, Durham, UNH Press, 2005). Interested readers should indulge in both sources.

Still, all of us need to use our imagination to the final step in the re-creation of the first Falmouth and I know firsthand that writing an historical novel is a difficult task. Chute makes it look effortless. *A Daughter of Francis Martin* rises above the genre because it remains true to the known facts while telling a compelling story that pulls the reader deeper and deeper into the circumstances of Mary Martin. We are convinced that the principals (characters) have lives beyond the tale. They are multi-dimensional characters; each has his or her own flaws and often lives or grows to understand or undergo the consequences. Even Michael Mitton "the great fowler" and a potential cardboard villain, if ever there was one, comes off as a believable character, someone we have all met. Virginia Chute has, to my mind, captured the soul of 17th century Falmouth before its fall.

William David Barry
Maine Historian

Editor's Introduction

*A*s my name may have suggested, the author of *A Daughter of Francis Martin* and I are related and we have shared, during the sixty-seven years of our marriage, a common interest in the early history of Maine, our native state. Virginia Hinds Chute was born, and spent the first two years of her life, in the port city of Portland, Maine. The house where she lived still stands on Forest Avenue. I spent my early years in Naples, Maine, about thirty miles inland. The main buildings of the Chute family homestead burned, for the second time in two hundred years, in the 1970s.

My Chute ancestors moved to Maine from Massachusetts in 1738 and settled what is now the town of Windham. You will meet, briefly, one of Virginia's maternal grandmother's ancestors in this book: John Libby who worked at the Richmond's Island fishing station in the 1630s. In our lives my wife and I have lived in five widely scattered states but we live now, and have for many years, within thirty miles of where we were born.

We were not world travelers but in our one brief trip to "the old world," a generation ago, Virginia spent several days in Plymouth, England. She had happened on the thread of a story and wanted to see how much of Plymouth in the 1630s she could store in her imagination. The Martin family and their relatives and associates, many of whom lived in Plymouth, populate the historical novel that gradually took form. Many were figures of historical record.

Another historical novel, operation of a used book store, other writing projects, intervened but, about five years ago a second, perhaps third, draft of *A Daughter Of Francis Martin* was finished. The author was still not satisfied with certain aspects and described and outlined proposed changes. But the planned revision never occurred. Any writer reading this will know that, at critical points, writing is largely revision, and that revision strains our capacity far beyond the original inspiration.

At this point in the history of this story Virginia's health failed to the extent she was unable to read consistently, research and organize the revision. For two years she tried repeatedly — and unsuccessfully.

While she still lived in that writer's purgatory and I decided, with the urging of family and friends, to offer, in her name, with absolute minimal editing, the completed manuscript as she wrote it, adding only this introduction, an epigram and an historical afterword.

Robert M. Chute

CHARTER FROM KING JAMES I.
TO THE
COUNCIL FOR NEW ENGLAND,
Nov. 3rd, 1620.

PATENTS FROM THE COUNCIL FOR NEW ENGLAND

To the Plymouth Adventurers, . . Jan. 13th, 1629. Fig. 1.
Company of Husbandmen, called
  also the Plough or Lygonia Pat., June 26th, 1630. " 2.
Richard Vines and John Oldham, Feb. 12th, 1630. " 3.
Richard Bonython and Thomas
  Lewis, ... Feb. 12th, 1630. " 4.
Thomas Cammock, ... Nov. 1st, 163·. " 9.
Ferdinando Gorges et als, . . Dec. 2nd, 1631. " 5.
Trelauny and Goodyear, . . . Dec. 2nd, 1631. " 10.
John Stratton, ... Dec. 2nd, 1631. " 12.

PATENTS FROM SIR FERDINANDO GORGES,

To George Cleeve, ... Jan. 27th, 1637. Fig. 6.
Robert Trelauny, ... July 12th, 1638. " 11.
Josselyn. No record preserved. " 8.

CHARTER OF THE PROVINCE OF MAINE,

To Sir Ferdinando Gorges, . . . April 3d, 1639.

PATENT FROM SIR ALEXANDER RIGBY,

Under the Plough or Lygonia Patent,
To George Cleeve, ... Feb. 20th, 1652. Fig. 7

Legend from Map FF-319
Collection of Maine Historical Society

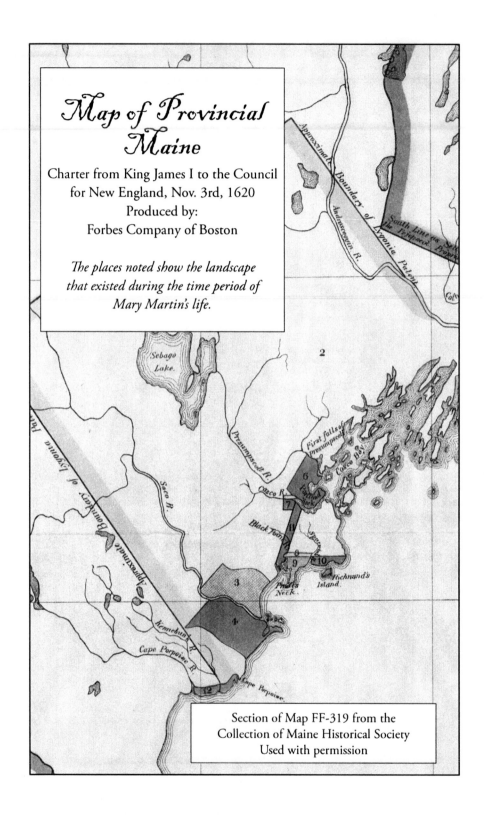

Map of Provincial Maine

Charter from King James I to the Council
for New England, Nov. 3rd, 1620
Produced by:
Forbes Company of Boston

*The places noted show the landscape
that existed during the time period of
Mary Martin's life.*

Sebago
Lake.

2

First falls of
Presumpscoit

Casco Bay

Black Point

Richmand's
Island

Purple's
Neck

Cape Porpoise

Cape Porpoise.

Chapter One

*I*t was an early afternoon in March 1637 and not unduly cold for a waning winter's day in Plymouth. Grey and damp the air certainly was, with only an occasional streak of pale light to indicate the efforts of the sun to make its presence felt. But the crowd that had gathered by the quay at Sutton's Pool could not have found unpleasant the slight sea breeze that blew fresh smells by noses long assaulted by the noxious odors of the streets.

Mary Martin, thirteen, and her seven-year-old sister, Frances, obviously young gentlewomen in their identical blue embroidered hoods, had paused a few feet from the edge of the crowd. Mary held a covered basket in one hand from which the tail of a fish protruded, suggesting that they were on their way back from the market when curiosity had drawn them to the quay—hesitantly—because they well knew they were not to stop at all, especially here. There was a motley press of people, the girls and two well dressed gentlemen conversing on the other side of the crowd being the exceptions. For the most part there was a mixture of those with shady business or none at all. Beggars of both sexes, in colorful rags, pushed their way about aimlessly, not sure why they were here watching the unloading of this particular ship among so many that came and went every day at Plymouth docks. The rumor of some special event had always the effect of drawing to the spot all the thieves, beggars and whores of the town—leading, in the case of a false rumor, as now, to a gathering composed almost exclusively of those who could hardly have found less profit, monetary or otherwise in each other's company.

Crowds of onlookers along the quays of Plymouth were unusual now, and this present one much different from the ones that gathered here to welcome a John Hawkins or Francis Drake back from one of their trading/ pirating ventures. Then there would have been richly dressed gentlemen with their belaced and embroidered ladies, impatient merchants and officious dignitaries—the mayor among them—their respectable members peppered throughout, of course, with the above noted thieves, beggars and whores—all waiting to welcome the adventurers and, hopefully, a large and sumptuous cargo. They were seldom disappointed. The quay, more often than not would shortly be strewn with an assortment of plates and chests of silver, pearls, diamonds and rubies, gold, drugs, spices and Turkish carpets. And, here and there amongst these treasures, living curiosities—black Africans left over from the sold or dead on one of Puritan John Hawkins slave trading ships, surly Spanish prisoners and chattering gesticulating monkeys. All this and much more to dazzle the eyes and make the fingers itch. That the itch often proved unbearable was evidenced in the night by occasional "hunchbacked" shadows that crept out of the city.

A crowd came, too, in 1605 to see five natives that Captain George Weymouth had stolen from their homes in the New World, and on an autumn day in 1620 to watch 102 separatists set sail in their ship, the *Mayflower*, bound for settlement in this same New World. Ships heading for America were no strange sight in Plymouth even then. Departures of fishing and trading vessels for Newfound and the New England coast were such common occurrences as to draw no spectators at all, excepting of course, the families of the departing fishermen and traders. But on the *Mayflower* were whole families going to start a new life. That was something to be pondered and considered by many a poor town or country wight who had before no thought of any way to escape from the poverty that hemmed his family in with hunger, cold and futile backbreaking work—work that, hard as it was, barely served to keep him out of debtors prison or off the rolls of known beggars and vagrants. Many pondered and decided, so that after 1620, and especially after 1630, so many loads of emigrants had elected to follow the Scrooby Separatists and Puritans that such departures were little more noted than those of the trading vessels. Hence the curiosity that this crowd aroused in the two maids and also in the two well dressed gentlemen.

Frances, the littlest of the two young maidens, had small pert features below busy dark eyes and a mass of black curls that refused to stay trapped under the cap and hood that were supposed to keep them in ladylike seclusion. Her head reaching barely to her sister's shoulder she pulled impatiently at her cloak. "Mary, oh please Mary, canst see what happens?"

"No, nor am I sure there is aught to see or if there be that we durst stay to see it," Mary said with some concern. Unlike her sister there was a dreamy look about her face—especially in her deep-set heavy-lidded blue eyes—and her thick, brown hair stayed where she had put it, almost invisible under her hood.

At this moment, out of the general mass just in front of them, a thin grizzled little man appeared. He was dressed in rags, once red now dulled down to a grey brown by the dust of many roads. He sidled up and looked at them with a mocking elfish face. Mary grabbed her sister's hand and started backing away.

"Now, now pretty ones, there be'ant cause to take fright of Tom Tutt," said he.

"Why he hath not e'en a bit o' harm about him. Prithee ask any o' these gentle folk." His arm swept out to indicate all the gathered crowd. "I did but think to tell thee of yonder ship—for a pence or two—little ones, to help take off the hunger that hath been a' gnawing at me vitals these two days past."

The girls didn't answer but neither did they move farther away. Encouraged by this small concession Tom Tutt hurried on. "'Tis a strange and fearful tale of knavish pirates, shipwrecks and other like calamities." He paused judiciously.

"We have but a ha'penny," Mary's voice was firm, but scarcely above a whisper. "'Tis as it must be then," said Tom Tutt, his hearing marvelously attuned to the mention and the sound of money in even its most minute amounts. He held out his hand, and as soon as the coin had passed from Mary's pocket safely to his own, he snatched his tattered hat from his head and made the girl's a low bow. "You had but a ha'penny, dainty ones, and, as for me, I have n'more of the tale than I have given thee already. I wot 'twas a fair exchange," and with a few hopping steps he disappeared in the crowd.

"Oh, Mary, what will our mother say?"

"Overmuch," Mary sighed. The weight of her responsibilities asserting themselves after the fact as usual. But almost as soon as she had acknowledged them they began to fade and her mind, as was its habit, slipped quickly away from the coming consequences of these last few minutes and her present surroundings to a daydream of pirates—eyes flashing, knives in hand—leaping on the decks of a captured vessel—one landing directly in front of her, his mocking face disconcertingly like that of Tom Tutt. And then came another image of sails, barrels and other bits and pieces of a wrecked ship. Wreckage to which clung men, women and young maids—one quite obviously herself—floating toward the trees of a far off island. A tremor of delight passed through her and a faint smile turned up the corners of her mouth.

On the other side of the crowd two females, well done up in petticoats and cloaks of assorted colors ingeniously layered on to conceal both dust and holes, walked up to the two gentlemen—one of middle age, squarely built, with short grey/brown hair and a wide but rather sharp featured face, the other younger, well proportioned with even pleasant features and dark hair that touched his shoulders. The shorter and weightier of the "ladies" waved a scented handkerchief under the noses of the gentlemen while suggesting that the four of them might take advantage of this lucky meeting and spend a profitable few hours in each other's company, an invitation the older man ignored. His younger companion merely laughed and assured them that

3

neither he nor his friend could afford such "profit" as they proposed. "A pox on both of you!" shouted the weighty proposer, shaking her fist now instead of her handkerchief.

"Ah that we happily leave with you," countered the young gentleman, turning his back. This answer caused the other female to let loose a small explosion of laughter which brought her a kick on the shins from her companion and might have progressed further into a full blown fight except at that moment an expectant murmur passed through the crowd and drew everyone's attention toward the ship.

Just coming ashore and barely visible over the heads of the crowd were, first, a man of thirty or thereabouts with a large ring in each ear and a long white scar running down one cheek. Behind him, with hesitant steps, came two young women with brightly embroidered shawls about their shoulders—an exotic covering to Englishwomen of the time—and, lastly, two men in the coarse woolen suits and Monmouth caps not uncommonly worn by fishermen came striding along, waving and smiling at the crowd. Word of who these people were quickly passed back and forth through the crowd like a wayward breeze and Mary and Frances heard it with the rest. All five had been prisoners of the dreaded Turks. The first man—plucked off a trading vessel some years before had somehow finally contrived his own escape. The other four had been redeemed by his great and compassionate majesty Charles I, the two women after fifteen years in captivity—they had been spirited off the shores of Devon when they were but maids—the two fishermen only eight or ten months after their ship and all its crew were taken. As they reached the end of the walkway and stepped ashore they passed down to the level of the crowd and out of the sisters' view. Suddenly a silence fell over the crowd, followed by the clunk of metal on stone and then a great shout from the crowd.

"Oh. Mary, what is't?" Frances tugged at her sister's cloak again. "If I couldst but see!" She bent quickly down and tried to peek between the legs of the men in front of her. As she was thus occupied two large hands encircled her waist and she was hoisted up above the crowd.

"Ayii!" she shrieked—Turks and pirates as visible in her wide open eyes as if the words had been written there.

"Tush, tush, Francie," said a familiar voice in her ear, "'tis no foreigner with a ring in s'ear that hath got thee, but only thine own father."

"Oh, Father," she turned and her brown eyes looked into his blue ones. "I was so frighted!" She dropped her head on his shoulder and his hand smoothed her dark curls reassuringly as he looked down at his other daughter's gentle upturned face, a feminine mirror of his own except that his was rather badly but not grotesquely scarred by small pox. In fact two of the pockmarks, one at each corner of his wide mouth, were so fortuitously placed as to give a permanent suggestion of a smile to his face and so enhance the general kindly look of it. Both father and daughter had thick chestnut brown hair though his, at fifty-one, was much streaked with grey.

"Thy mother hath thought something might have gone amiss and sent me to fetch thee."

Mary lowered her eyes and told him hesitantly of the ha'penny and where it had gone. He restrained a smile—even his frugal wife would not count that much loss—but he spoke soberly. "Well, 'twere foolishly done, but," he put his hand on her shoulder, "happily 'twas only your curiosity and dreaming hath carried you off again. Still we'd best get us home and collect thy scolding before I must face one too."

He set Francie on her feet, whereupon she began pulling at his sleeve. "Father couldst see what the crowd wast shouting about?"

Her father smiled at her quick recovery. "Ay little curiosity, 'twas for the man with a scar. No sooner had he set both feet on English soil again but he must drop down upon his knees and plant a kiss on the nearest cobblestone."

"Ugh!" exclaimed Francie, turning her small nose up even higher than nature had done already.

Mary looked out over the heads of the crowd and beyond the ship to where the sea was visible stretching out blue black to the distant horizon and on to strange hardly imaginable countries. She sighed—feeling but not thinking in any way she could have expressed, a kind of exciting but frightening sensation of disconnectedness—of separation from the regular pattern of family and friends, of ways of thinking and acting. It was a feeling akin to that of a nightmare when familiar things no longer behave in familiar ways. But this nameless feeling slipped quickly out of her mind leaving only a slight uneasiness behind.

Father and daughters headed obliquely away from the crowd and the quay toward Rag Street where lived merchants like Francis Martin, sea captains, and others of moderate means. Only a short distance and perhaps two or three lucky voyages away was Looe Street inhabited by many of Plymouth's very wealthy—men such as Sir Francis Drake and Robert Trelawney.

The houses these men lived in were larger and more luxuriously furnished that those in Rag Street but the streets themselves were the same narrow cobblestone ways to be found in every English city of the time. The same, also, was their acrid stench, like the noisome odor of an open sewer, and the hazardous footing—both the result of the foul assortment of garbage and other waste, including the contents of chamber pots thrown out, often from upper story windows with careless disregard for those passing below. Rakers were supposed to be hired by the town to clear away the accumulated filth, but this low-paying dirty job was hard to fill even in times of the greatest poverty, and those that filled it were no longer, if they ever had been, the most conscientious and reliable members of society, especially with a bit of money in their pockets and a supply of taverns to help them swill away remembrance of empty pockets, past and future.

Poverty, ever present in the streets of Plymouth, was increasingly visible in the 1620s and 30s. The plague of 1625 carried off many of the poor, but added others to its ranks, as did several bad harvests, a decline in the cloth trade and cattle business and three unsuccessful military expeditions, some of whose returning troops—starving, ill clad, wounded, diseased and bitter—were deposited in Plymouth and billeted on the inhabitants in and around the town. Efforts were made to reduce the anger and hostility of the townspeople by carrying their most annoyingly visible members—beggars, thieves and prostitutes to other towns after a suitable whipping. There is no record of how those towns reacted to being used as a dumping ground for Plymouth's worthless, nor, for that matter, of how long those designated worthless stayed away.

Many mercantile fortunes were made quickly in those days and some as quickly lost, so that occasionally among those ragged beggars of the street might be seen the formerly rich and influential. Francis Martin was more fortunate than these. Although he had had a number of unlucky voyages in the recent past, his had been a respected Plymouth family for several generations. His grandfather, his father and his brother had each been mayor of the city, and just last year his nephew had also held that office. This same nephew, John Martin, had been married four years before to Margaret Trelawney, sister of Robert Trelawney, one of the wealthiest and most influential merchants of the town. So, although the fortunes of Francis Martin were not at a high point, there were family resources and influence enough to carry him through to better times, He and his wife Prudence and their seven children—Grace, Mary, Marjorie, Thomasine, Frances, John and baby Nicholas—were able, by means of a family loan, to continue to live in the pleasant house they had rented on upper Rag Street with its three narrow stories, its carved oak door and small garden in back. The latter contained not only a prolific fig tree but a tiny cottage where slept the two servants they were also able to keep.

Prudence was standing by the door of this house as her husband and daughters approached. She was a sturdy attractively buxom woman with sharp black eyes and a warm rosy complexion. An equally rosy baby was on her arm and her two-year-old son held on to her skirts. With her was the aforementioned John Martin. A man in his early thirties, unremarkable in build or feature, but with something in the relaxed erectness of his stance and the way he held his head, slightly uptilted, that gave an immediate impression of substance. Close beside him, his small and fragile pretty wife, Margaret. Apparently they had been about to take their leave.

"Ah, there you are Uncle." John raised his hand in greeting, "We were just coming to fetch thee out of whatever dire trouble thou hadst fallen into and bring thee some good news withal."

"Ho! Solid John." The two gentlemen who had been at the quay were now walking up Rag Street toward the Martins. It was the younger one who had shouted the greeting. And, after a hardily perceptible hesitation, a look of surprised recognition passed over John Martin's round face. "Mad Michael! I cannot believe 'tis you. And yet verily methinks I recognize the same sly smiling face that did so often draw me from my books to roam the night streets of London these nine or ten years past."

"Not so often Solid John, else how hadst thou kept thy name! Howbeit, what is this I hear—that thou hast fallen from thy single state and taken a beautiful woman to wife? If this be she, the rumorers are no liars." Margaret blushed and looked somewhat uncomfortable if not entirely displeased. "And you are Mayor of Plymouth, too, I hear."

"Was, friend Michael, was. Last year. And glad to be out of it. Governing was to me more burden than honor. But I would know what hath brought thee to leave thy beloved London?"

"London? I escaped that beloved not above a year after you did—when my creditors became more numerous than my amusements—and betook me to the army where I stayed until I could dismiss my creditors with money. By then fair London had ceased to charm me as before. Mad Michael had disappeared and simple Michael Mitton taken his place." He bowed. "And in a few weeks time will make his way across the ocean with his worthy friend"—he indicated the gentleman beside him—"Mr. George Cleeve, just granted a fine peninsula in New England by none other than that noble friend of the new land—Sir Ferdinando Gorges."

A slight frown briefly deepened the line between his heavy brows and then George Cleeve smiled and the stern aspect of his face melted away. Expressions of surprise passed quickly across the faces of John and Margaret Martin, while one of sheer delight lit up the face of Francis Martin and was reflected in his daughter Mary's suddenly wide open eyes.

John Martin, quickly recovering—with an apology for his failure of courtesy—introduced the company to one another, whereupon their hostess suggested that they all come inside out of the chill and have som'at to refresh and warm themselves. "I durst say, Mr. Cleeve," she added, "thou wilt have need to fortify thyself against the many questions touching on New England that my good husband will afflict thee withal. Verily I do believe he is as much possessed by it as ever was that good Knight Sir Ferdinando Gorges."

"Possessed, thou sayst?" Francis smiled broadly at his wife. "That smacks of devilish involvement, and methinks would please those settlers of Massachusetts Bay as little as Sir Ferdinando or thy Husband."

Prudence sighed and shook her head. That her husband took the devil and his machinations too lightly was a continual cause of concern to her, as he well knew and took advantage of to vex her even as she teased him about his overweening interest in New England.

Unquestionably Francis Martin, merchant, was intelligent, hardworking and knowledgeable—though lacking in that final touch of shrewd aggressiveness that marks the masters in that field—and, as a husband and father was kindly and devoted. But neither can it be denied, as his wife had indicated, that the new world had occupied and preoccupied his thoughts and aspirations ever since that day in 1606 when he just turned twenty one, and his father and older brother had visited with Sir Ferdinando and the three Indians brought to Plymouth the year before by Captain George Weymouth—unfortunately for future relations captured, not brought willingly. Sir Ferdinand had taught the Indians to speak some English and Francis had listened with growing wonder to the tales of their land that came haltingly but with proud inflection from the mouths of these straight-backed men. They told of snow-topped mountains that watered the far reaching valleys below bringing forth abundant harvests of corn and beans from the fertile soil, of streams that wound into the deep still lakes full of fish as were the wide rivers that poured renewing water into the sea. They spoke as well of the vast stretches of forest land where the broad hot arrows of the golden sun were broken against the branches of the giant trees and fell in warm fragments to the ground, and of the animals that wandered in and out among those trees and the birds that flew overhead—both in such numbers that the natives never lacked for furs to wear or food to eat.

His father and brother were impressed and talkative about the opportunities for buying and selling that this land possessed. Francis, his ready imagination aroused by the images the Indians had evoked, dreamed of a vast country estate bequeathed to a long line of country gentlemen—perhaps even noblemen.

But, dreamer though he was by nature, Francis was by nurture practical. And after all perhaps, in conception, his dream differed from the schemes of his father and brother primarily in its base. They would buy and sell from England, he from New England. In intensity, however, the difference was as a match to a conflagration.

On many occasions in the succeeding years he and Gorges shared their enthusiasm for this land that neither of them had ever seen. And Francis's tall thin figure became a familiar one on the quays, questioning fishermen and traders back from their yearly trips to the shores and islands of New England. He eagerly collected whatever he could of the promotional literature that began to appear about 1610. Particularly interesting to him were the detailed descriptions and advice of Captain John Smith whom he met in the summer of 1616 when the Captain was in Devonshire distributing maps and pamphlets about New England which, incidentally, he was the first to call by that name. And in 1617, when Captain Smith set off for Plymouth with three vessels Francis was sorely tempted to sign on with him. But reckless adventurer he was not, and the plan which had begun to form out of his dream in 1606 required—it seemed to this son and grandson of merchants—a solid base of money which he had not yet built. In 1620 he watched the Pilgrims leave and envied them their destination but shook his head at their admitted shortage of funds.

Slowly, as the years passed, he built up a modest prosperity—more slowly than his shrewder brother but more steadily. He did not take the chances his brother took so, except for the occasional times when, dreaming, he let an opportunity for a good bargain or profit slip by, there were no lapses in his steady progress toward his goal of five thousand pounds—for land, transportation, trading commodities, etc. Part of the continuing pleasure of his dream was in the figuring and refiguring of what he would need to set up and maintain his "estate" and what each item would cost.

Though obviously a wife would be needed for the full realization of his plan he had not taken time to look for or even think about acquiring one. Then one day in 1619 he met twenty-year-old, dark-eyed, dark-haired Prudence Deacon and it suddenly became a wonder to him that he had not thought before about the great importance of a wife to his plan. Marriage and a family which, however ultimately important, might have been expected to slow, if not altogether stop his progress, did not. Prudence, if she could not share or understand her husband's enthusiasm for this far off wilderness never tried to discourage him, and, in fact, because by nature frugal and a good manager, she helped him.

Several times a year, even though he was not with them, ships containing at least some of his goods sailed off for New England. Times in the 1620s were not good. It was a period of depression and failure for many, which Francis Martin managed to avoid, so that finally in 1633 he could see that in three perhaps even in two years he would have that financial base he had been seeking. Then, as though the fate he had circumvented in the 1620s had continued to pursue him, one by one ships containing his goods were either shipwrecked or taken by the Spanish or the Turks. He watched the financial base that had taken more than twenty years to build melt away in less than three years time. But after each event Francis found himself to be quite calm, and when all was over, surprisingly neither bitter nor discouraged. Simply explained—his dream had not dissolved with his money. So long had it been a part of his mind that a mere reversal of his fortunes was unable to dislodge it. His wife it was who had to be comforted and wheedled out of her ill humor. Dreams were nothing to her—she had never really taken her husband's seriously—but comforts and security were much, not just security from poverty but from that loss of social position that came with being a successful merchant's wife. This was not shallow vanity. Social position, as she saw it, guaranteed a good future for her children. This was now threatened. But it was this very threat that brought her back to herself. And, in the past year, she had triumphantly managed so well on what they had allowed themselves from the diminished savings and a family loan that few of the old comforts were missed and social appearances, on which social position, once acquired, is judged, were maintained.

As soon as family and guests were seated in front of a good fire with food and wine before them John Martin proceeded to tell his Uncle the good news that had brought him to their house. He had that day been to see Robert Trelawney. "And 'twas just as I thought. He would be most pleased to have you take his brother Edward's place as one of his agents—especially since it now doth seem from his letters that Edward hath found himself, and a home, in New England."

"And Robert told us," Margaret smiled, "that he thought there was no more honest or knowing merchant to be found in all of Plymouth than Francis Martin. And my brother, as you know, is not given to over much praising of others."

Francis flushed with pleasure, and, by the door where she was sitting on a little stool almost hidden from view, Mary revealed herself by a sudden delighted exclamation.

"Mary!" her mother said sharply. "What dost thou hiding thyself there?

Get up stairs and help thy sister, Grace, mind the little ones."

Mary's face clouded over, and her father seeing and understanding, interceded. "Come wife, let her stay. She can take a turn minding the little ones later. She is the only one in this family that doth like to hear of the new world as much as I do."

"Methinks 'tis just her father's fancies she doth like to hear of," said Prudence, a testy edge to her voice, "or some dreamings she has conjured up in her own head. Howbeit, let her stay."

George Cleeve had looked startled and somewhat ill at ease at the mention of Robert Trelawney, but noticing Margaret's smiling face turned questioningly toward him he quickly recovered himself.

"I have had the honor of speaking with your brother Edward in New England on several occasions, Mistress Martin, and a most knowing and godly young man I have found him to be."

John smiled to see the flush of pleasure on his wife's face. "Well, Mr. Cleeve. You have surely settled a place for yourself in my wife's good opinion by these fine words about her favorite brother."

"Oh John," Margaret's voice was mildly reproachful, "'tis not a matter of favorites. Edward and I were so nearly of a mind in all things and were so much in one another's company when we were children. Robert was grown up and serious in his ways when we were but young and foolish in ours I fear. But Robert hath been always kind and forbearing. And though Edward did surely try his patience many a time he hath never failed to help him. 'Twas from Robert's suggesting of it that Edward decided to go to New England, where—in Massachusetts—he met the godly people who changed his life. In one of his letters"—she lowered her eyes as if seeing again those words she had read so many times—"he says that he accounts his going there the greatest happiness that ever befell him and that the conversations and sweet life of the people there so far wrought upon his conscience that he would not be in his former, as he says, 'base condition' for the whole riches of the world." Raising her eyes she smiled. "So you see, Mr. Cleeve, why it doth so please me to hear that you have seen in Edward this change he has written of. And tell me sir, dost thou see in the people of Massachusetts the same goodness my brother Edward doth? Robert is a strong Church of England man and sees in them little more than—how hath he called them John?"

"Trouble making, nit-picking fanatics."

George Cleeve smiled broadly. "I recognize the phrase, 'tis some'at apt, but no more than your brother's words, Mistress Martin It hath pleased me to converse with many men and women of the bay colony such as he describes and none more so, happily for them, than their wise governor, John Winthrop."

"And, verily, thou canst believe he doth mean it," Michael Mitton added. "He hath given a like report of this governor, not five days since, to none other than his majesty King Charles."

Cleeve shot an annoyed glance at his younger companion and the rest of the company gave short exclamations of surprise.

"Marry Sir!" Francis Martin looked concerned. "Was this not a dangerous thing thou didst? I hear there are those who, being exiled from the colony of Massachusetts, and blaming John Winthrop for it, plot against him. And in this Archbishop Laud doth see a way at last to bring discredit upon the entire colony. If this be so, methinks thou hast a powerful enemy."

Cleeve scowled. "It may be so. But I have much admired John Winthrop and would think it less than honest if I denied it. Besides," a wry smile displaced the scowl, "in a sparsely settled wilderness, we all have need of friends and I would not like to have made an enemy of John Winthrop. And, if results prove politics, it was not ill said. Sir Ferdinando Gorges, as thou hast heard, hath seen fit to name me as one of the commissioners to govern his province along with, among others, this same John Winthrop. 'Tis clear, those without prejudice—even staunch high church men like Sir Ferdinando—cannot but recognize the stabilizing influence this godly, if non-conformist colony might have on the wild fishermen and fur traders to the north. Further, I have obtained from this same good knight a grant for the land on Casco Bay, called Machegonne by the Indians, where I have been living with my wife and daughter these four years past."

John Martin had found his respect for George Cleeve growing as he talked. Respect that did not go well with what he had heard of the man before today. "You have had some disagreements with my wife's brother Robert over land and other things, is't not so?"

"'Tis so I am sorry to say, howbeit 'twas the doing of that rogue, his agent John Winter," he almost shouted, slapping a closed fist against the palm of his other hand. A flush intensified the scowl that had appeared again on his face. "Never have I had to do with such a humorless, knavish cozening offspring of the devil!"

"Sir," Michael Mitton put his hand on Cleeve's shoulder.

"Leave me be." Cleeve pushed Mitton's hand away impatiently. "I cannot play your sweet gentleman about that which doth so nearly concern me and mine!"

"Mr. Cleeve, do you suggest that this man hath been cheating Robert?" John Martin looked much distressed.

Cleeve sat for a moment staring at his hands and then looked up at John Martin, his scowl somewhat softened. "No." He spoke slowly. "I do not say that. I warrant that whatsoever John Winter hath done hath been done to further his own interests. Howbeit I do not doubt that he doth consider his interests and your brother-in-law's to be identical."

"Of our differences over land you did speak truly. When Winter came to New England with the Trelawney patent in 1632 he hath showed me that, in addition to Richmond's Island, the land across the water from it, where I had built my house and planted my corn was also granted in that patent to Robert Trelawney. Although I doubted not then, nor do I now, that land I occupied for two years was by this occupation legally mine. I did leave and count that dispute an honest one over titles. Further, since then have settled in at Machegonne and, as it doth seem to me now, that place is much finer than the other—as good for fishing and better for the Indian trade. And 'tis this excellence of the Indian trade, I believe, hath wrought the second trouble and brought that lying claim that Machegonne lies within the Trelawney patent, though the boundaries are so clear drawn as to admit of no such claim. But I am not the only one he practices upon thus. He hath further, and with no more proof told Robert Trelawney that a parcel of the neighboring land owned by his former friend, Thomas Cammock, is also part of the Trelawney Patent. So it can be said that Robert Trelawney hath been deceived in knowledge if not cheated of money."

John nodded. "I have met the man and have judged him to be cold and calculating, so this does not much surprise me. "But—" He paused, looking narrowly at the stubborn set of the features of the man before him. Stubborn and shrewd, but not, he guessed, either cold or basely calculating. "You spake of the Indian trade. Brother Trelawney believes that the Indians durst not come to trade at Richmond's Island because you have told them they might be killed if they do."

Cleeve looked him in the eye. "And so I have told them this past year, because 'tis true. When John Winter betook himself to England last year the Province Court hath given the man he left in charge at Richmond's Island the authority, as they have writ, to execute any Indians that were proved to have killed any swine of the English. Now what chance dost think an Indian would have if it fell out, as well it might, that he did cross the land of some planter who was missing a hog or sheep or goat—it little matters what—the wolves are wont to kill any of these often enough. 'Tis an abominable stupid law that is not likely to save a single swine, but could be the cause of much bitterness and, perchance, vengeful acts from the Indians whose friendship we need. You can name this reason or excuse, but the result will be the same. I have done and will so warn them again."

John Martin and his wife nodded as did Francis, but Prudence shook her head. "I know aught save what I hear of these matters Mr. Cleeve, but if these Indians be savages, as people say, are they not the same as wolves and no more to be trusted?"

"Oh my dear," Francis looked distressed, "to be a savage is in no wise to be a beast as I know from those I had talk with so long ago and have oft told thee of. Is't not so?" Prudence shrugged and Francis sighed. As he had long suspected she took in little he said about New England.

He turned toward George Cleeve, his face brightening. "I am minded, too, of the words of Mr. Christopher Leavitt, a man you may hap have heard tell of, Mr. Cleeve, being an earlier visitor to your Bay of Casco. He hath demonstrated by the kind usage the Indians gave to him as he to them, they can be trusted as much as we."

"Humph," retorted Prudence. "Methinks that doth not promise over much, husband!"

"Indeed," laughed George Cleeve. "I warrant I have had more cause for fright on the highways of Old England than in the forests of New England."

"Ah, mayhap 'tis true." Prudence shook her head again. "But if these savages be servants of the devil, as many say they be, and their brown skin seem to speak to close acquaintance with the fires of hell—?" She looked at Michael Mitton, "Dost this not make thee have som'at of fear, Master Mitton, to hazard thy soul as well as thy body in that wilderness?"

"Truth to tell, Mistress Martin, I had not thought overmuch of this before. But I durst say the soul has not so easy a time on English soil either. Indeed I could tell thee a tale would speak well to this point."

"Do, Master Mitton, do," Prudence nodded approvingly. "I doubt not 'twould be edifying for us all," she said, but looked particularly at her husband.

George Cleeve and John Martin exchanged skeptical glances. They were very familiar with friend Mitton's supply of tales.

Michael bent his head and parted his brown hair to reveal a long jagged scar. "'Twas given me one moonlight night on the road betwixt London and Cambridge." Mary leaned forward, chin in hand, staring at Michael with a fixed look of excited anticipation. "My horse was carrying me along at a good rate, doubtless being as anxious as his master for food and sleep, when, of a sudden, on a lonely stretch of road, I was hailed by an old man and a woman. I pulled my horse to a stop, with little thought of evil—even less as they bowed so courteously and spake in so humble a tone. They had traveled a long and a wearying way that day, they said, and were now but looking to find a house or tavern where they might rest themselves. No cause for suspicion in that. And yet—before the old woman meekly lowered her eyes methought, for a moment, they seemed to shine like a cat's eyes in the dark. 'Tis only the moonlight, thought I. And then my eye fell on the old man's cap, where it stuck up—so—on either side of his head as though 'twas covering two horns. 'Tis n'more than an odd shaped cap methought, and proceeded to tell them of a nearby farmer and his wife who would give them food and shelter."

"God be with you, said I by way of farewell. Hardly had I got the words out of my mouth when I felt a great clout on my head that knocked me from my horse and brought me senseless to the ground. When woke, all besmirched with blood, my purse and a goodly part of my clothes were gone. But most strange—round me in a circle were great paw prints like those of some monstrous cat, and beside these a narrow line burned in the grass like unto the mark a tail dragging along the ground might make." A muffled gasp came from the stool in the corner.

"'Tis likely, Mr. Mitton, that your 'God be with you!' hath saved your soul from the fate of your horse and your money!" Prudence exclaimed.

"Likely, Mistress Martin," Michael said soberly. "Most likely indeed."

John Martin and George Cleeve smiled broadly at each other. They had heard, from this same storyteller, a lewder version of this "edifying" tale.

"I do not deny," said Francis, "that the soul is as vulnerable as the body, wherever man may plant himself. But, methinks, fine air and clean water could do much for both." Unnoticed by her husband, Prudence frowned and then gave a sigh of resigned disapproval.

George Cleve nodded. "After sampling the stench and foul smoke filled air of London again I have no doubt of it." He looked at Francis Martin's eager face and felt the joy that came whenever he thought of his home—now verified as his by signature and seal. "The bright clear air and water of the bay, Mr. Martin—I know of none such anywhere in England. On a quiet day you can see the fish gliding just below the surface and, farther out, the irregular shapes of the islands, all of them full of wild berries and nesting birds in the summer." He paused, remembering it. "And, sailing in to the bay, the sweet smell of the land comes out to you, and the sight of the great pines—many of them more than 100-feet tall, and three- or four-feet thick, stretching back as far as you can see from the shore." He looked at Prudence and Margaret. "'Twould be a hard man that was not mindful of the lord in those surroundings Mistresses, and of his bounty. Truth to tell the fish are in such numbers that in little more than two hours and with only a few hooks my servant and I have caught upwards of thirty cod, most of them very great fish. And, as for game, there is a plenteous supply of water fowl, deer, rabbit, bear and naught to hinder your taking of it save your own excellence or lack thereof with a fowling piece."

"Ah," exclaimed John Martin, looking at his friend Michael Mitton. "If there be anything above the telling of tales and the charming of wenches that you excel in, friend Michael, 'tis surely fowling."

Michael smiled and shook his head. "Here I might seem to do well enough, warrant, but necessity in New England must needs have made many better fowlers than I."

"Marrie!" Prudence suddenly interrupted. "I have been forgetting the fish I did promise the Widow Pym. Mayhap 'twas your talk of fishing hath brought it to mind, Mr. Cleeve, thanks be—I hope the Widow had not wanted it for dinner. Mary!" There was no answer. Mary was staring at George Cleeve. But he and all else in the room had disappeared into the waters and shores of Casco Bay. "Mary Martin!"

It was sharp and penetrating, and her imagination gave way before it this time as on numerous other occasions. Watching her daughter go out the door with the basket of fish on her arm, Prudence shook her head and looked at Margaret. "I do wonder what the child is about, staring and strange like that. I fear me sometimes she is possessed."

Margaret smiled. "I durst say 'tis only dreaming she is about."

"Only? Mayhap. But, so much is she about it methinks she doth not see the world as it is at all anymore."

"Come wife," Francis said soothingly. "Mary is but thirteen and given to dreaming as our Grace was once given to silliness."

"'Twould seem, the world being what it is, a rare gift not to see it as it is," Michael said lightly.

George Cleeve turned toward his companion. "I count it a dangerous gift, my friend. Not seeing the world as it is doth naught to change it. And think you we can control what we do not see, nor doubt that what we cannot control will one day control us? 'Tis to the credit of Governor Winthrop and his people that their dream hath not blinded them to the practical world as it is. And they grow and prosper as a consequence." He paused, then added, "But all the same, 'tis true that a common dream, goal, whatsoever thou wouldst call it, hath done much to keep the people of Massachusetts working together, and 'twould help us in the northern provinces, as well, if we had such a common purpose."

Michael shrugged but said nothing. In the few weeks he had known George Cleeve he had become used to having what he uttered as casual polite conversation taken by Cleeve as a starting point for some polemic or other.

Francis, however, nodded vigorous approval of Cleeve's words. At which point Cleeve, apparently realizing that this talk of seeing the world as it is called for some addition to his former description of his home and dutifully mentioned the cold winters, the short summers and the not always reliable Indian trade. "Survival is hard work," he said. "A few have made a goodly amount of money there, in the fur trade, Mr. Trelawney for one. But most of us are more often in debt than out of it. Howbeit that is not so different, after all, from the way it is here. And there you can have land, Mr. Martin."

"Marrie—indeed!" Francis found it hard to contain his enthusiasm. Not since he spoke with John Smith had he heard such words about New England, and Smith had only visited there in the summer. Dreams and reality could, it seemed, have more than a tenuous connection. He saw Prudence looking shrewdly at him. She had but small skill in book reading, but much in reading husbands.

Cleeve stood up. "Well it must be somewhat after two of the clock by now and there are still merchants I must see in Plymouth before we set off for Bristol." Turning toward Prudence he started to thank her for her hospitality when, over his words another sound, by its chilling strangeness, unlike any of the usual street sounds, caught the ears of the group. Faint at first, it grew louder—a distracted cry that went from a high scream to a low moan, over and over again.

Cleeve reached the door first, closely followed by the others. Outside, not more than six feet from the door and with her back to it stood Mary, her eyes wide with fear, watching the screaming girl who ran stumbling and sliding toward her on the slimy cobblestones and stopped less than two feet in front of her. The girl—she appeared not much older than Mary—was a terrifying sight. Her matted hair, her face and what was left of her tattered clothes were stained with dirt and vomit and her legs and feet, bare beneath the few remnants of her gown, were streaked with feces. In her arms she held what at first appeared to be a bundle of rags. But, as she held the bundle out toward Mary, the rags slipped off revealing the body of an infant, not more than a few days old. Swaying and moaning she took another step forward, and Mary, as if hypnotized by this pitiful apparition, held out her arms to receive the bundle.

At that moment Michael Mitton stepped in front of her. She saw his hand drop down to the sword at his belt. The girl gave one more muted scream and then, staggering backward, fell to the street where she writhed for a moment and was still. There was a horrified silence as they all stood staring down at the frail figure and the tiny stiffened body that had fallen beside it.

The girl—Begette as she had been called—was well known to all the residents of Plymouth. She and her mother had been begging there since Begette was two or three years old. There was a certain tolerant sympathy for the mother and daughter who went so unobtrusively about their business, accepting a large donation or none at all with equal equanimity—unlike many, female as well as male, who shouted obscenities at any who did not give, and begged only when the circumstances were not favorable for thievery. Begette and her mother were regularly rounded up like the rest and carried to other towns, but only the mother had ever been whipped and that only once. In fact, one wet winter's day, the same constable who carried them out gave them a ride back to the edge of town and the small dirt cave where they lived.

Prudence broke the silence with a sharp cry. "Lord have mercy upon us all—the Plague!"

Apparently Begette had been trying to suckle her dead baby, because one breast was bare revealing several purple swellings rimmed with black—the unmistakable tokens of the plague. It was among such as Begette that this dreaded disease claimed its earliest but never its only victims.

Francis reached out and grasped Michael's hand. His voice faltered as he tried to find words of thanks for the quick action that well could have saved his daughter and possibly his whole family from the same fate as the girl at their feet.

But Mary, still standing where she had been when Begette fell, her hands now clenched at her sides, raised her eyes and stared at Michael Mitton with a mixture of horror and hate. "Thou hast killed her!" she said in a stiff hard voice.

"Mary Martin!" Prudence's black eyes snapped. To have spoken at all— but in such wise! If she had been close enough she would have slapped her daughter.

"Mary," Francis frowned, but did not raise his voice. He put his hand on her shoulder. "'Twas the plague did kill her. Mr. Mitton hath only tried to keep her from touching thee."

Michael looked at his sword and then at Mary with a sudden understanding "I did not strike her Mistress Martin, only pushed her away and she did fall."

Mary's fists came abruptly unclenched and her head dropped. She made no sound, but her shoulders shook and tears ran down her cheeks.

"Wilt thou look at her breast, Mary?" said her mother, subdued anger and impatience still apparent in her voice. "Such black-rimmed tokens are a sure sign that death was close upon her. She would have fallen betimes of herself. There was naught we could have done to help her. But had she touched thee 'tis likely thou wouldst have had that same death upon thyself. Now I would have thee tell Mr. Mitton thou art sorry for what thou hast said and thank him for what he hath done for thee."

Mary straightened her shoulders, and after a moment raised her head until her eyes were on the top button of Mr. Mitton's waistcoat. "I am sorry—and—I—thank you." She lowered her eyes again.

Michael looked down at the top of her head—a faint ironic smile briefly touching his thin lips. "I am sorry too—that this hath happened so and did so much distress thee. Methinks the tender-hearted are all too often paid with pain. But without such as thee surely this darksome earth would be a much crueler place than it is." The glib banality of his words that seemed to slip by habit almost unnoticed from his mouth was much compensated for by the kindly tone of his voice.

George Cleeve, however, raised his eyebrows and sent a disdainful look in Michael's direction causing John Martin to wonder how these ill-matched travelers had ever come together and how they would survive the close quarters of a long sea voyage.

Mary continued to stand as before, staring at the greasy cobblestones. Her father put his arm around her and she sighed and leaned against him. "Come, my girl," he said. "I will walk thee up to thy room. There is naught any of us can do here now."

One of the servants, coming just then to the door to see what had drawn everyone outside, was sent off for the constable to take care of Begette and her baby and, at Margaret's suggestion, to check on their cave and see if Begette's mother was also dead or perhaps lying alone and sick in what was, in those still damp cold days, hardly a shelter at all.

Prudence insisted that since those who were leaving had of necessity to go inside once again to fetch their cloaks they must stop for the sake of their good health long enough to drink a cup of sack, which drunk two or three times a day, she assured them was the best specific she knew for the "keeping off of the plague." Though some would have it, she affirmed, that ale with a bit of sugar had kept the sickness from them. John Martin wondered about the usefulness of burning sulphur, tar or other heavy smelling stuffs within a house to drive out the infected air.

"And the people too, I warrant," Cleeve interjected vehemently.

Prudence agreed and declared her preference for herbs and spices—the burning of which forced out the infected air as well as did those noxious fumes so far as she could tell and was sweet smelling besides.

Had there been signs of an epidemic outbreak of the plague, Cleeve asked. To which John Martin responded that there had been perhaps a few more cases than usual that past summer, but they were not taken to be signs of a major outbreak—perhaps because no one wanted to see them as such.

"There have been portents of the plague which I have heard," declared Prudence, "but until now have not told of, not wishing to have frighted my family—and for that my husband doth think but little of my source."

"The all-knowing Widow Pym, I warrant," Francis remarked dryly as he came down the stairs from his daughter's room.

"'Tis true," Prudence admitted promptly. "But do not judge the case until you have heard the portents she hath told me of. The first came in a dream she had, when she was, as it seemed to her, walking up and down the streets of Plymouth and in not one of them a sound to be heard nor creature to be seen. Then, of a sudden, right before her—so close that she hath almost stumbled into it—a great empty pit upwards of twelve to fifteen feet deep and twenty feet across. And out of this pit rose a bodiless voice foretelling a visitation of the plague so passing great there would be scarce any left alive to bury the dead. This dream she hath told me of last summer. But not above a week ago she came to me all starry-eyed and breathless. 'Twas just after dark and she had been hurrying up the street toward her house, most anxious to be away from the darkness and the thieving rogues that prosper in't, when—a little way ahead and suspended above her—she saw a long procession of wispy figures swaying and faintly moaning like misty offspring of the fog. But withal, to her, familiar shapes of friends and neighbors carried off in the last great plague."

"Well," sighed Francis, "I know not how to value portents such as these, but the two we have seen today, dead of the plague with winter not fully gone—a time that sickness doth seldom show itself—is a portent I do much understand and fear."

"As for the widow's portents," said John Martin, "she doth make, I believe, a goodly sum selling simples and other remedies for I know not how many ills. I doubt not that portents of the plague do much to encourage business."

"Her remedies may well be worth their price," said Prudence testily. "I mix up many of the same and have much faith in their usefulness."

"Yes, but thou dost give freely of yours to anyone who hath need of them," Margaret said soothingly.

"That I do," affirmed Prudence. "But remember you, the widow hath no husband to provide for her as I do, sister Martin, and so small an allowance to live on that I could never find it in my heart to blame her—even when she charge overmuch for her simples."

Margaret nodded. Her small pale face had an almost saintly seriousness until she smiled, and then the corners of her eyes tilted up, giving her face a mischievous pixie look. Her friends well knew how accurately her character was echoed in these two aspects of her face and were given a fleeting but disquieting reminder of the many that are contained in every gathering of appearances that we arbitrarily call one.

Michael Mitton, standing near the door as he and George Cleeve prepared to take their leave, stared at Margaret with unconcealed admiration until, catching him at it, she blushed and he, recovering himself, asked, "And you, Mistress Martin, what specific do you recommend against the plague?"

Margaret hesitated for a moment. "I can think of naught that would suffice save a pure heart."

"Verily I cannot believe that such a gentle lady wouldst condemn me and the greater part of the citizenry to sickness and death."

"Well, Mr. Mitton," said she, half smiling, half serious, "my brother Edward hath found true repentance a great specific for the ills that did beset him. You could make trial of it and see."

"Ha, my friend, thou hast been fairly caught." John Martin smiled.

'Twould seem, Cleeve thought as they walked away from the house, that the lady is of her brother Edward's religious persuasion. I wonder how Robert Trelawney swallows two such in his own family.

Chapter Two

That evening, having supped and tucked the littlest ones in their beds, Prudence and her oldest daughters, Grace and Mary, sat close up to the fire doing a bit of sewing before going to bed themselves. One of the ways that Prudence had decided to economize after their financial reversals was to start making all the family linen and clothes at home. And, since the family had been growing at a rate their needles were hard pressed to keep up with, the sewing time lost that day while the guests were there must be made up now. Grace sighed. Her eyes were not very strong and sewing by firelight was a special chore for her. She was fifteen, and at first acquaintance not judged attractive. She had a rather long thin face and small pale blue eyes that looked even smaller than they were because of the squint her nearsightedness forced upon her. Her hair was dark like her mother's, but hers was fine and straight, her mother's heavy and softly waved. But she was so pleasantly obliging in her ways and had such a ready smile that after knowing her for awhile most people wondered why they had ever thought her unattractive.

Prudence looked at her daughters with a loving indulgence that she usually kept carefully hidden from view. Not that this restraint was too difficult to maintain—there being minor frustrations and aggravations enough to keep her temper, for the most part, in a suitable state of irritation. But tonight she watched them and smiled fondly at their differences. Grace moved her needle in and out slowly and with much difficulty in the wavering light of the fire, but with a persistent steadiness. Mary worked for a time quickly and easily and then gradually slowed down, as now, the needle finally stopping altogether as she sat staring into the fire until her mother's sharp, "Mary! Mind your sewing," brought her back to another burst of speed.

Prudence's own needle kept a steady pace seemingly unnoticed by her, even as her attention shifted, turning inward and giving her—for a moment—as distant a look in her eyes as her younger daughter. And then, with a nod, suggesting some brief argument with herself, she turned to look closely at the girls again. "I do think," she said firmly, "'tis time I did tell thee a story

I have long thought to tell thee—sometime." She paused, sighing. "'Tis a hard, unhappy tale, albeit a true one and, methinks, can tell thee much I would have thee understand, and better, mayhap, than any preachment on morality that your father or I might ply thee withal. Though most certainly," she added quickly, "'tis always your duty, remember, to do whatsoever your parents tell thee is right to do, whether thou dost understand or no. Still 'tis better if thou canst know why they tell thee to do thus or thus. As for this story, I did think to tell thee of it just now for that the sad occurrence outside today—being its unhappy ending—hath put me in mind of it."

Mary looked up from her sewing, "What of Begette's mother? Didst find out what hath happened to her?"

"Ay," Prudence said, hastily brushing a tear from her cheek, then continuing firmly. "The constable found her in the cave already dead of the plague."

Mary felt her chest tighten and her voice shook as she asked, "Why had they to lie there so, sick and dying and all alone with none to tend them?"

"But Mary surely there was no one knew of it or methinks 'tis most certain a doctor would have gone to them," Grace said in a placatory tone, with no touch of doubt in her voice. "Is't not so, mother?"

"'Tis likely," Prudence said, and then realized that perhaps she was not so sure of this likelihood—rather the opposite.

"Thou dost not understand," Mary spoke with pained intensity. "Why were there none who knew of their sickness and why had they to live in such a place?"

"'Tis what I wouldst tell thee by their story," Prudence said impatiently, "if thou wilt listen. First—thou should know that Begette's mother hath been well known to me all my life. Louisa—" She paused as if savoring the sound. "When I was small I said her name over and over again to myself, wishing that my father and mother had given me a name with so fair a sound—such are the foolish envies of children," she added hastily. "But to continue, Louisa's story—her house was at the end of that same street where I did live. But 'twas, in largeness three or four times as great as our small house, and, withal, many times more handsomely furnished—as well it might be since my father, though, honest and of sufficient funds to keep us comfortable, was but a tailor whilst Louisa's father was a merchant—and none richer in all Plymouth." The girls gasped. "'Tis no wonder thou art surprised." Her voice took on a sermonizing tone. "Truth is not always as thou seest—'tis not always safe to assume our ends from our beginnings or t'other way about. Surely Louisa's beginning was as fine as any I knew of, save only that her mother died when she was but three years old and her father never saw fit to marry another. His trading, so it seemed, was pleasure as well as business for him, and the doing of it used up all his days and evenings too. Only Louisa—whom he did love, mayhap overmuch, could draw him from it. I say he did love her overmuch because, so far as I know of it, he did never say her nay nor denied her anything. Their house, as my child's eye saw it was filled with beauty and comfort. There were strange and wondrously carved chairs and tables, high down beds and soft cushions and, at table, such dainty and fantastical sweetmeats and rare fruits as I have never tasted nor even seen the like of since. Of learning she had, not only a knowledge of reading and writing, of fine sewing and of singing and playing the lute—as becomes a young gentlewoman—but, at her asking, she had also as much tutoring in Latin and Greek and numbers as, I warrant, any young gentleman at a university. 'Twas a wonder she did not contract some distemper of the brain from it all." Prudence shook her head, her common gesture of mild disapproval, and Grace nodded in agreement. Such a magnitude of learning seemed to her a grave affliction in itself. But Mary's face had a look of puzzled interest. What of the young gentlemen at the university? Were they often so afflicted? How important learning must be for one to adventure a distemper of the brain for it! She remembered the strange wild-eyed creatures behind the mad house gate.

"—her clothes." Her mother's voice overrode her thoughts and drew her into the story again. "Such foreign silks and laces she had choice of and what gold- and silver-bordered waistcoats, gowns and cloaks my father did make for her! Jewels she had a plenty, too. Not that her beauty needed such ornaments—so well set out was she in all her parts. Dark hair—more red than brown, eyes of a deep blue, flecked with gold and all her other features, as it did seem to me, regular and perfect in every point. I fear me, I did greatly envy her, not only for her beauty and her possessions, but because, though so much indulged and never chastened she was, unfailing gentle and good-humored to all she met—whilst I, loath as I am to admit it, was not." Prudence eyed her daughters. "Which, thou mayst be sure, did cause me many painful switchings," she said pointedly, pausing to rethread her needle and remind Mary to keep to her sewing.

"She did not lack for suitors, as thou canst well imagine. Her father's wealth, of course was no discouragement, but her person would have brought most of them to her door betimes. Howbeit, as surely as they came, so surely did they go again, receiving no encouragement at all. Many were fain to believe 'twas her father turned them out—finding none good enough to wed her, But 'twas not so, as I well knew, for when she did learn that your father and I were to be wed she spake to me of my good fortune in having so goodly a man and one I did like so well. Then, with much sighing, she hath told me how she oft times did wonder if there was not something amiss with her that she could not find, amongst all the suitors that had come, one that she couldst be fond of. 'I do envy thee,' Louisa said that to me! And, indeed, so happy was I in my choice of your father and his of me that it did not seem so strange that she should." Prudence smiled with satisfaction even then at the memory. "And so we were wed and I came off to Rag Street and busied myself with the care of my own house and the pleasing of your father—which last, he being so easy and forbearing, as thou knowst, was never hard to do.

But I thought no more of Louisa and heard nothing, until just after thy birthing, Grace, when my mother having come to help me with't, hath told me of Louisa's betrothal—to the eldest son of a Lord! I will make no mention of his name, sith 'twould profit none and might still bring pain to some. My mother did say 'twas an alliance most pleasing to all concerned. Louisa's father was proud that his daughter should be joined to this noble family, where he had no doubt she did belong, and from which his descendants would now form a distinguished line of noblemen and ladies stretching into the distant future. The lord of the manor being, as 'twas well known, so heavily in debt that he was in peril of losing all his lands and buildings was also well content, both with the marriage settlement and the beauty and accomplishments of his daughter-in-law to be. As for Louisa and her betrothed, it did seem they were even happier in each other than their parents were in them. The young man—though not as handsome as some of Louisa's suitors—had, so 'twas said, as good a nature as her own and shared her interest in scholarly subjects. Love, so it did appear, hath smiled generously on them all."

"And then of a sudden—like to a storm that doth sail without warning across a cloudless sky and brings destruction to ships and men that lie in its path—misfortunes came down upon Louisa. Not a month before the wedding Louisa's father lost his fortune." Prudence sighed, remembering for a moment their own slower slide from a much smaller fortune.

"How exactly it came about I know not. Some said he had never so much as did appear in all his fine possessions and did overspend on his daughter, others that his merchant ships, by his order, preyed so often and with such success on Spanish and Turkish ships, that they were especially sought out by other ships of those nations—three or four of his ships being taken in a matter of days at the last. However it was, all was lost. Even their house and all that was in it was forfeit for his debts.

They were left with scarce more than the clothes they wore and a small cottage that had before been the home of two of their servants. And, no sooner was the news of his loss abroad than a messenger came from the nobleman calling off the wedding."

Grace let out her breath in a long slow sigh, but her expression did not change. Mary, however, frowned and gave a sharp exclamation of disbelief. "Had he then no feelings at all?"

"Mary, mind your sewing," Prudence snapped, then she too sighed and patted her daughter's hand. "Surely he did have feelings. But dost think that feelings can always be given way to, daughter? Did I not tell thee he was in debt?"

"But why could not Louisa and her betrothed have worked together and saved money as thou hast done with our father?"

"Oh Mary, thou dost dream again. Think you either of them had been trained to any work or could work enough to pay off the debts of a great family? 'Twas the father's duty and the eldest son's as well, to take care for the future of their family, and to keep its ancestral lands together. How but by a wealthy marriage could this be done? Family futures can be arranged. Happiness must come as may be. The nobleman did what he had to do, things being as they were." Prudence pronounced this with a firm assurance that her face reflected.

"But for poor Louisa 'twas only the beginning of misfortune. Her father, not long after, discovered she was with child. And so deranged with rage was he that he drove her from the cottage." Prudence heard two sharp intakes of breath and an agitated rustling of gowns.

"Now daughters, before thou speaketh ill of him, think thee of his feelings. Had he not lost all he did possess save his daughter and the great pride he had in her? And though it may seem a hard thing to say—truth being not always soft and pleasant to the tongue—if a man hath not money or a woman virtue they are as naught in the eyes of the world. Howbeit, knowing well how great a love he did have for her, I doubt not that he would have repented his harsh way with her ere that day was over and himself have gone to fetch her back. But, from his losses, the violence of his temper or despair I cannot say, he died that self same day."

"What befell Louisa—how or where she kept herself in the next few weeks—I know not. Though I did try to find her out 'twas above a month before I heard she had been hir'd out as a servant by Goody Cloven, the butcher's wife. This did much surprise and trouble me, knowing how little she knew of any work and knowing as well that Goody Cloven had so mean a temper and paid so little that those most used to laboring were loath to work for her. But withal Louisa had not sought help from past friends, and others, I fear, did little desire for a servant a fallen lady big with child."

"But was there no one in her family would take her in?" Grace asked hesitantly. Her face had a strained look, as if she did not wish to admit into the quiet order of her mind the vagrant thought that this foundation of security could fail.

Prudence patted her daughter's head reassuringly. "Her family, if any there was, were far away in France. Her father and mother, 'twas said, were Huguenots who came to England, before Louisa was born to escape the Popish persecutions. But I much doubt, had they been here, that she would have called on them—her pride being so great. She would not take the help that some of us did try to offer her, nor would she e'en have conversation with us save to make polite reply to our questions."

"But be that as may be, she did give birth to her baby girl, still working—and by her looks too hard—for Goody Cloven and did the butcher's accounts for him too, I heard, until sometime after the outbreak of the plague in 1625. We had taken a cottage in the country to keep you children from the sickness, so I learned only later of the further trouble did befall Louisa. When the plague was at its height Butcher Cloven and his wife packed up their things, closed their house and betook them out of Plymouth leaving Louisa and her baby, not yet three years old, without food or shelter or aught else for their survival."

The girls stared at their mother in disbelief. Grace's weak eyes overflowed and anger as well as pity was obvious in Mary's flushed face. Her mother's eyes narrowed in a similar anger as she recalled the fat red-faced butcher and his wife. "I would I could see such mean-spirited rogues as these at the whipping post," she murmured under her breath, "Had I but known of their plight—" she said aloud her voice trailing off in a sigh. "'Twas then Louisa took shelter in a cave—lately vacated by the plague. Bur certain there was naught there to keep them from starvation, save such roots and herbs as she could gather, which would scarce have been enough. And, beggars being thought to be likely carriers of the plague, none would venture near them. So, marrie, what way was left to her but stealing and whoredom? Men, it doth seem having more fear of beggars than whores. Be that as may be Louisa chose the last or, mayhap it hath chosen her. She was, though much spent by hard work, still beautiful."

"When finally the plague was gone and the people back from the country Louisa turned quickly from that life to seek a job as a servant once again. But 'twas well known what she had been and none would have her—not even

Goody Cloven. Then it was that she and Begette, as people took to calling her little girl, began to beg—and so they have been doing ever since. As for Begette's baby, I can but think some one of the rogues that roam the streets hath taken Begette by force. The rest thou knowest." She broke off abruptly and stared dispiritedly into the fire until the dwindling flames roused her to her practical duties.

"Come, daughters. It is time to bank the fire and get thee to thy bed. As thou hast now seen the story is a hard and hurtful one, but I hope t'will teach thee a bit of what the world dost expect of thee and why thy mother and father watch thee so narrowly." Prudence said this without much force. Her sententiousness having given way to melancholy and a vague uncertainty about the results of what she had not realized would be so painful to recall in full. She looked at Grace's pale sad face and Mary's flushed and angry one and reluctantly admitted to herself, "Grace hath no need of such a moral lesson and, methinks Mary hath no ear for the moral I did preach."

As she and her sister walked upstairs to the small bedroom they shared Mary, confirming her Mother's thoughts, mumbled fiercely, "It hath taught me that the people of Plymouth are cruel and ungodly."

"Mary," Grace said in a gentler replica of her Mother's moralistic tone, "God Himself hath called what Louisa did a sin."

Mary said no more, but later, in her bed, she tried to think of sin and what it was, but could think only of Begette—seeing her pale eyes staring, first imploringly into her own and then vacantly out of the small heap of ragged clothes and body lying like any other pile of trash in the filthy street.

Chapter Three

By the middle of June there was no more need for portents or astrological conjuring of the plague. In the early days of spring hope and optimism had appeared as inevitably, and as fragile as the new leaves on the trees. The markets, like the meadows, came alive with color and the sounds of laughter and song. It was a hard time of year to think of death. But slowly, one by one, under the warm sun, the deaths began to increase—a neighbor, a friend, a member of the family. Until, all at once, all over the city, panic set in. As though in answer to some subliminal signal the streets began to fill with horses and loaded wagons. Those who could left the city for country homes. Others simply left, hoping to find some field or forest they would not be chased away from. Within a week only a few servants, deserted by their employers, and some merchants, tradesmen, doctors and town officials whose livelihood or civic duty demanded they stay, were left. The silence of the almost empty streets was a tangible presence—penetrated but not broken by the occasional sounds—pattering feet clacking now and then on the cobblestones, the intermittent and frightened screams of the distracted victims and their families and, finally, the chillingly regular clatter of the death cart on its daily rounds, the ringing of his bell and the repeated cry of the death cart driver—"Bring out your dead. Bring out your dead."

When the plague at last began to abate, in the fall of 1638, the death count showed that it had not been as devastating a visitation as those of 1603 and 1625. But this after knowledge could bring no comfort to anyone at the height of the epidemic. Nor at the end could it lighten the grief of those whose loved ones had been carried off.

John and Margaret Martin persuaded Francis and his family to stay with them at their commodious cottage near Robert Trelawney's country home at Ham, about two miles outside of Plymouth Wall. Partly by way of persuasion—knowing that, despite their strained finances, pride might cause them to refuse—but none the less truthfully, Margaret pleaded her need for Prudence's skill in midwifery and the easiness of mind her husband would have if her midwife was living right there. Prudence was easily persuaded since she would not in any way have let her pride jeopardize the safety of her children. Mary thought often now, and bitterly, of Begette and her mother and baby who had not had anyone to give them safe shelter.

This move to the country could not banish all risk and fear. Every Monday morning Margaret and Prudence must see their husbands off to the city. Trading was down, but still must be tended to—though this posed much risk for the men and some for their families also. To minimize this latter risk Prudence had the servants fill a large barrel with water every Friday, shortly before the men came home "Since 'tis well known," she reminded the others, "water hath power to kill infections." The barrel was placed at the edge of a small wood near the cottage and, on the way home John and Francis stopped there, took off their town clothes and deposited them in the water, putting on in their stead another set of apparel that had been left for them. Next day the water was poured off and the clothes laid out on the grass to dry. Like the herb teas and wines that Prudence plied them with, this operation much relieved the minds and somewhat lightened the hearts of both families. And such lightness of heart was itself extolled by many physicians as a plague preventative and even a cure.

For those not irrevocably wed to city pleasures, the cottage in its country setting was itself conducive to a light heart. At the end of a lane, bordered by a dignified procession of oak trees, the twelve room thatch-roofed cottage stood not far from the edge of a broad field where deer and other smaller animals came out of a nearby wood to graze. Well-designed flower gardens bloomed from early spring until late fall beside the cottage. And, in the back, a large herb and vegetable garden supplied the needs of the kitchen, while just beyond, in orderly rows, peach, pear and fig trees, berry bushes and grape vines provided a seasonal variety of fruit on the table.

Here, in the wood and the field, when she was not helping in the kitchen or minding one or another of the small children, Mary walked and dreamed, often alone, but sometimes with Francie who had not been much given to walking in the city. But freed from the treacherous smelly streets she delighted to run back and forth across the field and amongst the trees, her bright and darting motions making her look like a larger version of the butterflies and birds she chased. After her little girl was born, Margaret began to join Mary in her "aimless wanderings" as Prudence called them, and the two discovered a sympathy in quietness and talk that bridged the gap of years—though Mary felt somehow much older now that she had passed her fourteenth birthday and had been called to help at the birthing of her new brother and Margaret's baby as well.

As the weeks passed Mary found herself increasingly drawn to the beliefs of the "godly people," or Puritans, as others dismissively referred to them. This came not from anything that Margaret said of them. They did not talk of religious beliefs. Rather it was from the example of Margaret herself—her gentle humor and kindness—and because of what she heard of the people of Massachusetts from Edward Trelawney's letters so often quoted by Margaret: "If there were ever a happy people these are they…" and of their agreement "There is such a sweet community and fellowship on all sides."

And then, on several Sundays, Mr. George Hughes, a much respected minister of the non-conformist persuasion, came to the cottage to lecture to those of like mind who had gathered there. Mary sat listening with the rest to this sharp-faced intense man as he spoke of the elect and of God's grace.

"Do not think that because thou dost possess many worldly goods and have great learning that thou art assuredly among the elect of God. Know thou that we are all of us sinners in need of salvation. But none can buy or beg God's saving grace. It is a free gift—a gift that descendeth where He listeth—on the lowliest as well as the most high born of repentant sinners."

At these words Mary hugged herself and smiled with a feeling of righteous vindication. Then she noticed that the pastor's eyes were on her and she felt, and was sure that he could see, her sinful self-righteousness reflected in her face. Her arms dropped to her sides and her face took on an expression of thoughtful concern—which she did indeed feel!

On another occasion he spoke of true repentance and good deeds—"Good works open a pathway to the soul. Without them the soul is closed and barred against the entrance of God's grace. And so it is that the elect will be known for their good works, but not by them. For the cleverest hypocrites and dissemblers can put on good works as a cloak to deceive others and themselves."

And finally Mary was won when, speaking of the needs of the body that must be met so that the work of the soul, God's work, could go forward, he said—"Do not think thou need care only for thine own body and soul. All of us are God's creatures, and if thou wouldst glorify Him thou must care for thy neighbor as thou wouldst thyself." Whereupon Mary was sure that he would think as she about Louisa and Begette.

"I can see no ill-speaking in this nonconformist pastor," said Prudence, after one of the lectures, and with some surprise. "Nor do I see he differs much in what he says from our good Dr. Aron Wilson of St. Andrews." Mary disagreed but said nothing.

"'Tis mayhap more in deeds we differ than in words," said Pastor Hughes from where he had been standing just behind them. Possibly a trace of sinful pride could be detected in his voice.

If it had not been for worrying about her father and her cousin John, so much in the plague stricken city, Mary would have been well content with her country surroundings augmented by her new faith. Now when she walked out alone she more often used the time for praying than for dreaming. But, when Margaret was with her, prayer frequently gave way to talk. Margaret was full of stories of the days when she and her brother Edward played in this same field and wood when they were children. "I fear me I was as much for climbing trees and playing hide and seek as either of my brothers—more than Robert, surely." She laughed and then stared off dreamily toward the wood. "I remember how our nurse would, of an evening, tell us diverse adventures of King Arthur or Robin Hood or some such. In the morning off Edward and I to the woods to play out the stories." She nodded and smiled with a kind of playful despair at her own unladylike wildness. Then, raising her eyebrows—unexpectedly dark below her fair hair—she regarded Mary with a quizzical look. "Thy mother hath told me thou art the storyteller in your family and keep the little ones content with all manner of fantastical tales. Where dost get these tales?"

Mary blushed. "They are mine own imaginings. But they are not so very fantastical. Methinks the little ones like any manner of tale," she said, dismissing them, and then, hesitantly, looking with some distress at Margaret, "I suppose—'tis most sinful?"

"I cannot believe so," Margaret answered promptly. "Perhaps 'tis heretical to say, but I do not believe the good Lord doth blame children overmuch for these small transgressions. Mayhap I do but wish to think mine own and Edward's wickedness hath been forgiven or, being now a mother, that my little ones will not be harshly judged for their small faults. Which—I do hope—will not include wandering off into town as Edward and I were wont to do." She shook her head, but could not check the smile that spoke for her. "We would most often go down by the wharves where all manner of thieves and rogues still ply their evil trades." Mary looked uneasy at the mention of the wharves. "We spent hours watching ships taking on loads, setting out and returning. Once my errant brother did even propose that, when we were older, he should give me a set of his clothes so we could hire ourselves out on one of those ships and travel the world together. That at the least I did not—" She noticed the expression of delight on Mary's face. "Marrie! I hope have not encouraged thee to any wild adventuring," she said, only half facetiously.

Mary blushed again, as she was given to doing of late. "Oh no! 'Tis only something to think on. I wouldst be afeered of being soon found out and— sold to the Turks or some such."

Margaret laughed and hugged her. "There! Thy dreamings that thy Mother doth so much fear, do stand thee sometimes in good stead then."

Releasing her, Margaret said, smiling at another memory, "'Twas one of those times, down by the wharves, that I did first see my John. I was but ten and he fifteen and, as I remember, he did look with some scorn at my dirty face and tumbled clothes. He doth deny it now, but I mind well how he did turn away and start up talking to thy father. They were together, as they so often were when John was a boy. Francis, as I have told thee, was like to a second father or mayhap a brother to him. His real father, though most kind and well meaning, was so ill at ease with children that he did avoid being left alone with John, or so it seemed to him."

"Tis not hard to understand John feeling so," Margaret said. "Thou hast seen how it is when his father doth come here for a visit and the children gather around him." She stood very awkwardly stiff, and putting her hands behind her back, she looked down over her nose and said—"'Pray tell. What kind of a day hath it been for you children, eh?' And, after they have delivered to him a long and jolly account of diverse happenings, he doth take a deep breath–so—" her small chest took on a rooster like importance of curve if not proportion. "Then he doth nod and stare most solemnly and, presently, sayeth, 'Indeed. Indeed,' contriving betwixt one indeed and the other to take 's leave."

Mary could not stifle her laughter. The stance, the expression and even the voice was so like her Uncle's.

"Oh dear," Margaret said, lapsing into herself again, "I have been sorely lacking in respect. The dear serious man hath always been so kind to us. I know it doth pain him that he hath not a way with children as your father hath. Thou see how easily I fall into sinful ways; even now I am a woman and know better." She sighed.

If Margaret's ways are sinful, Mary thought, there can be no hope for me. But she could not at all believe they were—though she said nothing of it, knowing that Margaret would only say she knew not of what she spoke.

They talked also of New England and of her father's dream. Mary wondered how John, being so much with her father, listening to him question the sailors and exchange information and stories with Sir Ferdinando Gorges, had resisted the contagion. She could not believe he had never had the wish to go to New England too.

"Verily, I believe he did want to go for awhile when he was a boy," Margaret said, smiling at her cousin's unconcealed enthusiasm, "But, since then, he hath found too much enjoyment in buying and selling and trading—and enough of it to do right here in Plymouth—that he thinks of little else. 'tis hard for me to believe it, but 'tis true," she laughed.

"Ay," said Mary, her eyes taking on a familiar faraway look of excitement. "'Tis hard for me to believe that anyone would not want to go to such a country where there is so much new and beautiful to see—and naught of smoke and smells and plagues!"

"Marrie, methinks that no place outside of paradise could turn thy head or Uncle's from this wilderness of wolves and savages," Margaret teased.

"Paradise?" Mary looked quickly over at her cousin, the color coming into her cheeks again. In the time they had been there—and her fifteenth year approaching—she had begun to look more woman than child. Her face that had early been all eyes and mouth had filled out and developed an attractive mobility of expression that, to her frequent distress, quite accurately revealed her thoughts and feelings. But also whether from having such a sympathetic listener in her cousin, or from the more settled mind her acceptance of the Godly faith had brought her, she had a better command of words in her thinking and usually in her speaking as well. But Margaret's mention of paradise just then had been disconcerting, reminding her, though she hardly needed reminding, of a vivid dream she had had one morning, just before dawn. A nightingale, singing somewhere close to her bedroom window, had half awakened her. At first her mind had been filled with the song. Then, gradually, an image grew within it, and, expanding, took on color, becoming the lush green of islands scattered in a curve of water—the New England bay that George Cleeve had described! She felt her bare feet touching the new ground, hesitantly, as Adam and Eve must have done, stepping out of paradise—an ordered life already formed and regulated—into an unknown world. Another paradise waiting to be built and ordered and, far from anxiety or awe, she found herself full of joy that, as she awoke merged with the sound of the nightingale still singing. She had thought of this half dream many times in the days that followed, and several times almost spoke of it to Margaret. But she felt, vaguely, that there might be something sinful in it, and if so she was not saint enough to want to know it. Which thought, she sighed, was doubtless sinful too.

This thought of building and ordering a new life in New England, which she had never doubted they would do, caused her to think practically as well about how much she and doubtless her father too, must needs learn of the skills necessary to survive there. Her father on his weekends in the country, practiced shooting. But what could she do? To this she found answer upon going out by the garden on a late spring morning and discovering Jacob, the gardener, busily tilling and planting. She spoke to him, but so hesitantly and in such a low voice that he, smiling pleasantly, must ask her to repeat what she had said. Put at ease by his smile she plainly asked could he teach her how to grow a vegetable garden, since her father thought to go to New England one day. Which adventure Jacob nodded his approval of.

So it was that on a weekend morning her father came upon her kneeling beside a row of peas she had just planted. He frowned to see her gown, hands and even her face somewhat besmirched with dirt. "Mary! What hath brought thee to groveling in the ground like to a common servant?

"But, father," she smiled despite his frown. "Jacob hath been teaching me to farm. I have thought that we will have no gardener when we get to New England. And more! Agnes hath promised to teach me how to get milk from a cow and turn it to butter in a churn!"

Her face was so flushed with pleasure at the thought of the real help she could be that it would surely have been mean-spirited to scold her for it. Moreover Francis realized that she was right and further, found that he was proud of her. His frown faded away and he laughed and shook his head. "Methinks thou art a practical dreamer after all."

By the first week in September of 1638, the plague seemed to have so abated that John and Francis gave it as their opinion that if this abatement continued it should be safe for their families to return permanently to Plymouth in two weeks time. But, on a warm afternoon in the middle of the next week, when everyone was gathered in front of the cottage as Grace, who had a pleasant skill in music, played the lute for them, John rode up on his horse, alone, and with so sober a look on his face that they were all struck with fear. "Francis?" Prudence's voice, high and sharp, cut through their silence.

John nodded. "He was taken yesterday—and no one to care for him." Prudence was already part way to the door of the cottage, saying she needed but a moment to get her things. And that was all it took. There had been scarcely time to bring a horse around when she was back.

"Mother, I wouldst come with thee." Mary's face was stiff and white.

"No!" Prudence snapped and then after a pause, more quietly. "I need thee here to help Grace take care of the little ones." She mounted the horse and with no more words they rode off.

That night Mary dreamed no bright dream of nightingales and the waters of Casco Bay—but woke in a terror with the image of the black entrance of a cave and her father being carried in.

That was on a Tuesday, and for four days they heard nothing. Inside the cottage the quiet and tension of waiting affected even the babies, who ate, slept and cried erratically, keeping their young nurses gratefully busy. And Margaret, though fearing she could not, found she had no trouble suckling two infants.

They conversed little with each other but much with God. And the servants also joined in the worry and the prayers. Mr. Francis Martin was a favorite—his way with servants being much like his way with children: he forgot that they were different from him.

Mary, as the Godly people were wont to do, tried to understand the hand of the Lord in this affliction. In an anguish of fear and guilt, she pleaded that, if aught in her own sinful ways or thoughts had caused Him to lay this sickness upon her father, He would instead inflict her and let her father live. And then the fear would strike at her heart that this unwillingness of hers to accept what the Lord had ordained was a further sin. And so she sat desperately concentrating for hours at a time, trying to condition her mind to an unwavering acceptance of God's will.

It was on a Saturday morning while she sat by the window, so engaged, that the same horse and rider that had appeared before in the lane appeared again. Her concentration, her acceptance both were dispersed in an instant as she leapt to her feet and ran for the door. John was coming up the walk by the time the others got there—a wide smile lighting up his face.

"All is well! He is recovering!"

Mary, Margaret, Grace and Francie were upon him before he had finished these words, deluging him with a torrent of happy tears. The which prompted him to observe that he had not taken time to drop off his clothes in the water barrel. "But," he smiled again, "it doth seem there was no need—that is if salt water has as good effect as fresh."

There was now as much talk as there had been little for the past four days. Grateful prayers were said, and Grace, being not much given to words played hers on the lute. This soon brought forward the youngest girls—Francie, Marjorie and Thomasine—who let out all their fear-stifled feelings through their dancing feet, which would have to be judged, by all except the most pure of puritans, as prayer. As fine as any that had gone up that day.

Not only were there now fewer cases of the plague each week, but also, many fewer deaths among those who were afflicted. The disease, John said, seemed to have lost much of its virulence. All the same, Prudence thought it best they wait out the usual twenty-day quarantine period before coming back to Plymouth. There was a general round of sighs and then John said

36

he thought he had a bit of news that would make at least one of those days pass swiftly by—he looked at Margaret. "Edward hath returned from New England."

Margaret gave a short cry, then put her hand over her mouth. Her eyes sparkled and the color rushed to her face. "Oh why is he not with thee. Hath New England drawn off all the love he bore his sister?"

Quite the contrary, John assured her, he was as anxious to see her as she him. But Francis being sick, Robert had need of his help. Because, in proportion as the plague abated, business increased. Indeed he was, that very day at Looe in Cornwall buying supplies that would go out on the next boat for Richmond's Island, the site of the Trelawney fishing enterprise in New England.

"He bade me tell thee, though, that on his first free day he would ride out so early in the morning as to get both the sun and thee out of thy beds."

Margaret laughed. "I durst adventure my good name that the day when brother Edward will wake me of a morning will never come. Full many a scolding I did deliver him from when we were small by dragging him forth protesting from his bed just before our father hath come angrily to fetch him."

Edward came the very next day and, as she had supposed, Margaret's good name was in no danger. It was almost ten o'clock when he came riding up protesting that the darkness of the clouds that day had made him mistake the hour.

Mary got much pleasure observing the obvious joy and affection with which these two railed at and chided one another. She hardly remembered Edward at all having seen little of him when she was small and it being now four years since he had left for New England. Margaret had said they were of a mind in many things. They were also, Mary noticed, similar in appearance. Edward too was of a slight, though muscular build, and his face, like Margaret's had finely-chiseled features but of a larger size. He had as well dark, and in his case, heavy eyebrows, contrasting with fair hair. And he combined a scholarly aspect with the same look of mischief that his sister so often wore. Mary felt at ease with him at once.

Margaret looked puzzled. "I thought thou meant to work for Robert there as thou hast sometimes done here?"

"And so I did tell him that I would. I planned to be an actor and not a spectator only in the business of his plantation. And, to deserve his consideration, I did act as agent for the plantation in Massachusetts. But John Winter who is, as you know, our brother's manager on Richmond's Island, and in whose discretion and trustworthiness he hath unshakable faith, informed him that the cattle I bought in Boston proved poor. Though, so far as I could tell, they were neither worse nor better than the other stock. Winter also would have it that the trade in clapboards I did recommend was much overrated—though such a seasoned observer and traveler as John Josselin pronounced it good. Then, lastly, when I did make it clear I would stay on as a permanent agent for my brother, he gave me to understand that the plantation had no need of any agent save himself. From that day he spoke not at all to me of business nor showed me any accountings of what was needed or already bought or the like. Though, before that, I had on diverse occasions assisted and once, whilst he was absent in England, did all the inventory of goods on Richmond's Island and the Maine. Now all the books were hid from me." He shrugged. "So there was naught for me to do but leave."

"But what did our brother say to all this?"

"He did not believe me. Some past actions of mine giving him good cause for doubt, as thou dost know well enough." He smiled wryly at his sister. "But, as well, this John Winter hath climbed most high in his esteem."

Margaret nodded. "So we were told. We talked to Mr. Cleeve, when he was in Plymouth above a year ago, and he hath said John Winter was a knavish rogue, but doing well by our brother because he did see his interests and Robert's as the same."

Edward laughed. "That is George Cleeve indeed! Contentious as a bull, but always honest—a good man. And he is right of course. To do Winter justice, and Robert too, our brother does, in most things, have reason for the trust he has in this man. But, as for me, I think John Winter sees my interests as quite contrary to his own. And I do not doubt he doth believe that I would have his job." Edward hunched his shoulders, narrowed his eyes and somehow stretched his mouth wider so that suddenly he did take on the look of a stocky, short necked man. "'Twas thus I would catch him scowling at me," he said in a deep hoarse voice quite unlike his own.

Mary gasped and then collapsed in laughter with Margaret and Edward. When they could talk again Mary wondered how it was possible he could become so much like another quite unlike himself—and of a sudden remembered Margaret's similar talent.

"'Tis called acting," Edward said. And then a look of mischief crossed his face. "Methinks thou didst never suspect I was an actor on the stage in London—didst thou sister?"

Margaret's face alternated between shock and disbelief. "Edward, no!"

He smiled. "Do not despair of me sweet Margaret. 'Twas but once—in my wild student days. My friends, having seen me put on the face of one of the dons, or some other, for their amusement, dared me to adventure my skill with real actors. And so, nothing loath, I paid a poor actor to let me take his place one afternoon. And that was all." He paused and smiled wistfully. "I do admit I did enjoy it—in the doing and afterward. The applause and the praise, even from my fellow actors."

"Edward! Didst not think how unseemly and frivolous it was to join thyself with those lewd ungodly people?"

Edward restrained a smile at Margaret's vehemence. "Thou must remember, sister, I had not then encountered the godly people and was, I fear, little better than those you name with scorn."

Later on that same day, it being the Sabbath, Reverend Hughes came to them again and, as fate, coincidence or—if you wish—providence would have it, that day spoke to them of the prodigal son. Mary noticed Edward trying to catch Margaret's eye, but she steadfastly refused to look in his direction. However she was much mollified when she later heard Reverend Hughes and Edward talking with great animation of the Massachusetts people—of the minister John Wilson who was a friend of Reverend Hughes—and of John Cotton and other divines who felt the call, or in some cases more the push of persecution, to join their godly brothers across the water.

As John had predicted the days when Edward came did indeed pass swiftly. He joined Mary and Margaret on their frequent walks, the children trailing along behind as though he was a kind of pied piper. They seemed to enjoy the musical sound of his voice. Certainly they could have understood little of the content of what he said that so fascinated his sister and Mary. It was talk full of knowledge of books and distant places always touched with his own kind of deprecating humor, making fun of the world and himself as part of it with words and the mimic faces that even the littlest children loved.

On one of these days they took a basket lunch to the lake at Weston Mills. It was a bright breeze swept day in early fall, the air full of the pungent smell of harvest. Edward and Mary had fallen behind the others, waiting while Mary's four-year-old brother John explored an empty bird's nest. As they walked on Mary talked with Edward about New England and found that he spoke of it much as George Cleeve had done: its abundance of beauty and life-sustaining food sources first and then, in dutiful afterthought, of the harshness of the cold and the importance, nay necessity, of hard work. He looked surprised at the intensity of Mary's interest in what he had to say.

"Not all young women are so captivated by New England." He frowned briefly. Mary, blushing, explained about her father's preoccupation, and Edward nodded. "Of course! I well remember his abiding interest though, because of his sickness, have had no chance to talk to him of it since I returned." He smiled. "Thou art then of thy father's mind on this." He looked with a wistful admiration at her radiant face, an admiration plain enough to cause her to lower her eyes in a confusion of embarrassment and pleasure. He put his hand on her arm. "I hope thy father can one day take thee to New England, and that it will not disappoint thee."

Mary felt the warmth of his hand spreading through her and was suddenly overcome with shyness and relieved when behind them young John, his short legs having given out, began to whimper. Edward stepped back and tossed him up on his shoulders. Then, grabbing Mary's hand, he began to run toward the lake where Margaret and Grace were already setting out the food, young John bouncing ecstatically up and down.

That evening, as they sat around the fireplace singing, Mary several times caught Edward looking at her. She quickly looked away hoping he wouldn't notice that she had seen him, and wondered why she felt so lightheaded. Later as they talked of returning to Plymouth, Margaret asked Edward what his plans were for now and did he plan to go back to New England some day. He replied that he hoped to but, like Mary's father, planned now to save enough money first so that he could buy his own land.

"I would not be subject to another's whim again. And—" he hesitated. "I hope thou wilt be pleased to hear I plan to marry—someone I met in London. She is the sister of a friend I stayed with when I first got back from New England. She is very beautiful, Margaret, and of the godly faith. It only remains for me to convince her that New England is not the frightening place she doth fancy it to be."

Mary did not hear what Margaret replied or aught else that Edward said. Her heart sank, and fearing that her thoughts might show too well on her face, she abruptly left the room. She was fully aware now of the foolish hope she had been nurturing since the first day Edward came. She, a silly girl of not quite fifteen, thinking she might attract an educated worldly man of almost twenty-five years! She felt a tremor of bitter disgust with herself, followed by an intense feeling of mixed shame and longing of a kind she had never felt before. Her head ached with the strain of holding back the tears of self-pity she refused to cry. If you are pitiful, she admonished herself, it is only because you are foolish—but this had no effect on her longing.

The next morning she pretended to be sleeping when Grace got out of the bed they shared and did not come downstairs until after she heard Edward ride off. Margaret was worried that she might be sick, but Mary insisted she had only a foolish small headache and was now quite well again. She said it with such firmness that Margaret told her she sounded as though she was scolding a wicked child, and did she always treat herself so when she got sick? Mary blushed and smiled in spite of herself. Whereupon Margaret declared her fully-recovered by reason, she said, of her very pink cheeks. And a good thing too since, if she had not forgotten, today they must start packing up their things, for in two days John and Francis were coming to escort them back to Plymouth.

The two days went speedily, and no one worked harder or so gratefully as Mary. Grace watched with some surprise her sister's unwavering attention to work that even she found dull. And Margaret said, as she supposed in jest, that Mary's "small sickness" had the unusual result of increasing her energy, and she thought she could use a touch of such a sickness herself, if she knew how to catch it. Mary laughed to herself and had to admit that she was feeling, as well as seeming, much better than she would have supposed possible in so short a time—which realization caused her to look upon herself with considerable disdain. How young and silly she must indeed be, she thought, if her feelings could be so quickly turned about. But it pleased her that she showed no sign when Margaret began to speculate aloud on Edward's coming marriage.

"Methinks 'tis the kind of settling he hath need of. As for his bride—" she kissed Mary's cheek. "I only hope he hath found him one I will like as well as I like thee." Then her father was there and the joy of seeing him again and the worry at finding him so thin and hollow-cheeked made her, for awhile, forget about herself altogether.

The wagons were duly loaded and the bumpy miles back to Plymouth traversed. They had barely passed through the North Gate when Francie wrinkled up her nose and exclaimed in disgust—"Ugh! I had forgot that home did smell as bad as this!"

"Thou wert just accustomed to it before, little one, and will be again, never fear," her father said. But he did not laugh with the rest of them.

How Mary had expected the city to be, after all the fear and death they had heard of, she did not know. But surely it should not seem so much the same. The buildings, the cobble. The people they passed—even those in black—were chattering, laughing or railing at one another as always. The dreaded red x marks of the plague were still prominently visible on many doors, but they were beginning to fade or were in the process of being rubbed off. A sudden chill memory of what had been passed over her. She tried to turn her thoughts to God and His people, but failed. The sights and sounds of the city would not be displaced.

Turning into Rag Street they passed the Widow Pym, all in black, sweeping off the doorstep of her house. Francie looked surprised.

"Why doth the Widow go about in mourning dress, Father?"

"Old Heming hath died of the sickness, in despite of all the widow's simples."

"In mourning for a servant!" Francie's tone was scornful. "And such a crazy muttering creature."

"Gentle, my girl. 'Tis best we do not judge. Though methinks 'tis not seemly to go in such excess of mourning for a servant. Still old Heming was all the family the widow had these many years since her husband died—and the closest friend too, I warrant, despite his muttering these last years. He came here with her, a young man, when she came a bride above fifty years ago."

"Fifty years!" Francie, trying to comprehend the passage of fifty years, could only sigh and shake her head. "But father, if the widow's simples did naught to save old Heming and she there to see to him, dost think there be any who will buy from her again?"

"The physician's nostrums do not work every time—nor the minister's either." Francis added in a low voice.

"What sayeth thou, father?"

"Naught, little one. Just muttering to myself like old Heming."

Mary noticed how the black cloak and black-pointed hat emphasized the pallid thinness of the widow's face, making her look even more like the witch it had often been whispered she was. She spoke of this to her father.

"Ay," he sighed, and then almost sharply. "But 'tis not a good thing to speak thus—of anyone. There are those who never cease to look for someone they can blame for the ills that nature or their own weakness hath thrust upon them." He lapsed into a sigh again. "But mayhap the widow cares little for what others say. Such rumors have, methinks, brought more customers to her door than they have frightened away."

Chapter Three

His sickness seemed to have wrought more changes in Francis than the obvious physical ones. This hitherto good-humored man no longer laughed and scarcely ever smiled. Loud noises and trivial inconveniences that he would not have noticed at all in the past now caused his body to stiffen and a look of annoyance to pass over his face. The plague seemed to have rubbed all of his nerve ends raw. He didn't shout at anyone—but it was not necessary. The servants, as well as his family, easily read the signs of irritation in his expressions and responded more quickly and fearfully than they ever had to the angry shouting that Prudence sometimes gave vent to. The former atmosphere of the house—a natural though unintentional extension of Francis Martin's character—had dissolved, leaving the members of the family in an uneasy vacuum with their own reactions and emotions.

Grace, her weak eyes frequently full of tears, worked at whatever she was given to do even more quietly and steadily than before, while Mary, taking refuge in her old habit of daydreaming that she had learned to somewhat control in her year at the cottage, worked less and more carelessly than ever. The younger children played more vigorously and cried more often and louder than usual, so that someone seemed always to be hustling one of them out of sight and hearing of their father.

Francie's temper, a replica of her mother's in quickness and vigor, but without the control that Prudence, over the years, had learned to have over hers, grew more frequent and violent. She slapped a small unruly brother on more than one occasion, and kicked Angela, their seventy-year-old maid servant in the shin when, upon being ordered by Francie to go up to the third floor to fetch her cloak, Angela crossed her arms on her ample and righteous bosom and gave it as her opinion that Mistress Francie was better able to do that herself. Prudence, happening upon this little scene, promptly escorted her daughter out into the garden and, without a word, cut a short switch from a handy bush and applied it to Francie's bare legs, then sent her, tears still streaking her cheeks, to find Angela and apologize, which she did willingly enough, her anger having quite disappeared by then. Besides she knew she would be comforted not scolded there.

"Tush, tush, my pert and copped little one," Angela murmured, wiping Francie's cheeks with the corner of her apron and hugging her. "'Tis all forgiven and forgot already."

Prudence, for her part, was so taken up with the problem of restoring her husband to full health—which she had no doubt would bring him back to himself—that she failed, except in unusual cases like Francie's mistreatment of Angela, to exercise her usual firm control over the household or even to get angry or to shout at anyone. All this, of course, served only to increase the general unhappiness. But she was too preoccupied to notice. Almost every morning she went herself to the market—instead of sending a servant or one of the girls—in search of special items of food to tempt her husband's appetite. She sought out and brought home the choicest joints of mutton, especially plump geese and fresh, pink-fleshed salmon—the latter a particular favorite of Francis. She also made sure he had his favorite wines and fresh fruit every day. When he wasn't eating he was being plied, as quietly and unobtrusively as was possible, with cups of herb teas and spoonfuls of herb infusions concocted from a carefully selected assortment of medicinal herbs—like feverfew, rosemary, valerian, pimpernel, basil and foxglove—that she gathered or grew. She also fastened a little bag of herbs under the edge of his doublet. This last "treatment" finally prompted Francis to remark, with something of his old amused tolerance of the world and his wife, that she was likely to put herself in grave suspicion of witchcraft—her poor husband being a walking witness to her potions in the aura of herbs that emanated from his clothes, his breath and the very pores of his body.

"Verily," Prudence laughed, "and if I be taken so, I shall bring half of Plymouth with me on the charge of consorting with a witch—not the least of which will be my ungrateful husband." And well she might call him ungrateful, she thought happily, since it was clear that in the few weeks since she had begun her treatment there was a noticeable lightning of his dark humors. He seemed more relaxed and undisturbed by his surroundings once more. What had not changed was a quiet sadness of countenance He was still rarely moved to smile and but seldom—except in a sort of forced and awkward way—to his former gently humorous conversation. It was as though his close encounter with death had so chastened his spirit that the hopes and dreams that once animated it were driven out like some childhood fantasies.

His family, again following his lead, became easier with one another, but without the playfulness that had in past years enlivened their living together. Prudence continued to seem preoccupied, often shaking her head or wrinkling her brow in concentration as if she were, with difficulty and a measure of reluctance, weighing one thing against another in her mind. She was not much given to indecision. Recipes and rules, learned so early that they seemed as much a part of her as the workings of her body and as little to be questioned, made her decisions for her. Logical analysis of problems did not come easy for her. But happily in her case her feelings had always served her well.

One morning, coming upon Mary where she sat by the window staring at but not out of it—her needle and thread lying idle in her lap—Prudence said sharply, out of old habit, "Mary!" Whereupon Mary started, reached for her sewing and, in her haste pricked her finger. All of which her mother seemed not to notice. "Dost still dream of New England?" Her intently serious tone sounded stern.

Disconcerted, Mary again dropped her sewing. Hastily recovering it, she once more punctured her finger. "Some—sometimes," she murmured, almost inaudibly and blushed not knowing, what or rather whom she most often dreamed of now. His face could not be banished, especially from her dreams of New England.

In the past Prudence had been disturbingly perceptive in observing and accurate in deciphering the reactions of her husband and children, but lately, as that morning, she had become oblivious even to her most readable daughter's reactions—to that daughter's relief.

"And thy father. Doth he talk to thee of it now?" she said with the same serious intentness.

"No, not since his sickness." Mary remembered the times she had tried to speak of it. Her father had waved his hand in dismissal. "Some other time, my girl, some other time."

"So—" Prudence murmured. She patted her daughter absentmindedly on her head and walked slowly out of the room with no further word, leaving Mary staring perplexedly after her.

That evening, just after they had climbed into bed. Prudence looked for a moment at the almost somber face of her husband, as if giving one final weighing to a decision she had already made. "Husband," she said hesitantly, and then more firmly. "How much money hath thou saved now?" Francis looked up, frowning, and then down at his hands, his shoulders sagging. Prudence would have liked to hold him in her arms and to caress his tired head. But, if she was right, the plan she was now pursuing would be better than any such comforting.

"Not above eight hundred pounds, I fear."

"'Tis a goodly sum, methinks," said Prudence, putting even more firmness and conviction in her voice.

"Not for my purposes." Francis's voice trailed off.

Prudence did not acknowledge she had heard this last. "As thou knowest, I have, from the will of my Uncle Fownes, the sum of six hundred pounds, which thou hast said I must keep for myself to do with as I please. I have now decided what I wouldst do with it, husband."

"Yes?" Francis looked up, trying to show some interest.

"'Twill serve to keep me and our family in Plymouth for a year or two whilst thou dost get settled in New England."

Francis stiffened. His face turned pale and then red as he struggled to contain the unaccustomed rage that welled up inside of him at what or whom he would have been unable to say. "There is not money enough. 'Tis too late." The rage and color disappeared and his shoulders drooped again.

Prudence's eyes lit up with the almost triumphant look of a physician whose diagnosis has been confirmed. From now on the conviction and determination in her voice were natural and no longer a resolute effort to convince herself as well as her husband.

"Too late—for what? To plant some great estate that thou hast dreamed of? But husband, must thou have all of the dream at once? Thou art yet alive—thanks be to the heavenly Father. Couldst thou not take what money thou hast and begin to plant? And might not the rest of your dream be passed on to thy children?" She saw the almost imperceptible lifting of his shoulders, and said more lightly—"dost think thou should be so selfish as to leave no portion of that dream for thy children?"

Briefly the old absent-minded look came into his eyes and he gave a long slow sigh. Then he turned toward his wife, a skeptical half smile on his face. "But dearest wife, what of the wolves thou hast been so afeared would make an end to us all?"

"Tush," said Prudence, her eyes widening only briefly. "I have had conversation with Mr. Edward Trelawney about these creatures and he says that while they be a deadly menace to such sheep and pigs as roam outside a fence, never a one hath attacked a man or even a little child. So 'twould seem, husband they are not so much a menace as the horses that do trample men, women, and small children in the streets of Plymouth."

"And the treacherous savages—hast forgot them, beloved?"

Prudence gulped twice. "Indeed I have not," she recovered quickly. "On this subject as well have I consulted friend Trelawney, and he—even as Mr.

Cleeve hath said—they give no harm to those who treat them well. And further sayeth they have been good and faithful friends to many." This last was said with less than complete conviction. And then suddenly—"Oh, my dearest husband, dost thou not know that nothing couldst seem more treacherous to me than that devil plague that hath almost taken thee from me forever? And since, so it hath been told me, there is none of that in New England, what are wolves and savages to me?" Francis took her in his arms, and there seemed naught else to say that night.

Later, as he lay awake while Prudence snored softly by his side, he smiled to himself at the thought of her goodness and wondered at the love that had made her push for an undertaking that he knew, despite her urgings, was completely alien to her. She was happy and at home in the familiar—improving little by little and in various ways what they had. Adventure, the new and unfamiliar, repelled her. It was, as it were, an attack on the order she had created and established. And yet, not only had she insisted on this adventure, he knew she would not even be happy if he refused to go. A feeling of amazed joy spread slowly through his body, intermingled with a faint wisp of regret. He would soon relinquish to reality that dream he had made and remade as it pleased him. And reality, he knew, with a brief twinge of panic is not so easily manipulated. But regret and panic were soon dispersed by a great assortment of descriptive phrases that crowded one after the other into his mind—in the very words and tones he had first read or heard them. And he slipped off into sleep remembering these words of John Smith. "Who can desire more content that hath small means, or but only his merit to advance his fortunes, than to tread and plant that ground he hath purchased by the hazard of his life, if he have but a taste of virtue and magnanimity, what to such a mind can be more pleasant than planting and building a foundation for his posterity, got from the rude earth by God's blessing and his own industry without prejudice to any."

In their discussion that night and in the days following neither Francis nor Prudence spoke of a time for his departure. It was accepted, though not specifically mentioned, that nothing would be undertaken until after the birth of the child Prudence was expecting the following February.

At first they told no one of this new decision. When the emotions of that night had subsided Prudence discovered she did not want to think of the inevitable leave-taking she had set in motion, while Francis found himself afraid to believe it would really take place. But so much like his old self had he become that the children and the servants could not help but notice and wonder. John and Margaret, visiting a week later, noticed too and wondered aloud what witchcraft Prudence had practiced on her husband to so perfectly restore him. Prudence shook her head in mock dismay, while Francis laughed.

"See wife, did I not tell thee what suspicions were likely to fall on thee?" He paused "Well dost think we should tell them?" Prudence nodded, smiling at the note of excitement he could not keep out of his voice.

So, with his eyes on his nephew's face—hoping to see in some expression how John reacted to his enterprise—Francis told him of what they had decided to do. But, good businessman that he was, John's face reflected only what he wanted it to—in this case pleasure. Admittedly it would have been difficult to have been other than pleased when confronted with the obvious delight and enthusiasm that Francis no longer even tried to suppress.

"Well," Francis added with as much question and hesitation as he was able, at this point, to get into his voice, "I warrant thou can but think I have slid into my dotage that durst adventure money, life and family in the wilderness at my age."

"Nay, Uncle!" John rejoined. "Nowise do I think such. Verily, many a man older than thou art hath set off to plant himself and his family in the New World. But, e'truth, I hope 'tis not your decision to set out on this venture straight away." Seeing Francis's questioning frown he hastened to add, "I would not have thee wait over long, Uncle, only mayhap, until the end of next year. Methinks thou could, by so doing, add a goodly sum to thy savings. Business still recovers from the plague year and will doubtless continue to improve, further now that Edward is soon off to London to marry and live, at least for a time, leaving Robert in much need of your services."

Francis nodded. The practical side of his mind could not but be in full agreement with his nephew, while the other side, being taken up with its renewed habit of dreaming and planning was not concerned with the practicalities of time. Prudence sighed her happy agreement with this suggestion that put off the day of her husband's departure to a more forgettable distance.

Later, as he walked home, the doubts and fears that John had ably suppressed while talking to his Uncle, returned to trouble his mind. A barely adequate supply of money and physical strength were detriments enough, but more troublesome than these was Francis's lack of experience or even real knowledge of life in the wilderness. John had grown up so much in his Uncle's company that he knew the kind of information Francis had got from the sailors and explorers he had talked to, and the mound of promotional literature he had read—much about climate and kinds of animal and plant life—almost nothing about methods of survival. Knowing all this and feeling, as he always had, even as a boy, especially fond and somehow protective of his Uncle, John was much distressed about what might befall him if he set out on this adventure, as he was now so obviously bent upon doing. At the same time, remembering the almost childlike excitement he had seen in his Uncle's eyes, he not only became more fearful for him but also realized he could never try to dissuade him.

That evening, half hoping he might get a more optimistic opinion, he expressed his doubts to his wife and to Edward, who was spending his last few weeks with them before leaving for London.

Edward, however, only confirmed his doubts. "'tis not his age that troubles me, John, or his ability to work, as a merchant. I have ofttimes found it hard to keep up with him. What he wants as a bargainer he doth make up for in the quickness and sureness of his eye in detecting value. Whilst others are yet examining the goods he hath already bought all the best. But, I fear me, he hath but little practice in the skills necessary to survive in the wilderness. He hath never been given to fowling, I believe, and but little to fishing. And 'tis sure he hath never been a farmer! Nor, methinks, will he have money enough to hire others to do these things for him."

Margaret looked perplexedly at her brother and then at her husband. "It doth puzzle me to hear all this dolorous talk of fowling and such like. If Uncle Martin is so good a trader as thou sayst, brother, why should he not work for Robert in New England as he hath here?"

"Dear sister, thou hast forgotten what I told thee of my experience there— of our brother's trusted agent—the taciturn and immovable John Winter." He hunched up his shoulders and narrowed his eyes in a brief reprise of his imitation of the man; ending with a wink at his sister. She forced a frown on her face, so she would not seem to have in any way lessened her disapproval of his, however brief, employment as an actor.

"Such jealousies hath this man of his position," Edward continued, "that, I warrant his suspicions do extend to everyone save his own family and mayhap to them too. I deem it no disparagement to say that your gentle Uncle is no match for a man like John Winter. Even such a bull as George Cleeve hath but barely kept him at bay."

"Nevertheless, Uncle shall be a trader." John's quick mind had already taken up a variation of this idea, examined and accepted it, and now he spoke with determination and finality. "He shall go into partnership with me."

"Of course, murmured Margaret," smiling.

"Even if we do not make our fortunes thereby I see no reason why we should not do well enough to provide a living for my Uncle and, mayhap, a small profit for me as well. And brother Edward, if fortune doth smile but a little, we might have a place in our enterprise for thee, if thou canst bring thy bride to think as you do." A wide smile of relief made his round face take on the look of boyish good spirits that had misled so many of his business rivals. He clasped his wife about the waist. "I should always bring my problems home to thee sweet Margaret."

Edward, less sanguine than John, wondered about the competition with his brother Robert. "Not in the way of troubling him, there is room for many more traders there, and I'm sure thou wilt receive his blessing and more advice than thou from him. But remember he hath all the advantages of money, ships and established trade. And—though I do mislike to bring it up again—he hath also John Winter who will hinder your business wherever he can. Mayhap he might spread a rumor of your Uncle's dishonesty to discourage anyone who thought to buy, sell or transport goods for him." Then, noticing the smile disappearing from John's face, he hastily repressed his doubts.

"Marry! Pay me no heed. Methinks I have got me so timid I wouldst find danger and discouragement lurking in my own shadow, Besides there is another side to this John Winter that you might make profit out of. He doth so over charge the settlers for the goods they have of him that he hath angered many, and some have even threatened to take him before the court. 'Twould seem that anyone selling goods for a fair price would soon have his business from him. But that's as may be. Risk there be in any enterprise and I would rather cast my lot with you and Francis Martin than any others I know."

That same day Francis gathered the children together and told them of his plans, bringing down upon his head a great mixed precipitation of tears and laughter. Mary went from tearful joy to preoccupied thoughtfulness. The frequent wrinkling of her brow indicating that this was indeed thoughtfulness and not dreaming.

The next day, as she helped her mother and Angela sort the clothes for the monthly wash, she tried to think of words to rightly speak of what she had been thinking constantly of since the day before. Then Prudence, herself, gave her the perfect opening. Looking at the pile of her husband's clothes—cloaks, doublets and hose, handkerchiefs, cuffs, neckcloths and more—she shook her head and sighed. "How thou should take care of thyself alone in the wilderness, I do not see."

At this, the words tumbled off Mary's tongue in a rush, like soldiers over ready to leap into battle at a long awaited signal. "I couldst take care of him—if thou wouldst let me go." This last was almost inaudible. She closed her eyes, waiting for the angry words to come, and opened them again when she heard the laughter. Her mother and Angela were both looking at her and laughing.

"We wondered how long it would take thee to ask that question," said Prudence, lightly kissing one of her daughter's very pink cheeks. "But dost think that thou—scarce more than a snippet of a girl and a dreamer withal—couldst take care of thy father's house and cook and sew for him?"

"Aye! I do." Mary tried to talk slowly and keep the eagerness out of her voice. "And I could plant a garden for our food. I learned much of that whilst we were staying at John and Margaret's cottage."

"Well Angela, what thinkest thou of this petitioner? Such uncommon virtues as she hath and ready to deprive her mother of them all." Prudence was only half smiling and Mary's face beginning to fall at the thought that she might have hurt her mother's feelings, when Angela's solid voice gave answer.

"Tush! Thou hast, methinks, six or eight virtuous hands to do thy bidding now, so 'twould scarce deprive thee to do thy husband so much good."

"Verily Angela, thou art right," Prudence said, putting her arm around her daughter. "Thy father will have more need of thee than I. 'Twould be selfish indeed of me to keep thee if he is willing for thee to go, and truth to tell, I wouldst feel better in my mind if thou wert with him." Francis had not need of persuading. The thought of having with him the daughter who shared his own excitement was a great happiness. He hesitated only long enough to make sure she had no dreamer's fantasy that this New England life would be easy.

When Francie, who had almost never thought about New England at all, heard that Mary was to go there with their father, she began to sulk and stamp about the house, declaring it unfair that she be left to languish (or words to that effect) in this smelly city while Mary went adventuring. After scolding her display of ill temper, Prudence allowed she could see no reason why Francie should not go too. If Mary and their father were willing to bear with such a pettish wench she might even, in her better moments, be a help and some company for Mary when their father was off trading.

Prudence later confided to Margaret another reason she had been so quick to agree to her daughters going off. She could not but think, she said—what with the younger sons of good families going in increasing number of late to the New World—that her daughters might have better prospects for marriage there. Especially since the late unfortunate expeditions against France, along with the plague, had so much reduced the population of young men hereabouts. Francis did not like to think of parting with his daughters so she did not talk of this with him. Howbeit a mother, if she had a daughter's good matching in mind could not fail to think on't. "As thou wilt discover all too soon Margaret," she sighed. "I mind me of your husband's friend—Mr. Michael Mitton—a most likely young gentleman. He hath married Mr. George Cleeve's daughter soon after he came to New England." She sighed once more.

The day before he left for London Edward Trelawney came over to bid them all farewell. Mary, as she had done several times before, slipped quietly upstairs when she saw him coming down the street. But this time, Edward insisting he would not go until he had spoken to her, seven-year-old Marjorie was sent to fetch her down.

As he watched her come down the stairs in her blue gown and apron, her head high, her eyes lowered, he thought with, to his surprise, a sudden pang of regret, how much a woman and how self-possessed she seemed, this girl he had been thinking of as an attractive child. She, feeling anything but self possessed, thought with a renewal of the pain she had assumed was over, how wise and self-assured he looked.

"I missed seeing you on several occasions these past months," he said. "But could not miss this chance to say farewell and tell thee how much I did enjoy our conversations in the country. Thou hast a wit as fair as thy face, Mistress Mary, though, mayhap, not so barbed as my sister Margaret's." At which Mary looked up and smiled.

"So," Edward returned her smile, "Thou art to get thy fondest wish. I am pleased for thee, and thou should know that my prayers go with thee and thy sister and excellent father for a safe journey and a godly and prosperous life to follow in that place where I have spent my happiest days. Now thou must needs wish me well in my adventure too. For marriage doth seem to me no less an adventure than that which thou dost embark upon."

Mary hearing his sigh, realized, with some surprise, that he was not so sure a master of himself as she had supposed and felt suddenly easier. "Of course I wish thee well," she said softly. And then, surprising herself, added boldly, "but I doubt there is much risk for you in your adventure."

Edward shook his head and laughed as he took his leave. "A maid who turns words so easily to her use hath her future well made already." So, lightly, they parted, though Mary found that her heart was not so light as her words had been, and Edward had need of more than one godly prayer to get his wayward feelings back in order.

The months did pass. And in the preparation for, and prompt arrival of, lusty Humphrey Martin, plans for the journey were set aside. Summer came and went, healthy that year of 1639 for bodies and businesses alike. And, with Robert Trelawney sent up to parliament from Plymouth, Francis's assistance was especially needed, so that, as John had predicted, he was able to set aside more money than usual. It was decided then, business continuing good and voyages, by all advice, unpleasant in the fall and winter months, to wait until spring before setting out for that part of New England that had, in April of 1639, been designated the "Province or County of Mayne."

In early fall a letter came from Edward with apologies for his too long delay in writing. It contained the lists he had promised Prudence he would send, lists of the provisions, clothes and other necessaries Francis and his daughters would need on their voyage and afterwards in getting settled.

"Above all," he advised, "take care to be warmly clothed. Do not let the spring air in England fool you. The open sea in springtime hath cold wet winds that will chill your very vitals if you art not well prepared. For your husband, at the least, one hat, one Monmouth cap, three falling bands, one suit of frieze, one waistcoat, three shirts, a suit of cloth and one of canvas, three pairs of Irish stockings, four pairs of shoes and a long coat against the storms at sea—and land as well. I know not enough of woman's dress to name in detail what your daughters should have, but like in numbers and warmth to their father's would do well. Withal, be sure they have some pattens to keep their shoes and gowns above the mud. New England paths are not yet besmirched with filth like English streets, but neither have they cobblestones against the mud."

"For beds at sea and afterwards—two pairs of canvas sheets, eleven ell of coarse canvas to be filled with straw or feathers and two rugs or heavy coverlets. Of victuals for a year, until next spring's planting hath ripened and father and daughters have got some skill in fishing and hunting, twenty bushels of Meal, five bushels of Peas, four bushels of Oatmeal, one gallon of Aquavit and a hogshead of beer. There be, as mayhap thou knowest already, naught else to drink at sea. Howbeit, in the Province of Maine 'tis quite otherwise. I warrant you shall find the water there as pure and clear to drink as any beer."

At which point Prudence exclaimed her disbelief and declared firmly that water, at its best might be good enough for the washing of clothes and bodies, but, for drinking "only if you durst adventure the price of a fever or worse."

Edward further advised: "two hogsheads of English beef, a kental of fish, two gallons of oil and three of vinegar, sugar, spice and fruits." There followed after this a long list of household implements and tools—such as pots, kettles, a mortar, platters, dishes and spoons of wood, shovels, axes, hammers and the like. "Carry with you as much in weight as you be allowed, for excepting such goods as are made or grown in New England, there will be shipping charges added to the goods that are purchased there, as well as usurious John Winter's profit!"

"Be sure to have at hand for your cooking at sea," he continued, "two or three skillets of several sizes, a large frying pan, a small stewing pan and a number of vessels for eating and drinking withal. 'Twould be well to have a gallon of scurvy grass to take a little of now and again with some salt peter mixed in it and a little grated or sliced nutmeg. But, methinks, Mistress Martin, you will have bethought thee of this already."

"And doubtless considerable more!" Francis winked at his daughters, while Prudence ignored him and sighing thought how many more lessons in cookery her daughters would need before they left.

"And not the least important," Edward finished, "line and hooks for fishing and two flintlock muskets with twenty pounds of shot or lead. And for instruction in the shooting of game, you could find no better teacher than brother John's friend Michael Mitton, who hath settled near the bay of Casco with his new wife Elizabeth, the daughter of George Cleeve."

Mary frowned and said, in a barely audible voice, "I did not like him."

"Tush, such a pleasant, well-made young gentleman." Prudence emphasized the last word.

Francis, remembering Begette, said quietly, "Are you still some'at blaming him for what happened that day?"

"No," Mary reddened, half regretting her hasty remark, half in frustration at the difficulty she was having in naming what it was she did not like about this man. "'Twas how he did speak—it did seem—his words," she hesitated, "He spake prettily enough—but—methinks…" She finished in an embarrassed rush. "Methinks he did not mean any of the words he did speak."

Prudence sniffed. In her opinion that was a trivial objection. "I'm sure he did but try to be civil and obliging. Thou hast little knowledge of conversation amongst gentlemen and ladies in social gatherings."

"Indeed." Francis's eyebrows rose while his voice took on an ironical tone. "'Tis surely overmuch to expect that ladies and gentlemen should mean the words that they speak or worse, speak words of some meaning. Such finical requirements would surely put an end to all conversing in society."

Prudence dismissed her husband's words with a casual. "Humph," as she did most of the remarks he made in that tone.

Mary succeeded in holding her tongue but not her thoughts—'Cousin Edward is not like that,' slipped in, followed by 'nor Mr. Cleeve either!' Which last amused her so much that she chuckled softly, causing her father to assume, with pleasure, that she had detected and understood his irony.

Having now become, with the advent of Edward's letter, immersed in preparations for the journey, they all found the days had seemingly grown much shorter. Amidst the daily work of this household of eleven (counting the four servants—Angela, her husband Fred and their son and his wife) all the mending and ordering, gathering together, the making and checking of lists and packing of boxes must go on. Neither laughter nor quick tempers were in short supply.

John and Francis made plans for their small trading venture. What effect it would have, if any, on this venture John didn't know, but recently Robert Trelawney had been getting a number of complaints from those working at Richmond's Island. There were complaints about milk and beef rations being meager and about the beating of a servant girl by Winter's wife. So far, John told Francis, Winter had been able to answer the charges to Robert's satisfaction, and he remained, as he had contrived to be, indispensable.

Certainly he was in the continuing agitation over the two parcels of land claimed by George Cleeve and Thomas Cammock that Winter had convinced Robert were part of his patent. But at least, John said, Edward's accusations could not now sound so impossible, and Robert would perhaps think somewhat better of his youngest brother.

In December 1639 it was decided that the voyage would be made on one of the Trelawney ships, the *Star*, with Narias Hawkins master. It was scheduled to be loaded with goods and ready to leave sometime before the end of March. A sturdy well made merchant ship, the *Star* was like her sister ships the *Mayflower* and the *Arabella* that had successfully carried Pilgrims and Puritans, respectively to New England. It was about 250 tons burthen and able to carry somewhat in excess of 75 people without too much crowding. Compared to ships built some 300 years later, capable of carrying upwards of 1500 passengers in luxurious style, it seems as fragile and unstable as the paper boats that small children launch in ponds and streams and the passengers possessed of more temerity than sense in trusting themselves to such as these. But the vast and protean sea quickly reduces all such comparisons to absurdity, and twenty first century ships are seen to be only somewhat larger specks on that great encircling expanse of sea and sky.

With the coming of March, Prudence became increasingly busy and officious and Mary and Francie found themselves given to hugging whatever small brother or sister they came in contact with. Francis, in addition to a natural reluctance to part from over one half of his family, discovered a strong feeling for his native shores.

By the second week in March all the clothes the three travelers were not wearing, as well as the necessary provisions and tools were stored in the small spaces allotted to them. Mary and Francie shared one narrow bunk and Francis had another. Their bit of privacy was obtained by means of a blanket laid over a rope at the top. But so narrow were these 'cabins' that, with two people in one, they had to sleep feet to head.

The next two weeks were spent watching for a favorable wind, which kept the voyagers in a constant state of anxiety, impatient to go and reluctant to leave. At one point Francie heard that not above a year before the *Bonnie Bess*, a merchant ship—like theirs bound for New England—had been taken by Turkish pirates. She was ready to get off and stay at home, an inclination which the rocking of the boat and the answering roll of her stomach did nothing to abate. But she soon reluctantly thought better of it, not wanting Mary to be thought stronger or braver than she.

On a rare visit to the ship Margaret brought Mary a small box fitted out with writing paper, ink and pens. "By this means," she said, "your mother and I can keep close to thee and share whatever befalls. I know Uncle Martin will write, but you can be a second, different eye to see and tell us of the things he misses or tells too little of." She took Mary's hand and pressed it gently. "Goodbye, sweet cousin. I hope and fear you will be gone before I can come again. You will be daily in my prayers. May I be in yours." She stared beyond the deck at the familiar shapes of Plymouth buildings on one side, on the other the distant and empty horizon, and sighed. "Sometimes, cousin, with the rumors of Civil War growing ever louder and the plague, so it seems, scarce away before it comes again, methinks thy risky seeming enterprise doth often look the safest course."

They stood staring at each other in that awkward silence of leave-taking. "I never dreamed," Mary said softly, her eyes brimming, "how it would be to leave." She felt a cold wave of apprehension flood her mind. What else had she not dreamed?

Later Prudence, after rearranging her daughters' clothes, trunk, mattress and cooking utensils several times in a space which allowed only one possible arrangement, shaking her head and talking disconnectedly to herself the while about the unpleasantness of floors that never stayed still, of cooking on the deck in the wind, of she or anyone managing under such circumstances, raised her head and looked at her daughters in their bright colored gowns, each daintily set off by a white lace edged cap, fall and cuffs. They were both standing awkwardly stiff in their effort not to dissolve in tears again. Young gentlewomen, there could be no doubt of that, she thought, with an upsurge of pride that calmed the tailor's daughter who knew very well how nebulous but absolute was the distinction between gentlewoman and simply maid.

In a voice, steady now, with its usual firm tone returned, she said, "Thou must never forget that thou art the daughters of Francis Martin, gentleman and respected merchant, and that thy Uncle and thy Grandfather were both mayors of Plymouth."

This was the afternoon of March 29, 1640. The next morning, being favored by fine weather and a fair wind, the Star put up its sail and soon left Plymouth Harbour far behind.

Chapter Four

The moods of nature at sea are surely no more capricious or inexorable than those she exhibits on land. Our feeling that they are is probably an effect of the great scale on which they are played out, great at least as seen from the point of view of the players. Then, of course, there is no refuge. Although—as we all come finally to discover—there is no escape from nature anywhere. There are, on land, so many temporary shelters contributed by nature herself as well as man, that we are able to avoid some of her moods and preserve our emotional assurance of invulnerability—that is until that nature within ourselves finally catches up with us. But, even on a quiet uneventful voyage, the sea, and the sky, her companion in all her moods, surround and contain all there is. They are the visible world. Only the mentally and spiritually dead could remain unmoved and unchanged by the simple power of their presence.

The *Star*, reflecting the vagaries of the sea on this crossing—sometimes rolling and tossing, other times remaining motionless for days—moved, nevertheless like the rest of the world through the weeks of time if only erratically forward through the space, and sometimes, as it were, sidling toward the coast of New England. It was, in other words, an unremarkable voyage, by seaman's standards at any rate. To the Martins, of course, it seemed quite otherwise.

The good wind that had carried them away from Plymouth Harbor held for almost three days and then slipped quietly away during the night, leaving the ship marooned for two days, as incapable of purposeful motion as a drifting log, flotsam of the shore, pushed about by the sea, by tides and an occasional breeze.

Writing of these and subsequent days of the voyage to her Mother and Margaret, Mary saw but did not register in her mind the unremarkable facts she recorded. Her imagination was at its usual business of transmuting the world and, unlike her father's, her imagination knew no restraints. It soared and dipped as unmindful of the distance from solid earth as the flocks of birds that now and again appeared overhead, hundreds of miles from any shore. These same birds became as much creatures of her imagination as, at another time a poet's skylark became for him. They seemed like her own spirit, moving with effortless joy into the unknown. So a dove that landed on the deck and was found there dead the next day she mourned, for its own ended flight, but somehow for herself as well. Her mind, like the depths of the ocean, seemed to contain a limitless number of things she had not fathomed, and that rose as suddenly to amaze her as the great whale that appeared on the surface of the sea one afternoon, calmly spouting water as they passed not above thirty feet from its glistening back. What wonders there were in the sea—and if in the sea how much more so in the human soul? The sea, ever changing, yet remained the sea. Was the soul thus also? What possibilities for good or evil swam below in this constant changing. She trembled. How much control could one have over this changeless changing? Fear and hope edged their way up together in her mind, and lay there unresolved.

After two days of calm, a light wind arose and gradually increased during the night as did the heaving and tossing of the ship, causing many of the passengers, among them Francis and Francie, to take themselves moaning to their beds. Mary, to her great surprise and pleasure, felt only a brief discomfort which quickly passed, leaving her feeling better than before—actually invigorated. Doubtless this sense of well-being resulted from pride at her own sea worthiness. But the fresh air and even the fine salt spray, cold as it was, had much to do with it. She pulled her heavy cloak and hood tightly about her and stayed on deck, dreading the periodic trips she had to make below where the air was heavy with the smell and sound of sickness, and, even worse, the strident cries of the cattle tossed helplessly about in the hold. She emptied the slop pails and tried to give some comfort, particularly to Francie who, having suffered hardly at all from any sickness in her young life, was now convinced that she was about to die, and with so many sins on her soul that she was sure to be dispatched at once into the hot unfriendly arms of the devil. Having been assured by the captain and several members of the crew that the malady from which her father and sister suffered was almost never fatal, Mary tried to convince Francie to no avail. Their father—though sicker than Francie—assured Mary that, having survived the plague, he was not too concerned about an "uneasy stomach." He was, however, much chagrined that he had missed even a few days of this long awaited voyage—most especially the sight of the spouting whale! However, after several trips below, Mary noticed that they both seemed to find her healthy reassurances more annoying than comforting, and so she went down less frequently, not without some brief feelings of guilt. Might not the annoyance she detected be her own at having to go down at all? The godly habit of minute self examination, though it had been less exercised of late, had not deserted her.

After a day and a half of moderately heavy wind, clouds moved in, covering the visible sky. This was followed by a sharp rise in the wind, and, except for Mary, the passengers, not already below, went there at the Captain's orders. Because of the noise of the storm, or perhaps her old habit of shutting out the world around her, Mary had not heard the orders, and in the darkness of the storm, she was not noticed where she stood against the rail.

The wind grew higher and with it came rain that snapped sharply against the sails. The topsail was taken in and the mainsail furled, but the force of the wind was so great that the foresail suddenly split and was torn to pieces. Through all this Mary stood, her hands gripping the rail, feeling the roar of the wind surrounding her. And, occasionally, in a lull, the sound if not the content of a shouted order entered her consciousness. She felt no fear at all, only, and strangely, considering the cold, a kind of physical pleasure in the buffeting of the storm. She raised her head and the wind and the rain slapped at her face and dragged her hair from under her hood. She could feel the fingers of water running along her back and neck. Slowly a sense of power surged up inside her and with it a thought that reverberated in her mind like the tolling of a bell: "I am one of God's chosen, one of the chosen of God. I am saved!"

How long she stood there she could not later remember. What she did remember was a sudden consciousness of quiet—both wind and rain had ceased. She had barely time to register this abrupt change when a towering curve of water smashed down on the deck almost exactly where she was standing. It wrenched her hands from the railing and tossed her like a limp mass of sea weed against the main mast, and would surely have carried her along as it rolled heavily on, back to the sea from whence it came, just as it carried off a barrel of watering fish that stood in its path, had something not caught her gown and held it tightly.

Still gasping, partly for air and partly from a terror that kept her heart pounding, she shook the water from her eyes and stared up into the scowling face of Captain Hawkins.

Narias Hawkins was a tall broad-shouldered man with the dark weathered skin of his occupation. He had thick black eyebrows above small deep set eyes, barely visible when he was frowning, which was most of the time from the effect of bright sunlight or the effort of thought. The heavy set of his features made his unconscious frown look like an acceptable piratical scowl, and Francie had confided to her sister, with a shiver, that he did indeed look like such a one. Which comment, being overheard and reaching the Captain's ears, someway pleased him and caused him to make a special pet of the pretty and pert ten-year-old Francie. But what Mary found most remarkable was the difference between Narias Hawkins on land and Captain Hawkins on board ship.

On land he walked with his head slightly lowered and with somewhat of a stoop to his shoulders. There was almost a hesitant timidity in his "If it do please your worship," and "If your worship would be so kind," that he used to address any gentleman present but most especially his employer, Robert Trelawney. However, aboard ship, with the stoop gone and his head up, he became a visibly sharp and capable seaman watchful for the welfare of his ship, crew, cargo and passengers—as it appeared—in that order. He was sometimes given to colorful bursts of temper, but never a fawning word. One could only think that Captain Narias Hawkins was a man most unusually mindful of the correct order of things on land as well as at sea.

Now his whole face was contorted with anger. He jerked Mary to her feet and shouted, "'Sblood! Thou knotty-pated, clay-brained wench. Wouldst thou ride the waves to Neptune's bed? or more like into the warm belly of a passing shark? Get thee below. 'tis enough we have to do up here without keeping watch on the antics of silly wenches. And thou canst tell thy merchant father I have said it."

Mary, hardly knowing whether she was pushed or got there on her own, went below and sank down on her knees by the small cabin space against the wall where she and Francie slept. Her brain had scarcely registered Captain Hawkins words. It was too full, overwhelmed with what she accepted as the swift and almost fatal punishment for her overweening pride—her easy and weak acceptance of what could only have been a temptation of the devil. How could she, who had been reluctant to perform even such small good works as seeing to an ailing father and sister, and whose prayers had lately become no more than careless exercises, think the Lord had singled her out for blessedness? She writhed and shivered in her wet clothes. The cold that had been invigorating now numbed her body and spirit until she collapsed and fell asleep there on the floor.

It was a tribute to her young and healthy constitution that when she awoke in the morning, still damp and cold, the only ill effects she felt were some aches about her body and her spirit as well. She was grateful and somewhat encouraged by what she firmly believed to be a reprieve from death granted by God through the agency of Captain Hawkins. And, thinking of him, she was further embarrassed by her earthly pride in her seaworthiness. True she was only a silly wench, interrupting him in his struggle to save the ship. Even had she known that the ship was not in such desperate straits as she supposed, the principle and her feelings about it would have been much the same.

The wind by then had died down somewhat, and a warm sun emerging from behind the fast disappearing clouds soon dried off the deck and sails and raised the spirits of the crew and passengers alike. Despite the tossing they had received in the hold, only one of the heifers had died, and that one was to provide some welcome fresh meat for passengers and crew. Mary, remembering the terror stricken animal cries she had heard during the storm, could not accept the proffered chunk of red meat—pleading a still uneasy stomach.

The Captain "suggested"—his mildest suggestions having the tone of an order—that exercise on the deck might effect a cure for those passengers still sick below. So Francis willingly and Francie reluctantly were fetched up and instructed to hold on to a rope the Captain had ordered stretched from the rudder to the mainmast. Thus, looking like a wobbly company of mountain climbers, they swayed, stumbled, then walked up and down until they were warm. And, sooner than they would have believed possible, felt quite themselves again. In fact Francie became as bright and merry as she had been dull and sullen but a few hours before. She beset the Captain and crew with questions, which they good-naturedly answered—causing Mary to suffer more pangs of embarrassment remembering now, explicitly, the words that she had caused the Captain to spew forth. And, not wanting her father to hear those words from the Captain, she told him of the mishap she had brought on herself and of Captain Hawkins' rescue, omitting only her illusion of blessedness and the Captain's colorful language.

A quick look of fear crossed Francis's face. Death was common enough in seventeenth century families to be regarded with a certain fatalism, if not with any more acceptance than has ever been the case. But Mary, with whom he felt a closeness of spirit that he felt with no one else—even her mother— had always such a full bloom of health that he had never thought of her in relation to death. But now Francis held his daughter close and she, seeing the sudden pallor of his face and having no trouble understanding it, wept.

Later they went together to thank the Captain—which Mary admitted she had not done. And he, his temper as much improved as the weather, gave Mary and her father a rare smile. "'Twas foolhardy right enough. But, withal, thou be not a weak and whiny sort Mistress Martin." The note of admiration in his voice brought a flush of pleasure to Mary's face and a slight frown to Francie's.

For the rest of the voyage, although there was more rough weather, there was no more sickness nor very high winds. Francie, who had sighed fretfully after the first two days at sea and declared, with all the wisdom of ten long years of living, that there never had been in the world anything so dull as a sea voyage, now, having become the pet of the crew as well as the Captain, was kept alternately laughing and pleasantly frightened by their tales of pirates and shipwrecks and confided to Mary that had she been a boy she would surely have gone to sea.

Mary had taken up her neglected bible reading again and tried to send out ordered thoughts in her morning and evening prayers. She also tried to keep control of her thoughts at other times. Her dreaming, she decided, offered the devil easy access to her mind and she hoped to thwart him from now on. If she could not be one of God's chosen, she at least would not join the devil's company. She began to prize strength of mind and could not help envying her father, Edward and her Uncle John the opportunity they had had to strengthen and train their minds at the University. And she missed Margaret's quiet presence and easy conversation that made duty and virtue seem attractive. She could not talk of religion to her father. He was a member of the Church of England but wore his beliefs lightly. If he saw little to criticize in the godly people, it was not in his nature to understand their need to break from the practices of the mother church. But the two did have their long shared habit of imagining this land they were now approaching and it was enough.

Later that week, on the third morning of unrelenting fog, Captain Hawkins was standing at the rail with Francie at his side—he listening for possible sounds of land close by, she staring fixedly at a spot where a diffused circle of light, presumably the sun was just visible.

"'Tis said," Captain Hawkins broke their silence, "such fog be the spirits of them as died at sea with never a holy word to guide them on their way. Doomed they are to drift so from ship to ship in search of an innocent soul to pray them to their final rest. And some sayeth more. If any there be aboard who durst curse the fog the spirits, in revenge, casteth ship and all upon the rocks!"

Francie's eyes widened and she shivered slightly as a cold wisp of fog touched her cheek. But she had heard too many stories in the past weeks to be really frightened. Suddenly her nostrils flared and she lifted her head and drew in a long breath—"Oh Captain, dost smell it? 'tis like to my mother's flower garden!"

Soon most of the passengers were judiciously sniffing and exclaiming, and the Captain had redoubled his careful listening for land sounds. Happily, by midday, the fog, and with it the general apathy, had finally lifted and blown away. To the east and two or three leagues distant, to the Captain's relief, they could make out the rising hills of the mainland and in front of these many small islands.

Mary and her father stood hand in hand on the deck, smiling first at each other and then at the outlines of land. They passed the island the French called Mt. Desert before the fog lifted, according to Captain Hawkins, and should make their port at Richmond's Island before dawn the next morning.

All three Martins were up and on deck long before the sun rose, illuminating a cloudless blue sky. And with the sun the land as well rose into sight. Close at hand now details of trees and distant fields took shape. And then they were not one half mile from the main land and coming in plain sight of Richmond's Island, a small island about three miles in circumference. Now the faint odor Francie had noticed the day before was heavy and all around them, recognizable as the sweet smell of wild June strawberries intermingled and occasionally overborne by the sharp scent of pine.

The Martins looked at the approaching landscape with rising excitement as the shallop carried them ashore. Each in their own way absorbing the beauty that surrounded them.

Mary smiled to hear the birds singing and to see some of them dipping and gliding in and out among the trees with bits of grass or sticks hanging from their beaks. Several goats and two kids, in an elevated stretch of field, kicked up their heels in a surfeit of energy that echoed her own. Further off she noticed a cow with its head almost buried in a patch of tall grass. And, coming out of a house that stood on the highest part of the island, patches of red yellow and blue running and waving. A feeling of exuberant life communicated itself to her even in the air she found herself breathing in slow deep breaths in the same way that she might have rolled some new and delightful taste slowly around on her tongue.

Francis took note of the tall heavy-trunked trees on every side, raw material for uncountable numbers of houses, ships and hearth fires—and of fish jumping in the sea around them, a stream of fresh clear water emerging from the woods on the island, and thickly grassed fields that bespoke fertility.

As for Francie she could almost feel the soft white beach sand under her bare feet and the shallow water lapping at her ankles. She saw the shady woods where a hot sun would hardly penetrate and the open spaces where the taste of berries could not be far from the smell.

They murmured "how beautiful" to each other and were happily content in their agreement.

Chapter Five

When she first set foot on shore Mary lost her balance and almost fell to her knees so unused had she become to motionless ground. The picture flashed in her mind of the sailor returned from captivity, on his knees kissing the English cobblestones and she recognized a similar urge in herself to make some gesture to this soil. So much had she lived in her dream of New England that it seemed more like a return than a first coming. But regaining her balance, she only laughed in some embarrassment at her awkwardness, and then with her father and Francie, similarly afflicted, proceeded shakily across the beach. The men and one or two young women who had come down to meet the boat paid them little attention, being intent on the possible arrival of long awaited letters or supplies—tools, clothing and, of course, aquavit. One plump young woman about Mary's age, her cap askew and her cheeks quite red from running, did smile shyly when she saw Mary and Francie looking at her, but then she too turned her attention anxiously toward the boat.

A well-worn path led from the beach across two low grass-covered rises to a high one where a large thatch-roofed frame building stood. A man and a woman came down the path toward them. Mary smiled to herself as she immediately recognized John Winter. Edward Trelawney, slight and rather elegant looking, had yet given an amazingly accurate impression of this barrel-chested man, with his large round head and almost invisible neck. His coarse grey hair, somewhat shorter than Francis's shoulder length locks, was the only indication of his age. As Edward had noted his face gave no more clue to the sixty years he had worn it than it did to his thoughts and emotions. His wife, Joanna, however, showed her fifty years plainly in her face. The combination of a short temper and near sightedness had etched lines of her age and personality there.

It is probable that John Winter and his wife had begun their lives in Devon, the children of poor working class parents, like the majority of seventeenth century Englishmen. But at fifteen he had managed to escape to the sea, if escape it could be called with the abominable food, hard work and low pay that were a constant part of the seafaring life, in addition to the dangers from pirates and the sea itself. But while the rest of the crew blocked out the misery of their existence with drunkenness and brawling John Winter taught himself to read, write, and keep accounts with the help of the ship's captain, who counted on him to keep watch on the cargo—especially the casks of aqua vitae—and the crew. He had no friends. The rest of the crew didn't know what he told the Captain, but they did not trust this sharp-eyed, ambitious boy, and he had only scorn for them.

His wife had been apprenticed at twelve into a family of a prosperous merchant. She also worked hard, but of necessity, to avoid the lash, and her scorn was not for her fellow servants, but for the silk and beribboned women of the upper class who did nothing so far as she could see but clatter about on their pattens just above the filth of the streets, perfumed handkerchiefs against their sensitive noses.

John and Johanna had met and married when he was twenty and she nineteen. By that time he was a master's mate on one of Robert Trelawney's ships and rose in due course to master and then Captain of Trelawney ships that sailed out every year on fishing and trading voyages to New Foundland and the coast of New England. He and his wife and their son and two daughters, if not well-to-do, were by reason of the hard work and frugality of both parents, never in want. He was easily the most trusted and most frequently employed of Robert Trelawney's sea captains, and in the ordinary course of events could have expected no more than this. But then in 1632, when Thomas Cammock, friend of Trelawney and holder of a patent on the New England land next to Trelawney's newly acquired land was unable to take official possession of it for his friend or to manage it along with his own, as they had talked of, John Winter, being there at the time, took over both jobs. It was a lucky chance, but one he was ready for. George Cleeve and others soon discovered he was a good friend only where it was in his interest to be so, and that nature or circumstances had given him a devious stubbornness and patient tenacity that made him a dangerous enemy where he saw or imagined his interests jeopardized. He had also a calm willingness to lie—or perhaps to believe whatever it best suited him to believe

By way of introducing himself and his daughters, Francis handed Winter the letter he had brought from Robert Trelawney. And, after reading it through slowly, he replied in a tone of voice that could best be described as one of compliant disinterest:

"As Mr. Trelawney hath said then, you are to stay here with us until you settle on some land within his patent and have built a house upon it. And I am to help you in it."

Mistress Winter's back stiffened as her husband spoke, and her jaw visibly set in a look, in her case, of most uncompliant interest—as well it might be considering the upwards of sixty men she and one of her daughters and, at the moment, one maid servant were expected to cook for and clean up after.

"'Tis no inn here with fancy rooms and ladies maids," she said firmly. "We have little enough, and all must help in the getting of it."

Francis only smiled and assured her that after better than two months of ship's food and lodgings—which were as she surely knew, none of the best—any corner she could find for them would more than suffice. And, as for work, they had been idle too long, and needed to get used to the work that would be necessary when they were settled on their own land. Mary nodded, but Francie shifted uneasily at this unpleasant contradiction of her own inclinations.

Mistress Winter's nostrils flared as she looked at Mary and Francie in their fine cloaks and gowns, but she said nothing, nor did Francis, though he understood her look well enough.

The house to which they then proceeded had been described with some pride by John Winter in a letter to his employer, written in 1634 when it was first built.

"It is forty foot in length and eighteen foot broad, besides the chimney," he had written. "And the chimney is large with an oven in each end of him, so large that we can brew and bake and boil our kettle at once in him. And we have another house that I have built under the side of this house where we set our sieves and mill and mortar to break our corn and malt and to dress our meal in. There are two chambers in our upper house and all our men lie in one of them, and every man hath his close boarded cabin. And in the other chambers I have room enough to put the ships sails into and all our dry goods which is in Casks and I have a store house in him that will hold eighteen or twenty of casks. And underneath I have a kitchen for our men to eat and drink in and a steward room that will hold two tonnes of Casks which we put our bread and beer into. And every one of these rooms are closed with locks and keys unto them." Admittedly John Winter's style was something less than elegant, but it did have, at least, a compensating eloquence of detail.

What he did not note—although when the house was built in that exposed location he had considered it important for their protection—was that from the front windows could be seen the shores of the mainland or the "mayne" as it was called, and the sand bar that connected it to Richmond's Island, and from the back the entrance of the little harbor where the *Star* lay anchored. The eastern end of the island and the raised wooden stages on which the fish were laid to dry could also be seen from the house. This was of particular concern since the first year Trelawney owned the land, fishermen from Massachusetts, caring little for patents of ownership on places they were accustomed to use, carried off the stages in a gesture of defiance that Winter made sure was never repeated.

The accommodations, as Joanna Winter had warned, were not luxurious. In fact having been built by seafaring men they were not much different from the ones the Martins had just left. Francis's bunk was somewhat bigger, but such luxury as there was Prudence had supplied with a few pillows she slipped into his luggage. The girls shared the room where the ships' sails and dry goods were stored with the Winter's youngest daughter, Sarah, who was a year or two older than Mary, and Priscilla Bickford, the shy maid servant they had seen on the beach. They did manage to arrange the sails and casks of dry goods so that the large room was separated into three smaller ones. This was Sarah's idea, as she told Mary and Francie in a rare moment of communication. She did not appear to be shy, just quiet and wary and, like her father, little given to casual talk. She also shared his sturdy build and plain, scarcely mobile features. This arrangement of the room was necessary, she explained, to keep Priscilla from them—she being such a sluttish wench, very often not even bothering to take off her dusty clothes before she fell onto her straw mattress.

That she was simply exhausted, either did not occur to Sarah, or if it did, seemed no excuse. Although she too worked hard, she was not called out so early or kept working as late as Priscilla was—and Mary and Francie as well, as they found out soon enough.

Priscilla's term of three years was up and she had only to stay on until a new girl could be found. Then she was going—back to her home in England, poor as it was. "This Province of Maine is a hateful, lonely place," she assured them, her eyes filling with tears. She was very often on the verge of tears. Francie was too annoyed by her weepy sniffling to pay any attention to her opinions. Mary, however, attracted by her bumbling good nature, quickly developed an amused affection for her. Recognizing her weaknesses—of a kind that would most annoy the Winters—she understood what a very hard time she must have had in her three years working for them. Winters—a fitting name indeed! She grimaced, but also put little stock in Priscilla's opinions. She was in no mood to find fault with this place.

Mistress Winter was no less anxious for her removal than Priscilla herself. With all the work there was to be done a clumsy and unwilling servant often seemed worse than none at all. She plainly thought little of the possibility that the gentlewomen, as she scornfully thought of them, could be of much use. But there were two of them and they could hardly be of less use than Priscilla. So Priscilla was given permission to leave with the *Star*, probably in July, when Captain Hawkins hoped to have her loaded with dry fish, pipe staves and whatever furs they had been able to buy from the Indians. Until then Mary and Francie were told to work with her and learn the jobs they would soon be responsible for.

So they must needs get up with her—sometimes even before the early rising June sun was up—since at the first low tide the cattle must be taken across the sand bar to graze in the fields on the mayne. The first time they were hardly awake—a matter the chill morning air and the cold water lapping over their bare feet soon took care of. Overhead, terns split the silence with their screeching and the invisible air with their arrowed bodies as they dove for fish. On the beach the plovers padded fussily in the wet sand in the wake of the outgoing waves. And soon the sun slipping abruptly over the horizon and along the surface of the water began to warm them. It was a sumptuous feast. A feast that was better than dreaming, and Mary felt her spirit expanding in it.

On the other side of the long white beach, where the sand bar ended, was the house that George Cleeve had built and had been driven from when John Winter took possession of the land for Robert Trelawney. Behind the house was a four or five acre corn field protected by a tall pole fence from bears and the cattle that grazed in the surrounding field. They could hear the sound of the men already at work on the other side of the fence.

Then and until the time of the next low tide, when they went to fetch the cattle back, out of reach of the night marauding wolves, they found time to fill their mouths and their apron pockets with wild strawberries, while blue jays squawked and squirrels chattered their disapproval. Those were happy times. In between they helped to milk the goats and cows, fetch wood to carry back to the island for the kitchen fire and empty the slop pails. This last Francie would have refused had Mary not dragged her to it.

"Mother hath said to remember we be daughters of Francis Martin," Francie hissed. "And I cannot think you will find the slop pails any hindrance to your remembering."

Mary snapped back, as much to herself as to her sister. "Or" she added, "if you should find them so, this and other grubby work will leave you little time for remembering when we have our own house." Francie flounced off, pail in hand, while Mary suppressed a laugh and murmured to herself—"Here, methinks, such pride will fetch naught but starvation," and then smiled again in brief surprise at the pragmatic turn her mind had suddenly taken.

Companionship and the small feelings of importance that came from showing the two young gentlewomen how her work was done made Priscilla's face fairly beam with grateful pleasure. And, once shy and hesitant in speech, she now began to chatter, and regaled them with all the stories, gossip and complaints she had stored up.

"There beant no 'un about with me since Phebe Thomson hath drowned," she explained, as they crossed over to the mayne one morning before the last of the stars left the sky. She brushed away the tears that briefly filled her eyes. "She were coming over the bar after the cows, and very little water on't—not above a few inches—but her hat blowing off from her head and she trying to save it she slipped off in to the deeper water. And albeit I did shout and many of the company ran with all speed to save her, she were dead afore they could come to her. Everyone were hard taken by that—she was so much liked—most especially by me. She were the only friend I had, and she hath helped me so much Mistress almost never took after me while she were here." Her eyes filling with tears again she stumbled and would have fallen into the water herself if Mary hadn't grabbed her arm.

She told them also, and not without some perhaps pardonable pleasure, about the young minister Sarah Winter had pursued until he married a young woman from Saco. "She be after another minister now—Mr. Robert Jordan, who hath as sour a face as she hath, so 'twould seem they 'ud make a goodly pair," Priscilla giggled.

Of her own troubles, told at some length, the worst by her own reckoning— beyond the loneliness, and as unavoidable, given her own ineptitudes and Mistress Winter's short temper—had been the frequent whippings that had caused her, she said, to go ameeching in the woods. Once when she could not find one of the heifers and feared a whipping—which she got anyway, and a worse one when they found her but not the heifer. Another time after two whippings in as many days.

"But the wolves and bears?" Mary and Francie both shuddered.

Priscilla shuddered, too. "I were so distracted that I didna think on wolves and bears or ought else 'til I were well into the woods and lost, and then I were so frighted that when one of the men who were looking for me came sudden out from behind a tree I fainted."

"After that time some of men on the island wrote to Mister Robert Trelawney about the whippings and to tell him how little milk and meat Mistress Winter did give them—keeping overmuch to sell. Since then, Priscilla said she had threatened whippings more often than she had given them.

It could scarcely be doubted that Priscilla had some capacities that could have ignited a much less volatile temper than Mistress Winter's. Still her story of hard work, loneliness and whippings was more typical than Mary, or Priscilla herself, had any way of knowing. So though Mary was troubled by it and railed to herself and somewhat to her father about Mistress Winter's hardness of heart, it seemed remote enough from her own circumstances so that she was not disheartened by it. In fact her spirits continued to rise, especially when she thought of their own land somewhere not far beyond the trees that lined the shore. Moreover, and much to her satisfaction, she and even the reluctant Francie, could soon do all of Priscilla's jobs as ably as and faster than she could do them. So it was, well before the bright and breezy morning in July when Priscilla made her tearful farewell and Mistress Winter proved she could smile.

The mastery of their jobs did not mean that Mary had gotten over her habit of dreaming altogether. It had slipped back upon her again amidst the tedious rounds of milking, grinding and fetching despite her solemn resolve aboard ship. Nor did it mean that Francie had never sneaked off to talk to Captain Hawkins or to lie for a moment in a mossy spot under the pines. And it was these lapses, Mary noticed, rather than their hard work that Mistress Winter's eyes seemed adjusted to see.

Francis Martin had somewhat less to be satisfied about. Farming and fishing were not so easy or so quickly mastered as he had assumed when he thought about it at all. He had no longer the strength of his youth, even less since his battle with the plague, a strength that could have made up for what he lacked in experience. The days spent digging and planting or hauling in fish, though not without their pleasures, especially the latter, left him aching and exhausted, barely able to eat. If the thought came into his mind that the youth he had spent was more valuable than the money he had saved over the long years, he pushed it resolutely out again. After all, he was, by long practice a merchant not a farmer, and the sooner he could get himself back in the business of trading again the sooner he would be able to hire a servant to do this other work.

So, it was with the business of trading in mind, in particular the possibility of getting local opinions and advice about it, that Francis went, late in June, to the session of the general court about eight miles south of Richmond's Island in the town of Saco. It was at these court sessions, Edward Trelawney had told him, that the influential as well as the common people of the province gathered two or three times a year for the joint and mutually enhancing purposes of business and social exchange.

He made an agreeable journey by water in the boat of Thomas Cammock, of nearby Black Point, and his friend Henry Jocelyn and their two servants. The only other means of travel was by foot, since only farm carts and no coaches nor animals to draw them were yet available in the province, nor, if they had been were there any roads to run them on. Foot travelers walked along the beaches where they could and, only when it was unavoidable, through the woods where one might easily lose ones way or meet up with wolves who were feared because their appetite for sheep, goats and pigs might easily be extended, or Indians who were mistrusted because they had so often been cheated.

Cammock and Jocelyn were amusing and cultivated men—a welcome change from Winter's taciturn preoccupation with business. Cammock could even laugh, if somewhat ruefully, at the righteous seriousness of Winter's claim that part of the Cammock land belonged to Trelawney,

"The patent's clear enough, I trow, so his claim will not hold up in court, but the contention over it has cost me the friendship of Robert Trelawney, and that is a sore loss and one I cannot lightly forgive John Winter."

Henry Jocelyn had words of praise and affection for Edward Trelawney. "Not the businessman his brother is, but a sharp judge of character and good company he was. And, methinks, so well thought of by the settlers and even the Indians he hath done some trade with, he might, over the years have made a better manager of his brother's business. But there's none, I warrant, can pry John Winter from that job while he lives."

Francis nodded, well pleased to hear his own thoughts confirmed. But he was less pleased with their reaction to his plans for trading. Some competition for Winter's monopoly of local trade would certainly be welcomed by the settlers, they agreed. In fact they had heard that several charges of unreasonable profit were to be brought against Winter at the next court session at Saco. But money just now was very scarce; the inhabitants had little, and immigration having dropped off sharply that year, there were few new settlers with money to buy goods. It was hard to say how long this state of things would prevail. They were much influenced over here by what went on in Old England between the Puritan parliament and the King and his Episcopal supporters. When unrest and oppression threatened—never mind from whom—the immigration into New England and other parts of the new world tended to rise, tapering off in the brief periods of tolerance and calm. But, in the event—unlikely in the opinion of both Cammock and Jocelyn—of a full scale Civil War the influx of people trade and goods would almost entirely cease, severely affecting both the local business and the foreign trade in which they were engaged. Cammock shook his head and sighed. "'Twould be a hard time for us all and we can but pray it will not come to that." One prayer, Francis thought, that he would not neglect to send up regularly.

Returning to Richmond's Island he kept the unpleasant news to himself, not wanting to discourage his daughters and, by repetition, perhaps himself as well. Besides, he well knew that the ephemeral "ifs" of business were never solid enough one way or another to be a base for either despair or high hopes. Instead he brought out a rough map George Cleeve had sketched for him of some land in Casco. "'Tis on the Trelawney patent and not much above eight miles from here," he told the girls. "Good land for farming, 'tis said," and he pointed to two irregular lines—the longer one marked River of Casco the other Long Creek. "Here, Mr. Cleeve hath said, is good clear water to drink, to fish and to wash in and, for those who wish to trade, to travel by." His eyes were bright with excitement that he saw reflected on his daughter's faces. Such misgivings as each may have had dissolved in the general glow of anticipation.

Chapter Six

few days later, early in the morning before the mist of the night had risen, they set out in one of the island's skiffs with John Winter. He to confirm that the land Francis had chosen was part of the Trelawney Patent. They passed near a cluster of islands in the Bay of Casco that George Cleeve had described, their wavering outlines just visible through the mist, and turned into the Fore River—starting up several Eider ducks preening in the coves of the river. As they approached Long Creek the shifting curtain of mist rose and evaporated under the sun. Warmth and light invaded the air and infiltrated the wooded shore, giving shape and color to the trees and flowers, and piercing the surface of the water with slivers of light that glanced off the backs of several good sized fish that had been following the ripples they made with hungry curiosity. At John Winter's direction the two men pulled the skiff up on a sandy place below a sloping bank on the left side of the creek. At the top of the bank they stepped into a patch of bushy woods and then out into a large expanse of grass almost up to their waists.

"Good for grazing and growing of corn," John Winter remarked. And then added with a scowl, "and e'en George Cleeve agrees 'tis part of the Trelawney Patent."

Mary didn't hear that or the further conversation, concerned with boundaries and necessary acres. She had already begun to walk around the four or five acres of the field where the present occupants scurried about unseen in the tall grass. A curious cat bird peered down at her from a tree branch three or four feet above her head and on another branch far above her a small bird lifted its white throat repeatedly in the clear melodious notes of its song. It was not like her dream. She could not have dreamt these ancient towering oaks, elms and pines that surrounded the field. They bore no resemblance to the woods near the cottage where she had waited out the plague or to any other she knew of near Plymouth. Such trees had not been seen in England for perhaps centuries. There the small pleasant shade trees were in a comfortable human scale. Here the massive presence of these trees was both awe inspiring and intimidating but, also in some way, exhilarating. Nature here had more in common with nature at sea than with the English countryside.

As for her father, he found his dream already taking root here. His dream and the practical necessities were joined. He was that kind of practical dreamer—had his age and circumstances been right—that new lands are built by. This expanse of land already cleared was a welcome sight to him, though he had been told such would not be hard to find. In these early days of settlement there were many of these cleared areas burned over by the Indians who used them for awhile, some for planting, others as a base for their summer fishing and hunting excursions, abandoning them, perhaps, when the yield from the planting or hunting diminished. At one end of the field, close to the creek, was a rude shack, hardly more than a lean to, left by some subsequent occupant. Fisherman, fur trader or would be planter, his shack would make a shelter for a goat and perhaps a chicken or two as well as a man, if need be, while the house was being built.

The deed for these four or five cleared acres plus twenty more of forest land was duly made out and signed by John Winter as agent for Robert Trelawney, transferring this land to Francis Martin, gent, for divers and valuable considerations, including "the payment to Robert Trelawney or his agent the sum of six pence per acre yearly by the said Francis Martin or his heirs or assigns," etc.

The next two months were disappointing and frustrating ones. Francis, having no experience in carpentry, had counted on hiring a man or two to build or to help him build his house. The fact that Cammock and Jocelyn had told him that money that year was in short supply encouraged him to think that this would not be hard to do. But he soon discovered that most of the settlers used these summer months, after their gardens were planted, to fish or trade with the Indians. Finally, in late August, he found two men who, as it happened had just that spring finished their three years service for Trelawney at Richmond's Island. John Libby was a tall sober man of great good nature, and Nicholas White, his friend and opposite, short, jovial and quick tempered. Neither was a carpenter by trade, but both had worked with the carpenters on Richmond's Island, building the house there and more than one ship, and both were glad of the chance to make a pound or two to help them forward their own plans for settlement. They were honest men and worked well together. Against John Libby's unflagging good nature, Nicholas White's temper wore itself out harmlessly, and at other times his wit and humor cajoled John Libby out of his too sober ways. His wit also brightened this unaccustomed work for Mary and Francie as well—they having stopped working at Richmond's Island soon after a new servant girl arrived.

"I thought 'twould be thus—the work proving too much for thee," Mistress Winter said with a look of confirmed disdain. Mary felt her face flush with anger, but managed to say nothing. Happily Francie was not there. They had still to live at Richmond's Island until their house was finished. But whatever Mistress Winter might say or do, Mary was determined to work now on their own land.

At their father's request she and Francie began to gather wood for cooking fires and against the coming of winter. Everywhere in the woods there were fallen trees and branches—a veritable treasure of potential warmth to English eyes, especially the poor who, in their much divested homeland, could be arrested for stealing a fagot. But the treasure had to be gathered before the snows of winter buried it until spring. And the work was hard.

Mother Nature was not an orderly housekeeper. Branches of all sizes were piled one on another where they fell, many wedged in under others or too large to be moved. So they had to learn to use the cross cut saw, standing awkwardly and precariously among the piles of branches. On their first day and after almost two hours of work their arms were sore and their backs ached. Francie's face grew increasingly sullen, and at last, after losing her footing and slipping for the third time through a pile of branches and collecting another set of scratches on her arms and legs, she rebelled and, plopping down on a log, refused to move another stick of wood. "I shan't do such work," she shouted, glaring at Mary. "'Tis man's work, that neither you nor I hath strength enough to do. What think you our Mother would say to this?"

"Would she have us freeze or have naught to eat but raw meat?" Mary shouted back, sweat pouring down her face. "You shall see who is not strong enough!" So saying she grabbed a log they had both been pulling on and began jerking it angrily back and forth, until, loosening it from the mass, she slid it slowly forward inch-by-inch out of the edge of the woods where they had been working. The men, hearing the shouting, had stopped work and were watching as Mary emerged, pulling with her back to them. Suddenly one heel hit a rock and she fell backwards, ungracefully, onto the ground in front of them. Before she could get completely to her feet again, John Libby had reached over and pulled the log easily out of her way with one hand. Whereupon, covering her face, she began to cry with frustration, heat and weariness. Her father patted her shoulder and allowed he should not have set his daughters to do this work it being obviously too hard for them. Whereupon Francie began to cry as well and declared it was not too hard and they did want to have plenty of wood for the fire to keep them warm and cook their food. Mary was so surprised at this that she stopped crying at once.

Nicholas White, with good-humored sympathy in his voice said, "Now, now, young Mistresses—'tis not so bad as it seem. Strength be'ant everything, nor is't always greatest where it seem most." He winked at John Libby. "And if your father be of a mind to take a break for a bit of ale, I'll tell thee a tale of the smithy in the town of Looe, from whence I came, that I think you will find to the point, or, if not, 'tis merry enough to pass the time withal."

The ale having quickly appeared, and Francis nodding his approval, he began.

Bull Cane was the smithy's name and bull he did seem, with the muscles of several men—tho methinks, the brain of less than one, as thou wilt see. For wife he had a little peaked creature who had, withal, a bullish strength of mind to set aside of her husband's muscles. She were no great beauty, I wot, but Bull would needs have it that she were the most sought after wench in the town, and such jealousy and fear of horns he did have was as great as his fancies of her beauty.

Now, once a week four or five of us did meet for an exchange of good talk and high spirits as 'twere, and Bull Cane was one of these. Howbeit he did never share the cost of a pot when one or another of us was momentarily short of funds, as was our friendly custom. His business being good and his wife keeping close watch on his money, he never suffered from the flatness of purse that did on occasion afflict the rest of us, and so thought little on it, I wot. But it did rankle us sore that he would so gladly share our company, but not his purse. And railing on it amongst ourselves, as we did, ere long came upon a way to pay him back for his neglect. He, having, as I said, a great fear of horns, ne'er left his wife alone, save that he paid a young lad (having n'more than eight years) to stand watch and quickly to report to him did he see any man or ought else suspicious about his house. So far, through many months of watching, he had found naught to report and no trouble save to stay awake on so dull a job. But now we came to him and said that we would pay him double that night did he report some pretended trouble every half hour or so. The which he thought so good a way to liven his evening that he might have done it for nothing.

Come the evening and we all sitting at a table in the tavern with each his pot of ale—having each had but a sip or two—when in rushes the lad, his eyes convincing wide. "A handsome gent," quoth he, "doth at this moment knock at your front door."

Off went our smithy, and quick as a flash his pot of ale went down our waiting throats. And, full shortly, back our smithy comes. The man had vanished, being neither in the house nor anywhere around it. Then, looking in spot, "What ho!" shouts he, "And where is my ale?"

"Why," answered we all innocently, "dost not remember in your excitement that thou didst quaff it all before you ran in all haste to your house?" He shook his head but allowed it could be so and ordered another pot. Of that he had no more than a quarter when back comes the lad, with more excitement than before. Two shadows had he seen, says he, at the bedroom window. Off again dashed the smithy, faster than before, and his second pot of ale followed the first. And so it went for several more pots of ale—our smithy only wondering at the number of pots of ale he had put inside himself with no effects at all—whilst the rest of us grew wondrous merry. Just as he had ordered him one more pot, there was a great caterwauling in the street, and the lad came bursting in holding his head with Goody Cane—broom up raised—close at his heels. As soon as she did spy her husband she let him feel the weight of her broom upon his head.

"Thou knotty-pated fool! I did catch this boy peering in my bedroom window, and, upon my chasing of him and shouting the while for the constable, he hath in all haste cried out 'twas thou hast paid him to peer and spy on me!" Down came the broom again. "Thou lily-livered rogue shouts she and grabbing him by the ear she hath led him, doubled over, out the door and down the street amidst a very tempest of laughter—which he heard not, being so much occupied with whining and pleading for forgiveness. How it all fell out between them I know not, except we saw our smithy no more of an evening.

Three broad smiles and laughter gave good thanks to Nicholas for his efforts, To the which he added—with a bow—"'Tis but a tale like many another I told when I was for a short space a jongleur and a storyteller and traveled about to many a country town singing and telling of tales until my friend John Libby hath beguiled me with a tale of New England and would have it that I accompany him there.

Mary saw the smile for a moment disappear from her father's face and then come hastily back with a nod. "'tis our good fortune," he said, "that John hath thus persuaded you."

Nicholas bowed again—then looked at Mary and Francie. "So, as 'tis plain to see, there be more to strength than meets the eye! And as for thy aching muscles, I do not doubt they will stop complaining in a day or two when 'tis clear it does not suffice to get them out of work." He winked now at the two girls and they smiled back—the tale and the ale having worked an excellent cure—on their spirits at least.

He was right, of course. As the days past the work did get easier. Not more pleasant in the doing, but very satisfactory to see piling up in the shed. And with the steady work of the three men the house, such as it was, had begun to take shape. They had already put up the simple frame of timbers, with spaces left for windows and a door and had begun to cover the outside with clapboards that Francis had bought from some George Cleeve had left after building his house and barn. Mary and Francie helped to collect thatching for the roof from the banks of Long Creek and the River Casco—easier and pleasanter summer work than sawing and dragging wood for the fire.

One afternoon as the late summer sun hung sluggishly in the tops of trees and even the shadows lay hot and humid on their backs as they pulled still another long branch out of the woods, Mary looked wearily up to see a man in laughing conversation with her father. She could not help feeling an irrational twinge of annoyance at his cool relaxed manner. Then, despite the small beard and mustache he now wore, she recognized Michael Mitton.

"Ah, girls," their father smiled. "I have good news for you. Mister Mitton has come to offer us passage in his skiff to attend the court session in Saco two days hence." As anxious as he was to get the house finished and themselves moved in, Francis could not restrain his pleasure at the thought of a small respite from this work he performed so awkwardly.

Michael raised his eyebrows and looked appreciatively at Mary—her eyes bright and her checks flushed from work. She had always had a tendency to go about with her head and eyes lowered—an effect of dreaminess rather than modesty. It often caused her to pass unnoticed, especially beside other more flauntingly pretty females, even of late, her pert and volatile little sister. But when she looked up as now, it was as if a shutter had been opened on a spring morning. There was a fragile but indomitable beauty that few failed to notice in her large eyes and the mobile features of her face.

Michael Mitton was a connoisseur in such matters. His eyes traveled from the bits of leaf and twig in her becomingly disordered hair slowly down to her feet, while her jaw set in growing embarrassment and a renewal of the old dislike. She had no Puritan aversion to admiring looks. She had occasionally noticed the men on Richmond's Island looking at her with unabashed pleasure on their faces. And though she had blushed, she had also smiled and felt not at all displeased. But Michael Mitton's look had something of calculation—which Mary did not interpret, but which made her feel ill at ease and appear annoyed. Still, however it might be interpreted, Michael's look was as unconscious, in its way as those of the Richmond's Island men, and since it had pleased many women he was surprised at the annoyance he read on Mary's face and intrigued—briefly. He was a man of many interests.

Later Mary was disturbed at what seemed by then a foolish and discourteous reaction to her father's friend who, as her father had told her, was not only married, but himself the father of two small daughters. So while Francis and Francie talked with happy anticipation of the trip to Saco, Mary dreaded it. She need not have. When the day came she easily found a place for herself at the back of the skiff and Francie, in her excitement, kept Michael Mitton busy showing her how the sail was managed and fish caught, so that Mary was soon lulled into a pleasant drowse by the motion of the water and the cool breeze on her face. She thought of her mother and Margaret and wished they could be there out of the noise and dirt of the city—even, she smiled, pulling winter wood out of the forest. She thought of Edward—briefly— too, and the Godly faith he had come to here, and understood why. It was a faith, as it seemed to her, then, more in harmony with—more like—the awe inspiring uncompromising surroundings here.

She was suddenly startled out of her reverie by a canoe that appeared as silently as a ripple on the water and glided by not three feet from the end of the skiff. There were two men and a woman in the canoe, tawny-skinned, solemn and dignified. They wore almost no clothes. Mary's eyes widened and then she quickly lowered them, but not before she had cast an admiring glance at the several beaded-bracelets the women wore on her arms and the beautiful, intricately-patterned, beaded-band holding her hair. The first Indians they had seen! The men raised their hands in greeting and Michael raised his and nodded as they past. She heard him tell her father that they were seldom seen here this time of year, being busy at their summer fishing further up the coast.

There were some thirty or forty people gathered at the meetinghouse in Saco by the time the court session began; a varied assemblage in so many shades of red, brown, green, blue and orange as to challenge nature's most extravagant autumn displays. There were lace-edged gowns and doublets, and silken hoods and plumed hats of the gentle folk mingling with the leather jerkins, plain gowns, hoods and Monmouth caps of the commoner sort. On an ordinary day in the Province of Maine it would have been harder to distinguish one social class from another with any assurance, surely harder than it was in England. The rigors of life fell less unevenly in the wilderness and demanded plain serviceable clothes for gentle as well as common men and women. But, on social occasions, such as this court session, the divisions were plain enough. After the restrictions of everyday those who could put on a handsome display indeed, and none more handsome than the young Deputy Governor, Mr. Thomas Gorges, cousin of Sir Ferdinando. He wore an ostrich plume in his broad brimmed hat and a scarlet cloak draped loosely over his lace trimmed velvet doublet.

Though their clothes might show forth the common man, the demeanor of the various servants, laborers and fishermen showed little deference for their "betters." The younger indentured servants, on one of their rare holidays, were gathered together laughing and pointing at the passing dignitaries. When Mary and Francie walked by in their blue-embroidered cloaks one young wench with a pert snub-nosed face fell back against her male companion in a mock faint. "By cockes bones! Such proper trumperies as these do make me to swoon in very wonder."

Mary flushed, half annoyed, half embarrassed at being an object of attention. Francie aimed a kick at the shins of the speaker, that missed its mark by several feet—happily, as Mary, in further consternation, hissed in her ear as she dragged her even further away. "Dost wish to look as foolish as they?" Mary said snappishly. "You should now think on whose daughter you are!" Francie glowered peevishly at her sister, but said nothing.

The attention of the laughing group now shifted to a long-legged young man who had cut off a small pine branch and, having stuck it in his cap, was mincing about with his head high in a comical imitation of the dignified Deputy Governor. A stern glance and a cuff on the ear of the comedian by one of the province constables brought an abrupt end to the performance as well as the laughter that accompanied it, in which Mary and Francie had joined with the rest. Their father, walking just ahead with George Cleeve and Michael Mitton, turned around and frowned, motioning them to follow him into the meetinghouse.

The one-story frame building that served as a courthouse, church and tavern for the settlers sat in a small clearing on the western bank and about four miles up the Saco River. Several well-trodden paths led up to it and out toward the dwelling places of the more than 175 inhabitants scattered along both sides of the river, and as far apart as their staunch individualism demanded and the needs of safety allowed, the former seeming always to have the most weight. The settlements in the Province of Maine bore little resemblance to the close-built villages of the godly people of Massachusetts, where religious community was of the first importance.

In the single room of the meetinghouse there was a long table which for that day's court business was set at one end of the room for the Deputy Governor and councilors of the province as well as the various jurors as they were appointed. Rough benches, facing the long table were provided for the litigants and such witnesses and spectators as could be accommodated in the one room. Some stood against the walls to get a better view of the proceedings or, from the lessons of previous experience, to avoid the lurking splinters in the benches.

This court, like the one they left behind in England, had jurisdiction not only over such crimes as theft, assault, trespass, etc., but also over breaches of the moral and religious code. Swearing, fornication and working on the "Lord's Day" were not then thought to be private matters. But in exercising these extensive responsibilities the provincial court had neither the dignified surroundings nor the mellowness of age and long precedent that produced the intimidating atmosphere of its English prototypes. Its officers, however, were eminently conscientious, feeling no doubt the burden of supplying in their persons what the courtroom lacked in judicial atmosphere. And, presumably for this same reason, their verdicts were no more, and probably less subject to influence. John Winter, an agent for the influential Robert Trelawney, had been acquitted in the charge of unreasonable profit brought in the last session, much to the annoyance of most of the settlers who muttered that it would not have happened so in England, where no man was allowed to make more than a fair profit, as decided by the court. This session, however, Winter, and so Trelawney, lost twice to his old foe George Cleeve. First he was required to pay eighty pounds damages for the house and improved land across from Richmond's Island that he had forced Cleeve to abandon seven years before, and his attempt to claim Cleeve's present land on Casco Bay as part of the Trelawney patent was also denied by the court. But then the court again proved its judicious lack of bias by giving the verdict and five pounds damages to Winter in a charge he brought against Cleeve for slandering his wife six years before by calling her "the drunkenest whore in all the town of Plymouth." Cleeve later admitted to Francis, with his usual candor that he had, under the combined influence of anger and aqua vitae repeated a doubtful rumor passed on to him by a sailor out of Plymouth.

"John Winter had started by then to say that my new grant of land on Casco Bay belonged to Trelawney because"—his voice rose—"he would have it that the Presumpscott River at the eastern edge of my land was really the

Casco River named as the limit of Trelawney's patent," he scowled. "And he has a way of telling lies with such a calm assurance about his face he half persuades even those who know he lies! Marrie! I did grow so over weening angry I cared not what I said. 'Twas stupid!"

The meetinghouse had not been too full for these first cases and several others like them, of debt and slander, but it began to fill up rapidly when word got out that the indictments against Mary Puddington and Ruth Gouch for incontinency and adultery respectively, and the minister of Agamenticus, Mr. George Burdett, for seduction were about to be brought. The two women sat on the front benches, their hoods shielding their heads and faces from the looks of the curious. George Burdett, however, in his dark green doublet and light brown breeches, stood in full view against one wall giving, he may have hoped, an appearance of righteous innocence. He was of middle height, well built, with strong, narrow and one might have said eminently pious-looking features. Only his somewhat heavy-lidded eyes gave credence to the tales of his lascivious behavior, as blatant, if the tales spoke truly, as that of the bawdy friars of old England.

After the fourteen members of the "Grand Enquest" were appointed and sworn in, among them Captain Thomas Cammock, George Cleeve gent, and Mr. John Winter, Mary, the wife of George Puddington of Agamenticus, was indicted and convicted, "For often frequenting the house and company of Mr. George Burdett, minister of Agamenticus, aforesaid, privately in his bed chamber and elsewhere in a very suspicious manner." And, for this offense Mary was enjoined by the court to make the following confession before the court and later at Agamenticus—"I, Mary Puddington, do here acknowledge that I have dishonored God, the place where I live, and wronged my husband by my disobedience and light carriage, for which I am heartily sorry and desire forgiveness of this court and of my husband, and do promise amendment of my life and manners henceforth." This confession made, it was then the order of the court that she ask her husband's forgiveness on her knees.

Having been given a nod by the Deputy Governor and "assistance" by a constable, Goodwife Puddington rose to her feet and faced the crowd. Her hood fell back from her pale face, and looking straight ahead at the back wall of the room, she spoke the required words in a high thin voice that wavered and barely rose above the hisses and low shouts of "whore" and "bawdy wench" of the crowd. When she then knelt before her husband the hisses changed to laughter and such cries as "'tis where a wife belongs right enough" and "thou shouldest have seen her there sooner, Goodman." At which her husband turned and walked away, leaving her to rise and make her way as best she could alone through the crowd. Her exit was eased, as it happened, by the fickleness of the crowd itself. Its attention had already shifted to the next indictment which was, to judge by the fixed expressions of avid anticipation, the one they were most interested in, Mr. George Burdett, minister of Agamenticus, was indicted by the bench on four counts as "a man of ill name and fame, infamous for incontinency, a publisher of divers dangerous speeches the better to seduce that weaker sex of women to his incontinent practices, as 'a turbulent breaker of the peace,' for deflowering Ruth, the wife of John Gouch, and for entertaining the wife of George Puddington in his house." For the first three indictments he was fined a total of thirty-five pounds to be paid to "our sovereign Lord the King"; for the last, ten pounds to George Puddington for the wrongs and damages he had sustained from George Burdett. Why John Gouch had not by this reasoning sustained even greater wrongs, the court did not see fit to explain.

The scowl that now contorted the face of George Burdett transformed his narrow features, making him look more malevolent than pious and drew from the crowd new hisses and shouts of "rogue," "whoreson," "minister of the devil." To which he answered with a shake of his fist at them all as he stomped from the courtroom. Some in the courtroom shivered, and there were further murmurs of "wizard" and "minister of the devil in very truth!"

But once more their collective attention was drawn to the bench for the last act of this drama that had no denouement. Explanations and meanings being the province of orderly creations of art and religion not life.

"Ruth, the wife of John Gouch, found guilty by the Grand Enquest of adultery with Mr. George Burdett, is therefore censured by this court, that six weeks after she is delivered of child she shall stand in a white sheet publicly in the congregation at Agamenticus two several days, and likewise one day at the General court when she shall be thereunto called by the Councilors of this province."

The crowd groaned and mumbled—no doubt wondering at the lightness of the sentence which could have been death or a harsh whipping.

Through all these court proceedings—the first she had ever witnessed—Mary sat stiffly by her father, separate feelings of embarrassment, disdain and pity circling through her mind and somehow coming finally together in a dull anger against the court—the crowd—the women—she wasn't sure. They too seemed to have merged into one painful whole.

Behind her a righteous voice of firm conviction. "The court hath used them all as they deserved." And another with acerbity. "'Tis what comes of trying to make proper wives of serving wenches."

Outside the heavy atmosphere of the meetinghouse the air was doubly clear and sweet smelling. The sun had gone down behind the westerly trees, but the sky was still light, as was the clearing. All the shadows it seemed had withdrawn into the objects from which they had come. As they walked down to the shore Francie touched Mary's arm and asked in a puzzled voice, "Do you think the court hath used them all as they deserved?"

Mary hesitated, trying to sort out her own confused reactions and then sighed, "I know not." But to herself, "if the women be so weak as the court hath said…" The thought trailed out unresolved.

"I know little of justice or of judging others, but that man—" Francis shook his head. "In England, methinks he would have felt the whip."

Michael Mitton shrugged his shoulders and smiled, "For carelessness?"

George Cleeve, coming up behind them, overheard. "That does not surprise me—coming from you." His voice had a cold edge.

Michael smiled and shrugged again—"'Twas lightly said, but I think not falsely." Cleeve glared at his son-in-law, and then, with only a brief nod in the direction of the three Martins, turned and walked off.

"A very moral man, but wanting humor," Michael said ruefully.

The Martins' friendship with Cleeve and Mitton having become apparent to the Winters at this court session, the atmosphere at Richmond's Island became even cooler than before. A condition further aggravated when Winter, having neglected to pay Cleeve the eighty pounds levied by the court, Deputy Governor Gorges sent a boat with thirty armed men to the island to collect either the money, goods of equal value or the person of John Winter. It was an expression of Gorges' determination to reverse the lawless reputation of the province. However, Winter being absent, the deputation was refused admittance by his wife and the men who worked on the island.

Returning from their land that evening the Martins met the Court's men on their way back from this encounter and were warned to beware Mistress Winter's full-blown temper. "Think you 'twas a few carpenters and fishermen that kept us off the island?" they laughed. "What weapon could they have as sharp as Joanna Winter's tongue?"

All three Martins felt the force of that weapon in the days to come. "Thy knavish friend," and "that lying rogue, George Cleeve" or "Thy present thieving friend wouldst rob thy former friend and benefactor Mr. Robert Trelawney of land and money, too." Such was the angry chorus she sang morning and evening with many variations in tone and emphasis.

John Winter said nothing—in fact they rarely saw him after that. But on the crisp mid-November morning when they moved at last into their new home, he presented them with a carefully-itemized bill, so it was stated, of all the food and drink they had consumed at Richmond's Island. There was no counter entry for the two and a half months of work the girls had done.

Chapter Seven

Writing a letter to her mother and Cousin Margaret, Mary happily described their first days in their new home.

On November 14, 1640, we are come to our new home! The house is not over large, as I think our father hath writ. We have one large room with a loft above (a most warm and pleasant place for sleeping in the winter we are told). And below taking up a large space in the middle of one wall we have a great chimney for cooking. 'Tis not so big as the one at Richmond's Island, but Francie and I can stand together in it and see a patch of the Lord's blue sky above us.

Beside this room is another smaller one where our food is stored, as well as goods for trade—some only lately come on a ship from Cousin Martin. This whole house, father hath said, will one day be used for trading and another larger one built for you dear Mother and the little ones. We do miss you all most sorely. But until that day hath come this house will serve us well, methinks. Even Francie doth busy herself happily in it—putting the pots and dishes in their places and arranging our table which, for now is the packing box our kitchen things hath traveled in. And her tender nose takes much satisfaction in that good smell of fresh cut wood, the which our house is made of, as well as the sweet scents the fire in the hearth doth send forth.

This evening having supped on Indian corn—the which we did cook with water, salt and a bit of fat—and some fish (more of that presently!) we have sat sometime singing as we were wont to do at home. Father and Francie keeping better to the tune than I, as always, but each feeling the want of Grace's lute to fill our small voices in this wilderness and send our music thankfully to heaven.

But I must tell thee of the fish we did sup on. This day, November 16, being most unusually warm and pleasant, for this time of the year, Francie and I decided to go a fishing along the bank of the Casco River—just a short walk from our land—and caught more than ten fishes! Whilst Father busied himself with an inventory of the trading goods. If thou dost wonder how thy two silly daughters have become already such fisherwomen as this, 'tis first for that there be so many fishes here—the waters sometimes fairly crowded with them—so that 'tis easy work even for such as we. And further we have had to teach us a Kentish man from Broadstairs, John Libby, born and bred a fisherman. He it was who with his friend, Nicholas White, did mostly build our house. When John Libby hath told us he was born and bred a fisherman, Nicholas White maketh answer that he was himself born right enough 'as,' sez he, 'my presence here doth bear full witness to. But methinks I were not bred at all but grew like unto a weed unbeknown, and have turned my hand to whatever did present itself—of late to fishing and next, mayhap I shall try the life of a planter.' And withal he is most clever and honest and a hard worker as well as often comical. I do not doubt that he and his friend John Libby will do well here.

Prudence stopped reading Mary's letter here and sighed. "'Tis early days yet, but surely there be gentlemen as well as workers in this province of Maine."

"Or, as my brother Edward hath said," Margaret smiled, "Many a gentleman there hath found it necessary to be a worker as well."

Soon after we had come from fishing today," Mary's letter continued, "there came here, presently, and to our surprise, an Indian man and his wife. Have no fear! They were in nowise savage but rather very quiet and most pleasant. He was wrapped about in a cloak, made from a deer or some other like animal skin, and looked most solemn. She did wear a kind of coat made of trading cloth the sleeves decorated with pretty designs of different colors and the rest gathered in with a belt wrought handsomely of blue and white beads. 'Tis plain to see why they do so much like to take the English beads in trade! Once stealing a glance at her I saw she did the same at me with a look, methought, both curious and frighted—even the same as I did feel. But she seemed so shy and gentle I wished that we could have spoken (Francie said the same), but she looked with much haste away, and as I supposed, knew few if any English words as I Indian.

Her husband though did know some English and, discovering that our father was setting up to trade here, they did bring from their canoe some furs and three pairs of snow shoes. These last look like to our rackets for playing at tennis, but the Indian man hath said that when strapped to our feet they will let us go about with ease on the top of the deepest snow of the long winter here! I warrant they look not easy to me—but you shall hear more of this when we have made trial of them!

Your very loving daughter, Mary. Francie is practicing her writing and will write soon.

On another clear November day George Cleeve and his wife came for a visit and to trade. Mistress Cleeve was a jolly woman with silvery-grey hair and an ample figure. She was as amiable as her husband could be but, as it proved, without his over ready temper. They had brought with them a milk goat and a young pig, tended by Will, their indentured servant—a lean young negro man with an anxious smile. The latter being due no doubt to the necessity of having to lead the goat by a rope along the bank while carrying the pig under one arm. A method which, as, Joan Cleeve related, proved most unwise.

"Of a sudden, the she goat bestirring herself with much speed and determination in a direction of her own, Will must straight grab the rope with both his hands or lose her. Whereupon master pig hath dropped to the ground and fell then to squealing and running in another direction through the woods. So we must beach the boat and Mister Cleeve hold the goat whilst Will did give chase to the pig. He then bethought him to tie the rope about his waist and thus have one hand free for whatever might befall. This did seem a good notion until mistress goat hath taken it upon herself to go back from whence we came. Then before you could catch it with your eye Will was on his backside and piggy squealing off into the woods again."

By now everyone was laughing except Will, who was hunched over staring at his feet. "Tush, Will," Mistress Cleeve said lightly. "'Twere no fault of yours. No one could have managed those two contrary creatures any better than you have done. But to shorten the tale—the pig did ride the rest of the way in the boat with no further troubles save an excess of squealing in our ears."

The two animals were deposited behind the pole fence that enclosed something over two acres of land and also one end of the old shack—winter shelter for them as well as the wood supply. After that the Cleeves took some shoes, shirts and Irish stockings in trade. He also gave his advice about the Indians, which essentially was that their trade could not be counted on. There were too many going after it now. However, the settlers, already there and those still coming, should supply a continuing source of trade for clothes, tools and aqua vitae, barring a Civil war in England. Though he added ruefully they might like himself, at the moment, be more possessed of goods to trade than money.

Almost everyone that fall mentioned the possibility of Civil War but, as it were, in passing. No one seemed to seriously consider that the troubles between parliament and the king would be allowed to get out of hand.

Francis had watched with a smile Will's steady hold on the rope as the goat pulled first toward the woods and then the stream with no success. He asked if there were many settlers thereabouts who had slaves.

"A few," Cleeve allowed, "But Will is not one of them. I had his indenture from a friend in Boston who would have me promise that when his indenture years were I over would not keep him as a slave. Because, my friend hath said, he did think slavery was an abomination. I promised— but thought little of it then. Howbeit som'at later I remembered what I had said to John Winter when he hath told me the land I was first planted on had been granted to Robert Trelawney, but I could stay there did I consent to be a tenant of Trelawney. To the which I made answer—with some anger." Joan Cleeve smiled and shook her head at this understatement. "I did say I would never be a tenant to any man in New England! And forthwith I did think e'en worse a slave! And have since been much of a mind with my friend."

Some days after this Michael Mitton and his wife, the Cleeves' daughter, Elizabeth, as quiet and self-effacing as her parents were not, came by to welcome the Martin's to their new home and, like the Cleeves, do a bit of trading. She smiled pleasantly, but scarcely spoke at all, and Mary noticed that, for all the attention he paid his wife, Michael Mitton might have come alone. She found this an unpleasant contrast to the easy friendliness she had observed between George and Joan Cleeve, and it was another count against Mitton in her mind. He did bring several geese and ducks to trade, and those at least were welcome, she thought. Her irritation, like all emotions easily visible in her face, caused Michael Mitton to be briefly puzzled and intrigued once more.

Upon Francis expressing pleasure at the geese and ducks and some discouragement at his inability to procure his own, Michael offered to help him perfect his marksmanship. "Though," he added, "there are sometimes near as many birds in the air as there are fish in the sea, so that it does not require over much skill to bring home your dinner. 'Tis the forest animals that need the better aim, and practice will give you that. I go often hunting for food and trade and would be glad to have your company any day."

Francis smiled and nodded. "Since you live but a short distance from here you will doubtless find me trailing after you whenever I do not have trading business to tend to, which will be often enough I'm sure."

After the Mittons had gone Mary suggested, hesitantly to her father, that, after learning himself, "Mayhap you could teach me of it, and Francie too?"

Francis shook his head in mock dismay, his eyes smiling at them both. "What think you, your Mother would say did she know her young gentlewomen were sawing wood and firing muskets, eh?"

"Methinks a gentlewoman doth need to keep warm and fed as well as any other," Mary answered. "And safe withal. You cannot be here always to drive off the wolves and bears, betimes."

Francie's mouth dropped open and her eyes grew wide. "You are surely right," said Francis, putting his arm around his smaller daughter. "Even a queen must defend her castle, if need be, and no one count her less a gentlewoman or Queen for that. But still—'twere well to wait and tell your Mother of this 'til she is here."

Their last visitors and business before winter closed in around them came just the day before the first snow—the last week in November. Thomas and Elizabeth Page came by boat from their land—four miles up the Saco River. They appeared to be about the same age as John and Margaret Martin and reminded Francis and his daughter of them. He with his easy going conciliatory disposition—he had never been known to lose his temper, Francis was told, and was universally liked and trusted. Elizabeth Page resembled Margaret physically. She had the same kind of fragile prettiness, and her face had a similar almost saintly seriousness about it. But unlike Margaret, whose seriousness often gave way to laughter, Elizabeth's was seldom relieved and often deepened by melancholy. And her occasional laughter was thin and nervous, accompanied by an apparently unconscious wringing of her hands.

Thomas would have Francis show him the extent of his land and while they were out explained his wife's melancholy. Their two oldest children—born in England before they came here in 1633—were both taken from them by a fever two years ago, and for months Elizabeth had hardly spoken or eaten and had paid no attention to him or the two children that had been born after they settled here. But slowly, over many months and, perhaps, as her husband said, because they had so much need of her, she improved, until now she withdrew into herself only rarely.

Francis assured him that he well understood his wife's despair from the terrible fear for their children that he and his wife had felt when the plague came to Plymouth and how grateful they were for the home outside of the city that his friends had shared with their whole family.

There was little of sadness in Elizabeth Page's conversation that day. She seemed to appreciate Mary's company as much as Mary appreciated hers, and offered to tell her of several ways to prepare the Indian corn that the Mittons had brought them, "which," she said, "you will surely need, for tis, along with pumpkin, the food most regularly found on New England tables. Methinks the soil, from long habit grows nothing so well." She paused, then glanced upward. "I trust there be no harm—I recall a rhyme I think it 'tis like this:

"If barley be wanting to make into malt
We must be contented and think it no fault
For we can make liquor to sweeten our lips
of pumpkins and parsnips and walnut tree chips."

It was also she who suggested that, in payment for the supplies they bought, her husband, who was a tailor by trade, though able as necessity had shown to turn his hand at any number of jobs, should make them each a fur-lined cape from some furs they had from the Indians, "'Tis no luxury here," both Pages assured them." Nor thought Francis, looking enviously at their rowboat, is such for getting about.

The next day the snow fell, light and steady—depositing over a foot before it stopped. And from then until the second week in April the ground remained covered. And there were no visitors save on one bright calm day in December Thomas Page came with their beautiful and warmly-welcomed fur cloaks.

Chapter Eight

The first winter the Pilgrims spent in New England was one of great suffering—fierce cold that pierced their flimsy shelters, hunger, sickness and so many deaths. They recorded on March 24: "Of 100 persons, hardly 50 remain, the living scarcely able to bury the dead" All this must have sorely taxed their faith. They had left their human persecutors behind in England but failed to consider the blind persecution that nature can inflict. Yet when the *Mayflower* at last set sail, the fifth of April 1621, on the return voyage to Plymouth, the remaining Pilgrims and secular passengers elected to stay.

The Martins' first winter was not like the Pilgrim's, their expectations went unchallenged. They had their health and, should it fail, a large bag of herbs and instructions for their use from Prudence, as well as a good supply of food as suggested in Edward's letter, and quite adequate shelter. True, their diet was not so varied as it was in England, but it was ample. If the wind found unseen cracks in the walls of their new house, they were soon discovered and plugged with mud—dirt from their floor mixed with a little water and some of their goat's grass. There were no puppet plays or mummers—such as the dissenters frowned upon—no town musicians or dancing bears to brighten a dull day, but for the moment the newness sufficed.

There was ample time to master the art of snowshoeing, which they found to be almost as easy as they had been assured it was. It proved an excellent outlet for Francie's restless energy and for the need that Mary and her father felt to pace out the limits of the land and think what might one day be here—or there, There was also time for frequent practice in loading and firing the musket. Though she covered her ears and winced, Francie enjoyed its loud imperious boom—a sound of authority and protection. But Mary hated the shattering of the winter stillness.

The only other sound except their voices and the impatient squealing of the pig when they left her—she had from the start preferred their company to the goat's—was the almost nightly howling of the wolves. Frightening at first but, when there was no further sight or sign, not even tracks nearby, the sound slipped back to the edge of their consciousness, hardly noticed. But it was not in the nature of the relationship between these two predators that it should remain so.

Occasionally Francis went out to hunt with Michael Mitton or to visit and discuss prospects for trading with George Cleeve or with Cammock and Jocelyn at Black Point. On one of these occasions, a late February afternoon, Mary sat by the hearth halfheartedly pounding corn in a wooden mortar, while Francie parched some over the fire until, as she said, it popped up and turned itself inside out—something Elizabeth Page had told them of and they had practiced often for its good taste and to pass the shorter, but seemingly longer days of winter when blizzards and freezing weather kept them inside. Mary's eyes reflected the shifting red and gold of the flames as her mind projected yet another daydream of the future, their nature as orderly as the notes of a hymn—and as incompatible with the discord reality yielded up in its abundance. An excess of fruit and flowers spilled out on to the winding dream path where she walked. Birds sang, small children danced and in the midst of it all the male figure she had succeeded in banishing only from her conscious thoughts.

Francie, casting occasional sidelong glances at her sister, sang softly—with greater aptness than she knew—"Silly wench, forsake these dreams of a vain desire; bethink what high regard Holy hopes require…"

Suddenly these peaceful sounds were split by a shrill frantic squeal, almost like a scream—the pig, of course! But this wild sound was unlike any it had made before. Mary, after one immobile moment, jumped to her feet scattering corn on the dirt floor. Her hand briefly hesitated over the musket, resting loaded on the wall and then closed over it and she ran out the door. The glistening snow, crusted over now, easily held her weight but she slipped and fell to her knees twice before she reached the fenced in shack and saw what she had feared—a wolf inside the fence. It had caught the pig. The goat apparently was still inside the shack. So great was the late winter hunger of the scrawny wolf that it had not taken the time to drag its catch away or to kill it, but was already gnawing at one hind leg while the pig tried desperately to pull itself away. Mary raised the musket hastily and, scarcely knowing where she aimed, fired it. The recoil and her slippery footing sent her over on her back. The wolf with a yelp leaped on to the roof of the shack and down, as he had come on to the snow that was piled up almost to the low roof. There was no more sound from the pig.

Mary slowly picked herself up from the snow and stood beside Francie who, in the abrupt silence after the single shot had crept out of the house driven by a mixture of curiosity and real fear for her sister which almost turned to panic when she saw her lying flat on her back on the snow. Together they stared over the fence. A large area of snow was covered with blood, and in the midst of this lay the pig, her small eyes starting with terror. When she caught sight of them she began to drag herself—her half eaten haunch trailing limply and bloodily behind her—across the snow toward them, making a chilling pitiful noise—like a high pitched moan. The girls stared with horrified fascination at the immense effort and concern of the mangled creature to reach them. Francie began to scream and jump up and down in the snow.

"Oh Mary, thou must help it—Please, please help it!"

Mary continued to stare with increasing horror and incredulity, as though she had been asked to pull a star down from the heavens. Then, as Francie's pleadings did not diminish, she shook herself and ran through the door of the shack and over to where the pig was still inching her way along. Whereupon, with no hesitation, she raised the gun butt over her head and brought it down heavily on the skull of the pig. She felt the sickening crush of bone under the blow and knew she had killed it. For more than a minute she stared at the motionless form—her head throbbing. Then she turned and glared at Francie—her face red and contorted.

"Dost see how I have helped it? I hope thou art satisfied!"

Later, after they had cleaned and dressed the pig, as Michael Mitton had showed their father how to do, and hung it high in the back room to freeze, Mary apologized to her sister. "'Twas not your fault," she sighed, "but I did not want it to be mine."

Francie, who had scarce spoken since the incident happened, looked up now and also sighed. "Why is't that creatures must suffer so?"

Mary looked down at her sister's usually saucy face. Francie's brow was wrinkled with the fear and seriousness of this question that had descended on her like a cloud. "Only God can tell thee that, methinks," she answered.

And then her eyes fell on two large spots of blood on her apron and there rose in her mind, not only the image of the mangled pig, but the bony starving wolf. She had a rush of painful feeling, seeing again the image of Begette and remembering her rebellion against the nature of the world where there was so much suffering to be accounted for. Quickly suppressed it was followed by another of horror at her own nature that had given rise to what she was sure was no less than a challenge of the wisdom and goodness of God.

Her bible readings and prayers were longer that night. She prayed that her spirit might be chastened, that she might learn to accept what she could not understand. But even as she voiced these prayers she felt one part of her mind rebelling against them. She crept into bed at last full of despair.

Chapter Nine

There were no more encounters with wolves, nor any with bears, and by the end of April the gradual ousting of winter was nearly complete. The ground was clear of snow and dry enough to begin the hard and tedious work of preparing it for planting. For this was the first turning over of the soil—at least in the many years since the Indians had left. Francis decided to hire some help again. It was important that they get the ground ready for planting as soon as the frosts seemed over and the ground was warm, the growing season being so brief in this northern province. Money was still in short supply all over New England and had been for so long that, unlike the previous fall, labor was not hard to find. Men were even willing to take time out from their own planting to work a day or two for coin instead of corn which had, from necessity, become the most common means of exchange in the past year.

But once turned over the soil must be raked and planted. Thomas Page explained how the Indian corn they liked should be planted in hills, and under each hill, as the Indians had taught the first settlers, a herring placed for fertilizer. The herring, he said were easy to catch when they made their great runs up rivers and brooks in the spring and so it proved. Thomas also explained how to plant pumpkins and squash. But it was Mary, remembering what she had learned from the cottage gardener, who proudly explained how to plant beans in rows, neither too far from nor too close to each other. Though they did later discover that some of the beans they had planted close to the corn hills climbed up the stalks and ripened earlier.

However, the knowing and the doing were very different things. By the end of each day Mary, Francie, and Francis dragged their aching backs and arms to bed almost too tired to eat. Francie was even too tired to voice her peevish ill-temper at this joyless monotony of work and sleep, while all around her the sights and sounds of nature beckoned. The dreams that sustained her father and sister she knew nothing of. The future had no shape as yet. It was the present moments of joy she longed for and was missing that made the work seem so much harder to her.

Mary noticed that her father moved more slowly and seemed often short of breath. But if his body complained about the unusual usage it was being put to he did not, and only laughed when she inquired about his health, insisting he was getting stronger every day, and what she saw now was but the slight effects of greater age than hers and equally untrained muscles.

Then came warmer days in late May and early June and they were suddenly besieged by small black flies that attacked every exposed inch of their bodies and brought about almost unbearable itching wherever they bit. The second day of this siege the man who was helping them then, a planter of several years experience, brought a deer skin bag full of bear grease, the rank, rancid smelling Indian remedy which even Francie, her eyes almost swollen shut, was finally forced to sample and give thanks for.

The morning after the last pumpkin seed was put in the ground Francis stood with his arms around his two daughters staring out over the roughly cultivated earth.

"Well, my young gentlewomen!" he said smiling down at their sun-darkened faces still streaked with bear grease. "Methinks we have done a right noble work these past weeks, and I cannot think of any I have ever done that hath given me so much ready satisfaction now 'tis done—nor less desire to do again."

"Nor can I!" Francie seconded so quickly and vehemently that her father and sister looked at each other and laughed. But Mary's laughter ended in a sigh, remembering that indeed much of that work would have to be done again, year after year, nor was it finished yet, since it must be tended all the summer and harvested in the fall. But these thoughts were soon dispersed by a warm spring breeze that brought the smell of fir and fresh sprouted grass by her nose, leaving, for that morning anyway, only the sense of satisfaction in the work done and their capacity to do it.

"Now," said Francis, looking at his older daughter, "I have recently come by some news that I am sure you will be pleased to hear. There is settled now at Saco a new pastor, Mr. Thomas Jenner, one of the godly persuasion, just lately come here from Massachusetts."

"Oh father," Mary's eyes shone. She had not been able to banish from her mind the doubts and failures, as she saw them, that had beset her that past year, and she felt the want of spiritual guidance. True, there was Robert Jordan, now the minister at Richmond's Island, but he was a staunch defender of the established Church of England and she felt, though with some twinges of guilt at her presumption, that his was not the guidance that she sought. To her, as to others of like persuasion, such ministers seemed to bend too much before the world, to make too great allowance for the baser frailties of men. The ideal seemed to mean less to them than the real, and what Mary wanted was not smiling allowance, but serious help. She had also to admit the reluctance she shared with her father and sister to come again under the disapproving eyes of the Winters.

"And so we must go to the meeting at Saco! Is't not so Father?" Francie hopped on first one foot and then the other and clapped her hands. Sermons, orthodox or dissenting held little attraction for her, but the chance to go somewhere was a welcome one for her, as indeed it was for them all. Francis looked down with mock seriousness on his daughters' eager faces.

"As you know well I have not yet got a boat for us, so we must needs foot the long journey to Saco. What say you to that?"

"Yes. Oh yes!" shouted the girls together as they flung themselves into his open arms.

The going being settled there followed a flurry of activity by the girls. It was already Friday and there was much to see to before Sunday. Best gowns, breeches and doublets must be aired. Aprons, neck bands and coifs washed, and their own persons as well—bear grease being scarcely the perfume of choice for the meeting. Their vow to make no effort for two or three days after planting more than was required to set themselves down on the grassy bank by Long Creek, their fishing lines stretched out in the water, was joyfully abandoned.

On Sunday morning, all accomplished, they stepped out of the house well before the sun was visible. Francis had brought the musket, on the chance they might come upon some game along the way. Even Francie seldom worried about being attacked by wolves or bears. A winter's experience of the woods had shown them the truth of what they had been told before they came. These animals were most usually as wary of humans as humans were of them. Howbeit a musket was always welcome.

As they began their walk the pale light of the waning moon hardly penetrated the forest of grey and brown trunks—reaching up one hundred feet or more and some much thicker than the great columns of ancient temples. And a temple of nature it all seemed, with its dead and dying lying scattered about, some still putting out pale green leaves on prostrate branches, others moss-covered or crumbling in various stages of conversion into the soil and the process of life. Happily for the Martins there were often extended open spaces in these woods cut out by hunting Indians and exploring white men. And there was just enough light to make out the blaze marks on the trees made by one of the men who had come from Saco to work in the past months.

As they proceeded the sun slowly began to penetrate, in varying degrees and shapes. Sometimes, coming down through leaves barely visible above them, it laid down a bright geometric pattern on the ground around them and on their own persons. Sometimes it slipped a thin arrow of light through some small opening to illuminate and lend a momentary golden distinction to some heretofore undistinguished gathering of rotting leaves and scurrying insects. Other times broad openings overhead sent down yellow room-sized shafts that cast a brief unworldly glow on the people or animals that passed through them. Their path was also varied by occasional mossy patches, thick, soft and pleasant under tired feet, as well, now and then, by a brook angling and curving a cool careless path of clear water to splash on their faces and dip their cups in. And, every so often, they stepped out suddenly into a cleared field or natural meadow with, once, a house, but far enough from their path so they did not try to see who its occupants might be.

About four hours after they had started they came to a clearing that extended down to their left, disappearing into the dark gently moving surface of the Saco River. The meetinghouse, where the province court had been held that past fall, was diagonally across the river from this clearing. There were several boats on the river—doubtless others on their way to the meeting—so that the Martins had not long to wait for passage across.

The gathering at the meetinghouse this time was much more sober. Gentlemen and ladies, in larger numbers than before, stood about in their finery. Even the servant girls and young men, well represented, were dressed in bright broadcloth gowns and decorated leather breeches and had, for the most part, donned the same sober manners as their elders for the occasion.

Giving them a long look, George Cleeve, who had come down to the river to greet the Martins, gave a cynical snort, "Marry! It requires little wisdom to understand the source of this excess of piety in natures so contrarily inclined as most of these. A threatened court fine makes religious many a heathen whore and thief."

"Mr. Cleeve," his wife sputtered in a low voice, while Mary wrestled with a combined impulse of shock and laughter—the latter, as usual, winning out—her sense of humor having more Elizabethan than Puritan roots.

"Husband," Joan sighed, "Your tongue does surely outrun your head that you should assign so many sole property of Satan."

"And have I not discovered them on other days with their hands in pockets, barrels, and chicken yards and doubtless up skirts as well? But sole property of Satan? Nay." He smiled at the familiar expression of obligatory anger on his wife's face. He and she were much closer in their thoughts than her strong sense of propriety would allow her to show. "By no means did I intend to exclude their betters from that company." He paused his heavy brows drawn down briefly in a scowl that was echoed in the changed tone of his voice, "The thieveries their betters devise are only larger—as are their pious attempts at justification."

"I warrant, husband, your bitter tongue contributes more to your defeat than your enemies."

"Mayhap 'tis true. But if I find a man's hand in my pocket must I shake it? You know John Winter would still have our land and to that purpose, even now, seeks to have the court's decision overturned. And 'Trelawney' has still a fair sound and weight in the ears of many on the jury."

"Not, my father hath said, with Captain Cammock, nor with Mr. Page," Mary said softly, her instinctive liking for the irascible George Cleeve overcoming her timidity in the face of that irascibility. "Mr. Page hath said to my father that he favors your claim and thinks there are many others on and off the jury that would have your right upheld."

The last trace of a scowl disappeared as Cleeve looked at the earnest expression that had settled like a light shadow on Mary's face accentuating rather than dimming its attractiveness. A smile replaced his scowl as he thanked the now blushing Mary for this good news she had brought to him, and Francis verified.

"See Mr. Cleeve—is't not true what I have often said—it does not always pay to look on the dark side of whatsoever happens?"

"You do look most cheerful this morning, Mr. Cleeve," said Elizabeth Page who had just appeared beside Mary.

"'Tis the effect of the Sabbath day on his spirit, I warrant," commented his wife pointedly and with a suggestive nod toward the meetinghouse, at the door of which their new pastor stood—a man not much taller than Mary, with dark, grey streaked hair and a ruddy complexion. There was a look of earnest conviction and determination in the way he held his shoulders and in the set of his face, dominated by a rather large nose and a heavy jaw. But his small eyes looked out with a kindly, almost insistent good will on the gathering congregation. It was an interesting face and one that lead the mind to speculate. Was that look of conviction and determination an effect of the inner man on the outer or was it rather that those features, with their observable effect on others, had molded, in some part or all, the inner man? However it might have been, a short acquaintance was adequate to convince observers that Reverend Thomas Jenner's features did now most accurately reflect his inner state.

He was one who had never had a doubt about his calling. But, as a young minister, he had been troubled with doubts about his fellow clerics. Their self-indulgence disturbed him. Most of them, as it seemed, being more concerned with easy living than with saving souls and with God's worldly creation than with God Himself. They called him pious Jenny and even Puritan, which angered him until he heard a sermon by another one so named and found that he and other godly people, as they called themselves, were expressing his own concerns, He joined them in England, and when his frail wife died he took his three small children and sailed for New England, establishing himself in the newly settled town of Weymouth in Massachusetts. Then learning from John Winthrop that there was no minister of the godly persuasion in the Province of Maine, and having a missionary ardor that his like-minded Weymouth congregation could not satisfy, he took his two daughters—leaving his son to study at the recently formed Harvard college, and set out for the neglected province where he was now settled.

Beside the pastor in the doorway stood his two daughters. Esther, the eldest, perhaps fourteen or fifteen, had pale blond hair and small dainty features held in prim, tight-lipped order. Her sister, Hannah, about Francie's age had busy features, watching, sniffing and smiling at everything around her with obvious anticipation. Although their stimuli were quite different, Thomas Jenner and his youngest daughter had a similar enthusiasm. His older daughter had already acquired a fanatical zeal to replace the enthusiasm that was not a part of her character, as it had not been a part of her mother's, for whom devotion to her family had defined her emotions.

The new pastor was excited because he had found the challenge that had brought him here. Most of this congregation—quite satisfactorily large, he noted, as he stood before them ready to begin his sermon—had not been motivated by religion to leave the shores of civilized society behind them, but by the prospect of worldly advancement. It was a motive whose strength he did not minimize. Had it not, after all, brought them here even as religion had brought so many of the settlers to Massachusetts? Now might it not be, he reasoned, that a new motive, the possibility of eternal life, could motivate these settlers to live by the word of God? If they could be convinced—he squared his shoulders—that the easy path of the conforming church could be the high road to eternal damnation and, more, that every sin brought down the very tangible and immediate wrath of God upon the sinners, in sickness and death, failed enterprises or natural disasters, might he not win the strength of their belief to the godly way? He did not have for this effort either the intellect of a Mather or the eloquence of John Cotton,

But the first has seldom had much to do with conversions and, as for the latter, the disgraced minister, George Burdett, had been too well known for his eloquence—in and out of the church—for that commodity to be held in very high regard at the present. But what he did have, an earnest and unshakable conviction, absolute honesty and a visible goodwill, combined to make him perhaps the best and most convincing pastor the Puritans could have found for these isolated and often defensively independent settlers. Some who had smiled knowingly at George Burdett's eloquent haranguing, and put in their appearance at meeting with perfunctory impatience, now found themselves influenced enough by their new pastor's personality to listen now and then to his quiet voice—relatively quiet as compared to the average Puritan minister— and even to shift an occasional thought from the immediate to the eternal.

On this Sabbath Reverend Jenner had chosen to expound upon the sin of those who in their weakness—having something less than the patience of Job—presumed to question the justice of God. He began slowly, almost hesitantly, as though calling up each word and the thought it represented separately before them to be judged or to make its judgment.

"How often, my brethren, hast thou, in the very depths of thy proud hearts, cried out, when the wrath of God hath fallen upon thee, wailing and avowing thy innocence. 'Oh God, why hast thou visited thy tempest upon me, thy faithful servant?'"

Directing questioning eyes slowly on one after another of the congregation they fell on a young woman in the third row, leaning somewhat forward in her seat, her large serious eyes fixed on his face and seeming to express a special intensity of interest in his words. He continued to speak—his voice gathering strength and conviction from her unfaltering interest.

"What greater sin think you there can be than to call upon God to justify His ways to thy sinful self? Hath he not—despite the grievous sin of Adam and Eve and the continuing sins of their descendants, even unto the present generation—given thee life and, through his only Son, a chance of salvation that, in the depth of our depravity, none of us hath deserved?"

The sermon continued for two and a half hours and, despite her concern to miss no part of it, Mary had several times to forcibly rouse and redirect her attention. The air in the small building grew increasingly stuffy and the particular inflections of the pastor's voice became, as time passed, so familiar as to give a monotonous sameness of tone to his utterance. A minutely detailed and extensive listing of the sins of flesh and heart that man is too often guilty of was punctuated by a low snore, followed by a sharp grunt of surprise, the result of a well directed female elbow in the mid-section of the offending snorer. If Reverend Jenner heard, he gave no sign. The stifling air and the intensity of his concentration had their effect. His eyes, now seemingly fixed on some distant object, appeared glazed. His ruddy complexion even ruddier. Drops of perspiration stood out on his forehead—two or three drifting slowly down his large nose as he brought his sermon to a close.

"God hath done his part in making thee and setting thee upon this abundant earth. It is now thy task to justify thyself before Him, turning your actions from the sinful path thou hast followed heretofore."

Mary and Elizabeth Page walked silently together toward the river as the meetinghouse emptied quite a bit faster than it had filled. The Martins were to have dinner with the Pages and the new pastor before returning to Casco.

"I have before now stayed close within the circle of the Church of England," Elizabeth Page spoke her thoughts slowly, staring ahead at the river and their house directly across. "I had heard these reformers—the godly people—much mocked, but had never heard one speak before," she sighed. "Methinks he says much to the purpose, at least he has given me much to think on."

"And me also," Mary said softly, then briefly told Elizabeth of her cousin Margaret and of her own conversion.

Elizabeth nodded, "There is much to be got from them, surely. But do not think I am yet ready to take a path different from my husband's. 'Twas he did sustain me when I had, for so long, descended into a great folly of despair. She looked back, her eyes bright and full of affection, at the man who walked just behind them, his blond head bent in conversation with the small girl walking beside him. "But I am glad that Reverend Jenner hath come."

The Page's two-story frame house sat on a low hill facing the river. Close by on one side was a small shed, and on the other, farther back, a commodious barn. Two goats tethered to the far side of the shed were nibbling on the bright green grass.

The servant girl and the smallest Page children, two round-faced blond headed boys—one three or four, the other not much over a year—had come across the river in the first load and waited for them on the shore as they pushed in.

"Kate! Dost mind Sylvester yonder?," Elizabeth called. He seemed to be crawling aimlessly in the grass reaching out to pull up stray violets, the last of the abundance that had dotted the clearing with color a few weeks earlier. "I cannot chase him now that the time for the new baby is so near," she said nervously. "And he sometime does crawl about still when he would go speedily, and then the grass almost hides him, and I fear he will get away into the river before we see he has gone," She was wringing her hands and trying, as it appeared, to keep a wavering smile on her face.

"Our Christopher was not so adventurous a spirit," she said, relaxing again as Kate, a buxom but fast moving maid, started up the hill with a small kicking Sylvester under one arm, the older, Christopher, by the hand.

"Nor our Jane either!" She turned and smiled at the diminutive six year replica of her walking just behind them with her mother's pale blue eyes looking shyly up at them and the same light brown hair tucked under an identical white cap.

Later, after a meal of roast duck, beans and corn cakes—with the unexpected pleasure of oranges that Thomas Page had brought back from a recent trip to Boston—they sat together in one of the two downstairs rooms. It was large, but sparsely furnished with two wooden benches and a high backed chair, a cupboard and a narrow plank table, all made, Thomas said, by one of the other settlers, a skilled carpenter, in exchange for winter coats for his family. Through the oiled paper that covered the three window openings came a warm amber light that softened the rough simplicity of the room and lent its softening glow to the faces of the occupants as well.

Francis and Thomas were talking quietly together and, characteristically, Francis's interest enlivened his genial pock marked features, while Thomas's square jawed face remained impassive, only an occasional inflection of his voice giving any indication of his interest. They were weighing the merits of the pipe stave trade with England and, possibly, other European countries. Not one would have thought a very inspiring subject, as it was not for Thomas Page except as it absorbed his friend. The fascination of commercial pursuits was particularly far from his understanding. Not because of scruples derived from his religious principles, many a dedicated Massachusetts Puritan was an almost equally dedicated merchant, but as a consequence of a basic disinterest in material pursuits save for the tailoring and farming that supplied their necessities. But for Francis Martin, just then, it was an inspiration of the most important kind. His practical English mind knew that his equally English dream could not be sustained without solid financial support.

The Indians, it appeared, were not to be relied upon. The French paid better and cheated them less often. The other settlers were not to be relied on. The other settlers were, for the moment at least, too poor. They needed goods but could not pay for them. The alternative?—a reliable export product must be found. Fish, generally looked upon as the best commodity, required fishing boats and a goodly number of fishermen. So he had concluded, as he explained to Thomas Page, that Captain Cammock and the Deputy Governor were right when they suggested pipe staves as a second choice or perhaps even a first choice when the smaller initial expense was taken into account. A ship for transport would be wanted, of course, but that he thought could be arranged from the other end or smaller loads could be sent at first and whatever space was available on outgoing ships taken advantage of. Thomas nodded, but Francis scarcely noticed. He had started talking with some hesitations about the project in his mind, but these fell before his words or his need to be convinced. He was experiencing one of those moments of euphoria, rare of late and so all the more affecting, when the practical means and his dream came together harmoniously.

The pastor seeing the glow that animated Francis face—not unlike the glow of religious inspiration—shook his head and sighed. Though this seemed to him an inexcusable heathenism, he did not try to inject his own religion into the conversation. He preferred to pursue his conversions slowly and with, as he would have put it, "rational persuasion," rather than exhortation. His own limited eloquence played a part in this preference. Also, though his own belief was certainly passionate, he considered it to be based on, and eminently supported, by reason. Faith was the way of reason for him. He had no more been troubled by doubts about his beliefs than he had about his calling. The material and sensual obsessions that some men and women are prone to he considered, quite naturally, to be devilish possessions, but also examples of unreason. His wife, soon discovering that his physical desires were as minimal as his material requirements, tried to sublimate her own sinfully stronger ones, as she saw them, in religion and, in her last days was horrified by an erotic dream in which she found herself in an adulterous relationship with the devil.

Mary was sitting by herself now. Elizabeth having gone into another part of the house to check on her children and the servants. Noticing this, Reverend Jenner joined her. He had recognized her as the young woman who had shown such great interest in his sermon and had been looking for an opportunity to speak with her. He had hoped for an early conversion until her father mentioned that she had been of the godly persuasion for several years and deplored the lack of a minister of that faith in this Province. That explained her interest he supposed. He had quickly rejected a small twinge of disappointment. "By your face this morning I judge thee to be somewhat troubled in thy faith. Is't so?"

"Yes," she answered softly. "But thy words did much encourage me."

"Wouldst tell me what hath troubled thee?" He leaned toward her, studying her expressive features earnestly, although he knew such mercurial faces respond so quickly to so much that they are often as enigmatic in their messages as the quiet faces that scarcely even record the imprint of the passing years.

Mary, disconcerted, looked with awe and considerable diffidence at this spokesman for the Lord, who regarded her with such benevolence. "Suffering," she murmured in a barely audible voice. Further she could not go—discovering suddenly a reluctance or, as it seemed to her, an inability to find words that would express her thoughts. An agony of intellect and imagination possessed her at such times. What had seemed clear and profoundly moving was found, when it had been formed into words, to have become merely confused and melodramatic. Some, discovering this, wrap their deepest thoughts in a permanent and protective silence, others prate on, hoping, perhaps, that somewhere in their extended chatter the shadow of the truth they have felt will emerge. Mary was of the former sort. But this time her single word was enough—preferred even by the pastor who had more ready answers for general questions—though it had come to him over the years that general questions could always be found lurking in specific ones.

"Sin and suffering, it should be remembered, are handmaidens one to the other," his small eyes narrowed and his nostrils flared slightly, giving his face a look, not of anger, but stern austerity—briefly. Then his eyes widened again and a slight smile moved his full lips up at the corners. "And yet suffering is but a moment in that eternal life that God's elect will share."

Later, walking home with the warm spring breeze in her face and the signs of new life pushing up through the ground, chattering and singing in the trees and gliding with vibrant insect wings about their heads, eternal life did seem more real than suffering. So much do the moods of nature affect philosophy that it might be well to inquire of philosophers what month this or that passage—this cynical paragraph, that rising hope—was set down.

After dinner Esther Jenner had taken Francie and Hannah outdoors with her, promising primly that they would sit by the river and read the bible. The two younger girls had exchanged happy glances of mutual appreciation at dinner and were glad to get outdoors together. As Francie told it on the way home, her dark eyes snapping with self-righteous vexation, she knew that Hannah wanted to run down to the river as much as she did. So she started and Hannah, after a quick look at Esther, followed. But, only half way down, Francie stumbled and fell. She looked now, ruefully, at the grass stains on her gown. Worse, in her fall she had scraped the knuckles of her hand on a large rock, and as it began to sting and bleed, she had let out a sharp exclamation of pain. Whereupon Esther—her features set even more primly and her eyes

106

raised, had said, "'Tis God's punishment for thy un-Sabbath-like behaviors."

Francie, angry tears she could not suppress running down her cheeks, glared at the imperturbable Esther. "He hath never punished me afore when I did play games and dance on the Sabbath!"

"God punisheth where and when he listeth," Esther had answered as she turned her back and started off down the hill.

"Marrie! Now she will surely tell thy father that I am too wicked to be with thee." Francie said, fretfully, scrambling to her feet.

Hannah shook her head vigorously. "Nay, Esther will never say ought of this. 'God knoweth' is what she doth always say to me." Her sigh bespoke a long memory of unreported offenses. "All the same I wouldst rather leave it so with God—who knoweth all betimes—than to face our father withal."

"Doth he beat thee?" Francie's eyes became round and wide at the thought.

"Oh no! He doth sometimes switch me, but it scarce hurts at all." She sighed. Sin could not be exorcised, she knew without some pain, but she had never had a spirit penitent enough to call for a more firmly laid on switch as she had once overheard Esther doing. "He doth only look very sad and disappointed as if he were frighted that I might not be saved—and that doth make me frighted, too," she said soberly.

"And so," Francie finished in a peevish tone, "we did go down and sit by the river and listen to Esther reading from the bible for above two hours. Methinks the godly people are not very happy!"

Mary gasped, her eyes snapping.

"Tush, daughter," Francis looked at Francie and shook his head, his eyes smiling. "Dost think thou hast discovered the secret of happiness in dancing and games on the Sabbath?"

"Oh Father, thou dost know I did not mean that," she almost whined. It had been a very long day. Her bruised hand was smarting and her tired feet stumbled frequently as the shadows began to slip together through the trees, as if the sun's descent had released them from the limiting shapes of things they cast during the day into their own ubiquitous form of darkness.

"You are right little one. I know you did not mean just that. But methinks, though I have no great wisdom in these matters, that 'tis not this or that religion makes us happy or no, but our own natures."

"Father!" Mary's voice was sharp. "Surely you can not mean that it doth make no difference what we believe?"

There was real distress in her voice, echoed, as her father saw, in the expression of her face, lit by the glow of the stick of candle wood he carried. The dream that had possessed him in England still lingered and he would like to have sheltered both his daughters in it, especially Mary whose need for a dream he well understood, if not its content. But it was hard to speak convincingly about a passion whose depth and extent his pragmatic mind could not fathom.

"As I did say to Francie, I have small wisdom in such matters. But I know I did not mean to say that what we believe makes no difference in our lives. Hath not what they believed brought the godly people across the ocean to face hardships they had been warned of?" He ended, as he felt, inadequately.

"Ay, father," Mary's brief distress had abated under her own conviction, "and so didst thou and Mister Page come across the ocean"—and John Winter she added, but to herself.

Chapter Ten

The long days of summer that followed were full of pleasant activity. Fishing and berry-picking were necessary work, but hardly seemed so on a bright summer's day with birds singing overhead, flowers underfoot and the sunlight `riding on the waves. Even tending the garden was not much complained of, except in the hottest weather.

The rowboat was at last bought after a late spring ship arrived from Plymouth with a substantial supply of trading goods from John Martin. The furs got in trade from the Indians for these goods, English cloth, metal pots and tool, was ample for the boat, though there was not as much left as Francis would have liked. But, with the boat, trading trips were easier and Sunday meeting was a regular diversion—social as well as religious. Francie and Hannah became fast friends, Francie learning some measure of control out of her desire to keep the father's good opinion, while Hannah relaxed some of hers. Mary and Elizabeth grew close as well. On one hot summer Sunday, their usual midwife being at another birthing, Mary was called to help in the delivery of the newest Page son.

As for Francis, by the middle of the summer he had arranged for a ship bound for England to carry a thousand pipe staves cut by men from Richmond's Island, going thus, reluctantly, into debt again to John Winter. However, cousin Martin had assured him of the excellent price for staves in England now. Surprisingly it was well above the price of the year before—the price that Winter had asked. What little money he had left Francis decided to set aside for some emergency or a sudden drop in the price of pipe staves in England.

Happily, and unlike many in the Province that year, they had a more than ample harvest. Nature, scattering her early frosts with a capricious hand, missed their land and they were able to get in a large store of corn and pumpkins as well as dry beans before the hard hand of winter closed over them, and hard indeed it was. Even the Indians agreed that the like of that winter of 1641 had never been seen before. Fowl and fish lay frozen on the inland bays where few dared walk. And there was little visiting, thaws being brief and suddenly over. Those who did venture out did so at the risk of frozen toes and fingers which several lost to that implacable icy goddess of winter.

Like the other settlers the Martins spent most of their days huddled close to the fire, going out only for more fire wood or to feed the goat. This latter responsibility was unhappily ended when, one morning in mid February, they found her lying stiff and quite dead by the partly open door of the shed—the wind having ripped an old hinge off. It was a double loss since she had been bred. They had nothing now to guard from the wolves, if they had come. But, frozen or hiding from the cold in caves, the absence of their howling was noticeable and one welcome benefit of that winter. The silence, however, like an encircling vacuum, breached only occasionally by the sharp crack of a frozen branch or the high moan of the wind, seemed to dull their senses so that they like the rest of nature slipped into a kind of mental and physical hibernation.

Gradually, at last, the days did begin to grow longer, the sun warmer and the winter more feeble. Here and there a small greening twig rose above the melting snow and animals, of both the human and wild varieties stretched their cramped limbs and found they had survived. Francis, though his shoulders were not as straight as they once had been, had benefited from the quiet winter and felt stronger than he had for more than a year. Mary and Francie, too, were healthy. Their food, after the few fish Mary and Francie caught in the fall and the birds, few also, that Francis was able to shoot before the terrible cold set in, was all vegetable but ample and nourishing. It was their spirits that seemed not to have revived.

They went about their daily activities with a minimum of conversation and thought. Francis neglected to worry, Mary to daydream and Francie to complain. It was as though their minds had not yet thawed out. Then one warm morning in late April a veritable choir of birds awakened Mary earlier than usual. She lay quiet listening. The joyful medley of sounds seemed to surround her and lift her out of herself. Suddenly she laughed softly and, slipping from her bed, she dressed quickly, filled her apron with an assortment of brightly colored ribbons and feathers and hurried outdoors. When she returned her father and Francie were just getting up. She said nothing of her early morning activities until after breakfast. Then with a sudden "Come!" she grabbed a hand of each and pulled them out the door and down to the end of the greening field. There, standing alone a few feet out from the woods, was a well shaped young maple tree about ten feet tall. But what made Francis and Francie gasp were the lightly fluttering red, blue and yellow ribbons plus two large white feathers that this miraculous tree had apparently sprouted over night. It was impossible not to laugh at such an incongruous vision. Francie clapped her hands in delight.

"Mary, thou hast taken all the ribbons from our clothes and the feathers from father's hat! She laughed again and Mary smiled, her eyes bright with pleasure. "But why didst do it?"

"'Tis not yet May Day, nor surely is yonder tree a proper May pole, but methought we didst need somewhat of dancing and singing to wake us from our bearish winter slumbers."

"Oh ay!" Francie's feet began to move as though the very suggestion had motive power.

Francis, allowing that his eyes were better for admiring and his voice for singing than his feet were for dancing, began to sing—

"If joy had other figure than
sounds and words and motion
to imitate the measure…"

To which the girls added their voices as they began to dance, skipping and turning with light improvised steps around the tree. The feathers wavered and the ribbons fluttered more extravagantly as they circled. Even the birds were briefly silenced, except one absent-minded blue jay who inadvertently landed on the branches of the beribboned tree and, with a squawk and frantic flapping, departed from this unnatural roost. They had finished two merry songs and were beginning a third,

"See, see, oh see who here is come a Maying! "

When out of the woods in the direction of the creek someone, three in fact, did come, but certainly not a Maying. It was the pastor and his two daughters, and they stared wide-eyed at the singing and dancing Martins and their gaily bedecked tree. Hannah could not quite restrain a short muffled exclamation of delight. However her father and sister, the latter, her lips tightly compressed, stared in silence.

Francis caught sight of them first and stopped singing to bid them welcome. Mary and Francie—their cheeks bright red and their hair tumbling loose from their caps, went almost all the way around the tree again before they saw the new arrivals and stopped short. Mary saw on Reverend Jenner's face the expression of sad disappointment that Hannah had spoken of, but she could not feel contrite. Her numbed spirit had wakened and soared and could not be brought down so suddenly—even for good reason. And, defiantly, she was not so sure there was good reason. Could God who had filled the birds with song and given them bright feathers and graceful flight object to the joyful songs and dancing she and Francie had done? She could not at that moment, at least, believe it. And she did not lower her eyes as she usually did when she spoke to the pastor.

"We were but joining the birds in a welcome to spring," she said with a brief smile.

"I'm sure thou wilt go back to thy work and to the pursuit of godliness with added spirit." He returned her smile, thinking not so much about the dancing as the pride he saw in her eyes. Her will doth not yet belong to God. Her sister hath a quick and troublesome temper, but Mary hath the stronger will. Bent to God's service it might accomplish much, but he sighed, such pride doth surely tempt the devil.

"Perhaps we might go inside and say a prayer of thanks to God for yet another spring that he hath given us."

It seemed to Mary they might better pray out there with all the signs of the new spring around them, but she said nothing. The contrition she had not felt before was now beginning to come upon her.

Only after he was sure that the Lord had been properly propitiated for the Martin's failure and his own, he being their pastor and so bearing some share in their guilt, did Reverend Jenner remember the news that had prompted him to pay them a visit on that particular day.

According to word the Deputy Governor had just received, Robert Trelawney had been imprisoned by Parliament for some innocent remark questioning the power of that body. Francis's distress was somewhat relieved by Mr. Jenner's firm assurance that everyone was certain the problems in England were but trifling ones, causing short tempers, but promising easy and quick solutions.

However, in a letter he received from John Martin a few weeks later there were no such comforting reassurances. "The King, does try, it seems, to usurp the power of parliament—no small matter, surely. And Parliament in resisting, as it must, is trying to put more limits on the power of the King! Neither, methinks will give in, and compromise grows farther off each day, with cooler heads like brother Trelawney not listened to and even imprisoned. I cannot yet believe that it will come to war, but if it does I fear that whoever wins twill not be the English people."

George Cleeve left for England in June and they hoped to hear more of England and Robert Trelawney when he returned. "If he does return," Mistress Cleeve had said, shaking her head. Her strong good-humored features wore a combined expression of worry and exasperation. "The Deputy Governor, Ferdinando Gorges, hath threatened to cut off his ears and banish him from the Province for his treasonable language."

Francis expressed shocked disbelief that Thomas Gorges would do anything so unwarranted.

"Nevertheless 'tis so. But do not blame young Gorges overmuch. He hath been exceeding provoked by my husband. There is, when all goes well, no more reasonable and generous man than Mr. Cleeve. But when anger doth overcome him, as it hath been wont to do with much ease of late, he doth have a most loose and ungovernable tongue. 'Twas thus when he did hear that upon the Deputy Governor's court affirming Mr. Cleeve's ownership of the land at Machegonne Robert Trelawney did accuse Gorges of treason. Whereupon the Deputy Governor agreed to review the case again and hath given out that he doth think Trelawney hath been wronged."

Francis saw John Winter's devious hand in all this difficulty—stirring up Robert Trelawney. The matter, he exclaimed with sympathetic annoyance, had already been decided twice in Cleeve's favor, "I do not wonder he was wroth."

"Ay, 'tis true, 'tis true," Mistress Cleeve nodded. "But methinks he hath taken out his spleen on the wrong man. To call the Deputy Governor and his friend Richard Vines rogues who wouldst fain bow their heads before the rich and powerful and, betimes, cozzen the poor out of their land was scarce politic!"

Francis's eyes widened and he shook his head in agreement. He was admittedly shocked—but amused also—effects George Cleeve often had on his friends at least.

His reason had shortly gained control of his temper again she explained, and he realized that it would be best to absent himself from the Province for awhile and, further, that in England he might remedy his affairs which, as things stood, he could not do here.

Various and conflicting rumors continued to come throughout the summer with the fishing vessels from England causing Francis to look for a ship with room to carry more of his pipe staves. But there were none that had not already engaged to carry as many as or more than they could safely hold. Pipe staves, it seemed, had been judged a good commodity by a great many settlers, including the Deputy Governor. The price then would not be as good as he had hoped. Still, he was but mildly disturbed. He could afford—granted a good harvest—to wait awhile. But John Winter's hand descended again. He heard from his friend, Michael Mitton—now a local constable—that Winter was pressing for the debt that Francis owed the Trelawney plantation. He paced back and forth in an angry and futile agitation. He knew there was naught to do but part with a large part of the pipe staves at the current deflated price, many more than would have answered for the loan even the fall before.

Then, in late autumn, there came another blow that reverberated throughout the Province of Maine and all of New England. The rumors that the disagreements between the King and Parliament had now come to Civil War were confirmed. On August 22, 1642, King Charles had raised his standard at Nottingham. The certainty of drastically reduced trade and emigration was a hard blow indeed for the already tight-belted settlers. However much it had been talked of no one had seriously anticipated the reality—the drastic slow down, perhaps stoppage—of all those goods— cloth, clothes, weapons, tools, fishing gear, rum and foodstuffs like sugar and salt that they still depended on England for. Having the prospect of little but hope to sustain them they clung tenaciously to it and comforted themselves with the assurance that, while unruliness might be a trait of the French and the Spanish it was quite un-English and surely both parties would soon see the wisdom of compromise.

In addition to these economic problems there was now the frightening possibility of serious trouble with the Indians—incited by the Catholic French, or so many of the settlers believed. They forgot that ever since the first white man came upon their land the Indians had complained—with much truth and no result—of the cheating English traders who filled them full of aqua vitae and stole their goods outright or, in exchange for their furs, gave them spring water with hardly more than a smell of liquor to disguise it. One particularly flagrant exploiter had been murdered in 1631 by a party of Indians, but that was more than ten years past now; an isolated incident that was soon forgotten. Since then the general population had greatly increased and it can hardly be doubted that the percentage of dishonest traders had increased proportionately. But the silent Indian faces gave no sign of the anger that was building until it suddenly erupted that fall. They broke into three houses by Casco Bay (George Cleeve's house was not one of them) harming no one, but stealing many goods from those that were well known to have cheated them. That was all that was to happen for many years, but the settlers could not know that and it was a long time before the sharp edge of their fear and suspicion was dulled.

The Martins received a further confirmation of the outbreak of hostilities in England in another letter from John Martin. He, however, seemed more concerned about their diminished prospects for trade with England than about the Civil War. Robert Trelawney had shown him a letter from John Winter detailing their poverty, so he had enclosed some money, in the nature of a business investment, he added, dampening the flare of injured pride that had risen briefly in Francis's breast. It could be repaid from the overplus of some later transaction when business had improved. One had, after all, to expect such shifting fortunes in business even in the best of times. Francis sighed and nodded, quite mollified. Though, as John said further, he did not fully believe Winter. The man—they should be warned—scrupled not what lies he told. He had even, in the same letter, blamed the Martin's poverty in part on Mary and Francie who had never learned how to work. Now it was the girls whose ire rose.

"How hath he dared to write thus after all we did on Richmond's Island?" Mary snapped. "All the cows we herded and milked, the chickens we fed, slop pails emptied (Francie growled) clothes washed and meals cooked while Sarah and her mother went walking about the island with the Reverend Jordan."

Because, Francis thought bitterly, he little cares or fears what I might say or do. Wrath and injured pride alternated with a painful feeling of impotence against what his lowered condition had brought upon his daughters.

Margaret too had reacted angrily, John wrote. In fact this accusation had roused her—out of the melancholy humor she had been in since her brother Robert's imprisonment—to a spirited defense of the girls and their mother's raising of them. John also assured them that he had not shown the letter to Prudence and that she and the rest of the family were in fine health. A small tear slid unnoticed down Francie's cheek, and her mumbled, "I do miss them all," echoed in the momentary silence.

There was no mention in the letter of trading goods shipped or about to be shipped, which told Francis more than he cared to know about the present seriousness of the troubles in England. But he said nothing of this to his daughters. He could see that, after the usual wave of homesickness had passed, the generally encouraging tone of the letter had somewhat raised their spirits—though they continued talking angrily of John Winter's lies. Mary slapped corn cakes into the pan so hard that one flipped out again and was lost in the ashes of the fire. Francie stabbed viciously at a blackened log smoldering in the fire. "Would that that were John Winter's black soul lying there," Francie said sharply.

"Ay!" her father said, flushed with anger, suddenly stepping behind them. "And that fat stick next, his wife's, give it a jab too. She were so busy trolling her daughter around as bait to catch the Rev. Jordan as a son-in-law she neglects her own duties. If he sees she's the bait he'll be wise not to bite."

Never before had they heard such an outburst from their good-natured father and they collapsed with laughter.

"Oh, Father," Mary wiped her eyes, "Surely you need not be angry for us. We will be happy to forget, if not forgive them."

Francis hugged them both but his face still reflected his anger. "I suppose they know not what they do, trying to elevate their state. And I have, like our friend George Cleeve, let my tongue rule my head. I'll ask forgiveness, for myself. They may care for their own."

That summer he would have liked to go less frequently to Meeting. There was so much work and not enough money to hire someone to help. However he knew that did they fail to go they would be fined for every Meeting they missed. The fines were used to pay the Reverend who, Francis sighed, must have need of a servant to tend his vegetables and feed his cows and chickens while he was visiting parishioners. God's work now paid better than trading but did the war in England go on much longer the settlers would have naught to pay their fines with save vegetables and eggs.

Mary and Francie were happy to be going until they discovered they must leave for home as soon as the Meeting was over. Mary rarely saw Elizabeth Page then, but Hannah came with her father on his several prayer visits to their house. The two girls talked and laughed. However Hannah made sure they stifled their laughter when her father was praying. Her sister had told her God didn't like laughter.

On one of his visits Reverend Jenner told Mary and Francis that Elizabeth Page had that spring come to accept the godly faith. "She doth now work most diligently to bring her husband and children in that same path with her." There was on his ruddy face and in his voice an expression of honest concern so closely mixed with pride that he found he could not still the one without losing the other. It was a problem he had felt the pinch of before.

In one of their few meetings that summer Elizabeth expressed her fear that she would not succeed in the conversion of her family, because she sought it for the wrong reason. "Not for the greater glory of God," she said, her voice and thin delicate features reflecting the tension of an unceasing battle with herself, "but because I cannot bear the thought of an eternity without them."

Mary remembered her own struggle to accept God's will, whatever it might be, when her father lay ill with the plague. There were so many pitfalls in the godly path to salvation. It was not enough to turn one's back on sin. Kindness, love and duty, it seemed, had double faces to lead and distract. A wayward thought slipped into her mind. Heaven must needs be a sparsely populated place and a lonely one. She pushed out the thought—and shivered. The devil continued to find her easy prey, it seemed.

Near the end of the summer they had a letter from Prudence, written down by Margaret since Prudence had but small skill in writing. Grace, who married the year before, had given birth to a son. The other children were well and growing. She worried that they had not sufficient herbs for all that might befall in that strange place and was glad to hear that neither wolves nor savages had attacked them. "And," she finished, "'Twould seem with all the fishes and furs there are about, thou wouldst have enough for our passage soon so that this too long separation could be ended. 'Twould be better to live on little, my loves, than that this ocean should remain much longer between us."

Francis covered his face with his hands, a wave of despair that he did not often allow himself to indulge in, overcoming him. He well knew he had not near enough money to pay their passage over to join the poverty he had brought Mary and Francie to. In his own letters he had painted their life here in brighter colors than were warranted so she would not have cause to worry. But now she could not understand the long delay in sending for them—perhaps putting it to some fading of his love for them over the long time and distance. Of that at least he could reassure her.

Margaret added her own note at the end of the letter, telling of her trip with John to London to see what might be done for brother Robert who was still confined in "that wretched prison at Winchester house." They were anxious to discover if, as they had received word, Edward and his wife and small children were living now in extreme poverty. Mary's throat constricted and her voice was barely audible as she read, "It is most sadly true. How I have wept to see the small dark room they now live in with scarce enough food, I am sure, to sustain them and to know the truth of what we had further heard, that Edward has slipped from the godly path into his old ways of gambling and drink. I can but wish that he had stayed in New England."

A stab of longing for that same thing made Mary catch her breath.

"Or that his wife had been willing to go there. She is a pretty pious creature—overmuch timid though. But there 'tis wrong of me to put my brother's weakness on to her. I had better pray, and so I do, many times each day that he will find his way back to the path of godliness before it is too late. To supplement my prayers dear John sends to them regularly small amounts for food. Robert, too, hath from his prison instructed his solicitor to give such aid as is necessary to keep Edward's family from starvation."

"If one must needs starve 'tis surely better to do it in the merry streets of London than in this dull place," Francie muttered crossly, out of a vast experience of hearsay, having never been in London herself, but so low that Francis and Mary, each absorbed in their own memories and regrets did not hear. Her eyes snapped and glowed in the firelight as she banged the fire and its smoldering logs again with the poker.

Mary shook her head at Francie's vehemence, a wave of tired helplessness assailing her. Natural disasters—poverty, illness, these could be fought. But who would win, and at whose expense? She sighed.

"Cousin Margaret hath a wondrous quick and pointed tongue when she is angry. 'Twould be better, I warrant than thy poker in combat with Joan Winter." She sighed again. "Would that I had been born with such a weapon as that instead of the useless blushing and stammering I am afflicted withal!"

Chapter Eleven

The winter passed——not so cold as the one before—and spring came earlier. Francis's strength had declined further, but it showed little in his naturally gaunt good natured face. Mary noticed that he worked more slowly and paused more often. She said nothing, but worked harder thus assuring an increased effort from Francie also. However little Francie cared for work she cared even less to think that someone—particularly Mary—could do more than she. But, as hard as they worked they could not get as much planted as the year before.

Francie at thirteen, with her lively dark eyes and black hair, was blossoming into a bright rounded prettiness that caught the eye of several passing fisherman. On an afternoon in midsummer, one of these, a young fisherman from Richmond's Island, tall and red-faced with large hands and feet and wide seeming innocent eyes, strode up to their house with amazing self -assurance and did not ask but rather offered to marry her. Mary and Francie were standing just inside the door when the young man's encounter with their father took place. They could see the look of surprise, quickly replaced by an angry frown, as Francis sputtered, "The little one? What dost think thou rogue! She is hardly more than a babe!"

Whereupon the unperturbed young man, apparently noticing neither the tone of Francis's voice nor the unflattering reference to himself, said, "By the mass! If that be so then I had just as lief take t'other one. I will, afore the year be out, have a bit a land and some shelter and need of a wife, a good strong one."

"Thou knotty-pated fool!" Francis shouted. "Dost think thou art good enough to husband either of my daughters, thou who hast not brains enough to husband a sow? Get thee hence before I fetch my musket and embroider thy jerkin with't!"

A flood of adverse circumstances can overwhelm even those who have seemed safe on the high ground of some dream or other. Mary felt the cold edges of such a flood rising around them.

The harvest that year—despite all their hard work—was very poor. A late frost in the spring had caught many of the bean sprouts as they were just lifting their first leaves above ground, while an early one in the fall touched most of the pumpkins, so that they began to rot soon after they were brought in. The corn crop was reduced by half at least when several woodchucks managed to tunnel under the fence that Nicholas White and John Libby had helped them build the year before.

They were discouraged, but not overly worried. They thought of the abundance of fish to be caught in Long Creek on the warm fall days that were sure to follow the early frost. There would be, as well, the ducks and geese flying over Casco Bay testing Francis improving skill with his musket. And, always, the small but adequate store of money should they be short of food later in the winter. Though certainly it pained Francis to think that the money he had been saving to bring the rest of the family to New England was not only not to be augmented that year (that was an old burden) but might well be diminished.

The return of George Cleeve in September did much to brighten Francis's outlook. Although Cleeves' opponent Thomas Gorges had gone back to England, the planter he had appointed as Deputy Governor in his place, was no more favorably disposed toward Cleeve than Gorges had been. But Cleeve was unworried; he had come back triumphant, having persuaded an influential parliament man, Sir Alexander Rigby, to purchase an old patent that not only antedated the Trelawney Patent but included that land as well as Cleeve's holdings and the settlements of Blackpoint and Saco. Furthermore, Sir Rigby had appointed Cleeve deputy President of this his "Province of Lygonia."

"Though the tempers of Mr. Vines and John Winter have, so 'tis said, been much enlarged by reason of my husband's recent success," Mistress Cleeve declared cheerfully, "so much, as it seems they would fain transport the conflict in England betwixt Parliament and the King to these shores, Mr. Cleeve, forsooth, hath brought back, along with his good fortune, such sweet reasonableness and good nature as would pacify the devil himself."

"But not, methinks, Mr. Vines or John Winter," Cleeve smiled broadly, his eyes bright with unconcealed satisfaction.

However he brought unhappy news as well. The Civil War had spread to Plymouth. A brief attack on the outskirts of the city-by the Royalists had been repulsed but no one doubted they would be back. The citizens of Plymouth had voiced their support for Parliament, and the King's advisors were known to believe that "if Plymouth be lost all the west of England will be in danger."

Francis paced the narrow dirt floor of the house in an agony of concern and frustration. "All war is begotten of the devil," his voice was harsh with emotion, "but Civil War is the most damnable of all." He stopped and looked at George Cleeve. "I know you are a strong Parliament man, but for my part, I fain would support the King, unreasonable as he may sometimes seem, for I do deem his place and power to be a part of the divine order and a most necessary restraint on those of the meaner sort who, I doubt not, in the raising of themselves would bring down civilization." He raised his hand in a restraining gesture as he saw Cleeve frown slightly and open his mouth to speak. "Nonetheless were I there—and would that I were—I must needs defend my family and my home from attack, whoever the attacker might be. Such is the upheaval of right and the natural order that Civil War doth bring upon us! Ah, verily I do much fear for the safety of my loved ones." His face was pale and he swayed as if he would fall.

Francie shrieked and Mary rushed to his side, her hands reaching out to steady him. The fear and concern on their faces, followed by George Cleeve's quiet reason soon calmed him.

"The city wall is strong, my friend, and stands as always, between the citizens of Plymouth and their enemies," Cleeve reminded him, "And there are many to defend it. No harm will come to your wife and children. The endangered ones I fear for are in the unprotected farms and small villages."

If he was not entirely convinced, these reassurances did make it easier for Francis to get his feelings under control again and served him when Mary or Francie's fears overtook them in the months that followed.

However Nature, it was soon apparent, had another sore disappointment for the Martins that fall. The fishing they had counted on to augment their food supply proved much poorer than usual. And, as the winter months set in their store of food dwindled alarmingly. The pumpkins, usually in monotonous abundance, gave out first. Then all the beans, except those that must be saved for seed, were gone. By the end of the first week in January there was only corn to eat and what clams could be dug out of the frozen sand. Neither Mary nor Francie were very good marksmen and Francis's eyesight had grown poor along with the rest of his health so that when their store of shot and powder was used up they had but a few small ducks and a snowshoe rabbit to show for their efforts.

Francis decided the time had come when the money they had must be used to buy food. It was then they discovered how many others were in similar circumstances. A little money many had, but food to sell no one had. They walked slowly and soberly on the lightly crusted snow on the long miles back to their house, the winter sea being too rough for the boat. There was no break in the leaden sky. It seemed to surround and include the three travelers as well as all the stiff still trees around them. At least the wind did not reach this far from the shore.

"We must surely starve to death before the spring," Francie's frightened eyes and voice spoke for them all.

There was a long silence and then an angry flush spread over Francis's face. "No, we will not starve. We will be hungry, but we will not starve. There is corn in the storeroom and clams to be dug in the flats and shallows. And I will see Michael Mitton about some shot and powder for our musket." He looked stronger and more confident than he had for more than a year, and the girls caught the mood from him and went about the task of taking stock and rationing the corn with a kind of martial enthusiasm and dispatch. Though the mood did not last long it got them through the first bad days and the first realization that if the corn—with the untouchable seed corn set aside—was to last until spring their ration could be no more than a cup a day between them.

"Boiled in water with a bit of kelp and clams, when we can get them, 'twill do us well enough, I warrant," Mary said firmly.

Every day when the tide was low and it was not storming, they went out to dig in the clam flats where Long Creek met the River of Casco. The first week a January thaw made the work not unpleasant. But the warm weather abruptly ended as the temperature dropped well below freezing and stayed that way for three weeks. The holes were more chipped than dug, and yielded fewer clams than before. Their faces and feet grew numb with cold before they were through and their hands were raw and painful. Also the short rations and hard work caused them to slow down without realizing it, so that they must stay out longer to get even a minimum supply.

Though they were, after the first week, seldom ravenously hungry, they suffered often from stomach pains and sudden weaknesses in their legs and arms that were not relieved by any of the herb teas that Mary had from her mother. She worried about their father and watched him closely, but he seemed, at least, to get no more weak and tired than they did. She was surprised but much relieved.

Francis went to the Mittons, as he had said he would, in the hope of buying some shot and powder. Michael was not there, but his wife promised to speak to him of it though she was afraid he had scarcely enough for his own use.

It was now mid-February and for three days there had been no sun and the air so cold that for several feet out the salt water of the Casco river was ice. They hadn't had the strength to challenge the cold and the hard frozen flats. It was noon of the third day and Mary sat, after a few spoonfuls of corn meal and water, wondering dully if she would be able to keep that bit of food in her stomach. A wave of nausea came over her now after almost every meal and made it difficult, in her weakened condition, to keep the food down. Nausea had become identified with the tasteless yellow paste she must force down her throat. And the first time it had come she rushed outside and threw up on the snow, but the sharp ringing in her ears, the dizziness and cold sweat made her realize that death lay close in that direction.

After that, when she swallowed she concentrated all her remaining strength and will on suppressing the nausea and retaining the food—a matter of several minutes—until the nausea gradually faded away. She glanced at her father staring fixedly at the fire. And, just beyond him, Francie, her lips set tight. She wondered if they were having the same problem as she. They did not complain to one another. Even Francie's peevish tongue was silent. Perhaps they sensed that talking of their problems, naming them, only sharpened and gave more life to what was already almost more than they could bear. Or, mayhap at that moment they were simply silent out of the general lassitude and dullness such hunger brings with it.

Their lethargic shells were abruptly broken that day by two heavy knocks on the door. They started and Mary shook her head as the sounds penetrated her silence. But not until a muffled "Hello" and two more knocks followed the first did meaning become associated with the sounds.

Mary responded first—going to the door and inquiring who it might be. "Michael Mitton," was the answer.

A look of annoyance and dislike settled on Mary's face, but she hastened to lift the latch and let him in out of the cold.

"Ah-h," Michael exclaimed, as he took off his gloves and felt carefully of his nose. "'Tis a life saving stop this. Without your fire, methinks my nose and perchance a finger or two besides would have been kin to icicles before I got me home." His eyes gradually became adjusted to the dim firelight and he began to take in the room and its occupants. The one empty pot on the hearth, the three empty well scraped dishes on the table and, most of all, the three pale, hollow-cheeked faces. Below Francis's now thin white hair, the pockmarks stood out against the bones of his face. Mary was all eyes and mouth again as she had been as a child. But it was not a child's strained frown that stared back at him. And Francie's bright black eyes were dull, her small features pinched.

Michael had heard that the shortage of food was widespread in the province that winter, but he had not seen such sad evidence of it before. His carelessly good-humored features clouded briefly and then his proficiency in polite conversation came to his rescue.

"You have showed good sense in biding by the fire today," he smiled. "I, however, have let my love of fowling carry me too far from home. Howbeit, so good hath the fowling been, I could scarce bring myself to stop."

"For you, mayhap, it hath been good, but not for all of us I fear." Francis commented, trying to keep his voice light.

"Marry!" Michael exclaimed. "I had almost forgot thy want of powder and shot. 'Twas in part for that I have come this way today—to tell you that my wife hath spoken true. I have not over much left myself. But, I can, at the least let you have a little to protect yourselves."

Francis nodded his thanks, his face expressionless. He had not expected even that much.

"Now for the other purpose of my coming here—beyond the benefit of your fire. Yonder bag," he nodded toward a bulging deerskin bag he had set down beside the door, "contains a plenitude of fowl—the most, as you will see, being ducks, and of a goodly size!" He held up his hand as Francis opened his mouth to speak. "Nay, I do not want your money. So good hath the fowling been today I have already sold, at Richmond's Island, several times the number I have here, and would have cast the rest away had I not thought 'twould but serve to keep the thieving wolves alive. I would deem it a kindness did you take them and thus lighten my bag for the journey home."

"And what of your own family?" Mary asked stiffly—trying not to show how his smoothly worded offer annoyed her. Or, perhaps it was just that his well-fed presence seemed to patronize and mock them in their misfortune.

"By reason of many such days as this one, we have already an overplus."

"You could, in weather such as this, keep them frozen until you have a need for them." Mary felt Francie plucking frantically at her sleeve as she spoke, and her own heart sank at these foolish words that had not risen even out of pride, but from simple dislike of this man.

"Ha, I fear you have caught me," Michael laughed, seeming not to notice either Mary's frown or the edge of resentment in her voice. "Like to a gambler, a true fowler is never happy save when he is pursuing his sport. And, I warrant, if the storeroom be full Mistress Mitton will set me to chopping wood or some such dull pursuit."

Francis shook his head and frowned as Mary seemed ready to speak again."My daughter doth not speak for me." He had no use for the kind of pride he thought he saw in her face, and even if he had, the sight of his daughters—everyday, it seemed, weaker and paler than the last—would have overcome it. He even managed a smile with some of his old good-humored spirit at the thought of quiet amiable Elizabeth Mitton overruling her husband in anything.

"I warrant 'twould be unneighborly to resist such a call for help as this. We will be glad to take your overplus of fowl, friend Michael, and thank you for it."

Before he left Michael took Mary aside, "'Twould be wise, methinks, to make a broth of the first fowl so as not to offend thy stomach with overmuch food at first."

Mary smiled. It was kindly said. A heavy wave of weakness flowed over her and she felt close to tears. She was beginning to feel her dislike diminishing.

Michael raised one eyebrow and a corner of his mouth turned up, giving his face an appealing look—half sly, half boyish and quite innocent. The effect of this, much more than the flattering speeches—which he credited—had brought him his reputation as "a charmer of wenches." He made a slight bow.

"I count my gift of fowls amply paid for by thy rare smile, Mistress Martin, and see now why thou hast kept thy smiles so close—knowing their power."

Mary felt another twinge of aggravation, but suppressed it and managed to hold the smile on her face until Michael was out the door—a feat she could not have accomplished a few years before. A fleeting doubt of this accomplishment assailed her mind, but she had too much else to think about to bother with it.

A week of ample food had a miraculous effect on their bodies and spirits. Even Francis's face had a pinker hue. And now the daily trips across the bright crusted snow to the clam flats became outings filled with laughter at their frequent slipping and sliding.

In two weeks time Michael Mitton was back again with another bag of "excess" fowl and many compliments for "your charming daughters, Francis." Mary discovered that she now felt only an amused indulgence at his language. It was his way, a minor fault that could not detract from what was surely, she told herself, a generous, even sympathetic, nature.

One of the effects of increased physical and mental vigor was to set Francie complaining again. She did not want to distress their father, so Mary was the recipient of all her grievances, usually whispered in rapid succession just after they had slipped on to their mattress at night. "I see naught in this terrible place," she said one night, "but freezing, work and starving in the winter and, in the summer, sweltering, work and supplying flesh for the insects to feed on withal! I know not what you and father can dream of that would make you wish to stay in such a place!"

Mary could not have given an answer, even if Francie had expected one. There were times when she had had these same thoughts, but not for long and not seriously. On the other side there was always the beauty and the wildness—invisibly joined. And even the struggle she thought.

As her eyes closed, the streets of Plymouth came vividly into her mind—bustling with carts and horses, gesticulating vendors and merchants talking animatedly to one another. She saw Cousin John's round face flushed with the excitement of a trade. The city was always an exciting challenge for him—but—for others—like Edward—she slipped into a dreamless sleep.

Chapter Twelve

On a late March afternoon Michael came again. It was that time of year when the ground, almost bare of snow, except in the deepest parts of the forest, freezes stiff each night and thaws to a slippery muddy state during the day—in short it was the time when winter and spring have their yearly battle for the land. The Martins had just come in from yet another afternoon of clam digging to find Michael waiting for them by the door. There was no smile on his face this time—only a distressed expression as he handed Francis a letter.

"The news I have brought you in that letter is not good. I have heard of what it tells from the captain of the ship that brought it, so prepare yourselves."

They were prepared for an escalation of the war, even the fall of Plymouth, but not for the blow that was delivered. The letter was again from Prudence, but written in a different hand—Grace's small and careful one.

"Oh, my dear ones, such a grievous loss we have lately suffered. 'Tis hard for me to tell thee of it knowing what a sadness my words will bring upon thee. Just two weeks past on December 3, the King's men did unexpected attack the Plymouth garrison on the northern slopes of Lipson. Although our men did finally drive them off, the sounds of battle were in our ears for many hours, and we, safe inside the walls, were much frighted for the safety of our men. In the midst of this fighting must go thy cousin John to carry some rations to our brave defenders. And the cavalier fire, knowing not the armed from the unarmed man, hath caught him as he crossed the last field before the garrison. He never rose from there."

"Oh how we have mourned him, our dearest friend and caretaker, and how we mourn again thinking of you reading of it."

Francis could read no further. The paper dropped from his hands. He stared at nothing, the tears running slowly and steadily, unnoticed down his cheeks. Another son, a brother, a friend; John Martin had been all of these to him. Beside him Francie sobbed and Mary wept silently, sorrowing for John, but even more for Margaret in her loss.

Michael Mitton's face was sober and his voice rough as he spoke to them.

"I know whereof you grieve. John gave me friendship when I deserved it not." He was silent. For once his glib tongue failed him.

It was Francis who finally broke the long silence as he handed Michael the letter. "Please, I have no voice for this, wouldst read the rest of it to us?"

Relived, Michael took the proffered letter and began to read where Francis indicated. "But sadder still is it to see poor Margaret. Thou wouldst not know her. She is habited all in black, as is proper, and 'tis not that I mean but her manner and her way of living that is so much altered as to make her seem another than herself. Her face is pale and still and she doth go about her tasks with ne'er a word—unmindful, as it seems, even of her little ones. She doth spend most of her days on her knees or in reading of her bible or else in seeking out of sermons about the city—several ministers having come inside the wall since the siege began. The King's soldiers showing little sympathy for ministers of the godly faith."

"If thou wert here, Mary, mayhap she might speak with thee, thou hast so much her ear in times past. But, in truth, I could not wish thee here now. How many times since the siege began and John was lost have I for once been glad, my loved ones, that you were not here. But, withal, I would not have thee trouble about our safety or our comfort. We have, by means of dear brother John's forethinking, enough of food to last many months. He hath had, before the siege began, such quantities of food and drink brought in that our storeroom is full and bags and barrels line the walls of divers other rooms. Our only worry being that we may soon have hungry rats for guests, the garbage in the streets being much diminished since the siege began."

"How long it will take to get this letter out and on its way I know not. Almost every night there are some who creep forth from the city by boat or on foot but it is a matter of finding one and an honest one to trust this letter to."

When the first pangs of grief were past another desperate result of John's death filled Francis with despair. The siege of Plymouth had temporarily disrupted trading. But now, with John Martin gone, this temporary disruption would become permanent. There were, of course, other traders, other men of business in Plymouth who would welcome trade with New England but none, as far as he knew, who would carry him and his family for however long it might take for him to get established here. For days he gave way to deep despondency, scarcely moving from his chair. The specter of starvation had rallied his spirit and his strength—but not now. Emptied of hope he lost all motive power. His strength ebbed away, his body seeming to have caught the sickness of his spirit.

His daughters knew about his trading enterprise but not of his dependence on his cousin. This was surely just as well since there was nothing they could have done with such knowledge except share their father's desperation. What they feared, seeing how sick he had become, was that the weight of grief had added to the strain of near starvation was taking its toll and they were frightened for his life. Mary, knowing nothing else to do, followed her Mother's all purpose prescription for ills of the body and spirit and plied him with the usual herb teas. She gave him broths and stews of the fowl Michael Mitton had brought and, occasionally one, of fish as the days grew slowly warmer. After almost a week of this self indulgence, as he later thought of it, Francis roused himself.

He was a kindly, gentle man, but not a weak-spirited one, and the sight of his daughter's surreptitious frightened glances penetrated his despair. He watched them work about the house in their now faded, often-patched gowns, splitting and carrying wood, tending the fire, cooking. They had no time to sit and brood. He was proud of them and angry at himself. He was no better, in fact worse, than a child sulking and pouting because the world did not give him his way in all things. So he could not trade, for now at least. Others had survived off the land and so, somehow, could they. And once the siege of Plymouth was raised he would contrive, one way or another to bring the rest of the family here. It would be hard at first—his pride quavered at the difference in what he had planned to bring them to and the reality. But he reassured himself. There would be ten pairs of hands counting all. And, with such a number of workers as this, what could they not accomplish.

So he harangued himself out of his despair. If he was over sanguine, their survival depended on it. This trance is, after all, what we all practice more or less successfully. In this case his own success was passed on to his daughters as his despair had been before. Mary, joyfully noting his revived spirits and returning strength, said a prayer of thanks that the herb teas had worked again. Who is to say they had not played a part, the human body and mind having such a myriad of subtle communications.

The spring and summer of 1644 passed much as the year before. They did manage to plant more that year, owing much to a visit from their former helper, Nicholas White. He stopped by one day to see "if that house I did help thee build was still standing." He laughed—his sharp black eyes quickly assessing their present state. But so quickly was this accounting taken that the Martins never noticed. He offered to help them plant for the day in exchange for his supper and a corner to lie in for the night. Almost a third more of the garden was planted that day.

Nicholas White's quick hands and humorous tongue eased the work and made the time slide by on several other days as well. His jongleur self, it seemed, had always a joke or story ready-made for every happening. When one midday the black flies were at their worst and, despite the layer of grease they had applied, invaded ears, hair and even mouths—Francie, slapping and spitting, yelled her frustration at the sky. "May a plague take thee all!" Whereupon Nicholas, with mock severity, shook his head and cautioned her against such hasty words. They had put him in mind, he said, of a poor farmer tormented, even as they, by the black legions, as he hath called them, so that he did at last, half mad with slapping and scratching, cry out to the Devil, "Thou mayst have my soul if thou but takest the black demons from hence forever!"

"So frighted was the servant at his side by these terrible words that he did quickly get his feet in motion and put some several miles betwixt himself and the farmer. On the following day, the servant's courage being only somewhat restored, he did fetch a neighbor to go back with him to the field. And great was their fearful wonder at what they did see there or, more like, did not see. In the whole length and breadth of the field there was never a one of those black demons, though there were withal no lack of them still in every other place, But the farmer, alas, was also missing, nor was there ever sight or sign of him again."

"As for that field, the black legions were seen no more. But, since no one durst adventure their life and, mayhap, their soul, to plant there it hath, at the last, as I hear, grown up to wolfsbane and witches elm." Francie shivered pleasantly.

Later in the day a large flock of crows settled themselves, in orderly rows in a nearby tree, watching as each kernel of corn was dropped into its appointed hole. It was Francis's opinion that a little of their precious supply of powder and shot should be expended on "those feathered thieves lest they devour all the seed corn in the ground!"

Nicholas shook his head. "Methinks they would be gone ere thou hadst thy piece in hand. They and their cousin the Raven be so smart, 'tis said, if thou dost plant three kernels of corn together they will eat but two and leave the other and so preserve the crop alike for thee and for themselves. I know naught for sure of this," he hastened to add, noting the skeptical smile on Francis's face, "but I have heard much of how they can be taught to speak—to mimic wondrous well one human voice or another. A most useful trick, as one Simon Yogge, a peddler, hath discovered. This peddler, so 'twas told to me, was cozened by a greedy farmer who hath sold him sundry baskets of fresh picked vegetables and eggs and then, whilst Simon was at his lunch, filled all, save the top layer of the baskets with rotting stuffs—the which Simon did not discover 'til he wast many miles away at market. Farmer Totwell, so called, admitted naught of this and would in no wise make good the peddler's loss. Putting it off on Simon that he did spend the day in the tavern drinking and wenching, leaving the vegetables to rot in the sun. As for Simon, liking not at all to look such a gull, nor to lose the money he had given Farmer Totwell, determined he wouldst somehow pry his money loose from this lying old cozener and, mayhap, teach him a lesson withal."

"Now, as it chanced, our peddler had a raven that he had bought to keep him company in his travels. And, to amuse himself and others along the way, he did teach the creature sundry words the which it would repeat in just the tone and pitch Simon had spake them. 'Twas this did put in Simon's head a way to get his due and more back from Farmer Totwell."

"There lived in a small sod hut, close on the farmer's land, an old woman, Betty Stamp by name, that some thereabouts did deem a witch. Simon held not at all with this but thought 'tmight serve his purpose. He and old Betty were friends, by reason of her giving him shelter in her hut on more than one stormy night, and his repaying of her with a bit of wool, a turnip or mayhap some eggs from his baskets. He had betimes spake to her of his trouble and learned that she too had been cozened by this farmer who did oft, most conveniently, forget to pay for simples that he had of her. So he set forth his plan to her and she did quick agree to it."

"On a moonless night, some weeks later, Farmer Totwell sat a dozing by his fire when he was of a sudden roused up from his dreams of future cozenings by a furtive tap, tap, tapping on his door. Stumbling and grumbling he did hie himself to the door, but when he opened it there was nare a soul to be seen. And then, as he was about to close it up again, supposing he had been still a dreaming, out from a nearby bush came a voice, 'Betty Stamp hath put a curse on thee.' It was the very voice of that personage."

"Ha! Dost think I wouldst be frightened of thee thou ridiculous old fool? Farmer Totwell shouted, now thoroughly wakened. And, grabbing his cane from beside the fire, he ran from the house and began to beat the bush from whence the voice had come."

"'Betty Stamp hath put a curse on thee!'" This time the voice came from a tree on t'other side—to which the farmer hastily betook himself. Then the voice did seem to come from the front gate, then from the bush, then the tree again—and the farmer went will-he-nil-he back and forth shouting and swinging his cane as he went."

"In the meantime our Simon had crept into the house and fell to searching for the farmer's money box which he quickly spied under a mattress. From this box he took only the money he and Betty Stamp had been cozened of and a small bit more to cover all the trouble they had been put to by the cozener."

"The next day Farmer Totwell, in full ire, did ride the five miles to town and, stomping into the constable's house hath told him that the night before Betty Stamp, the witch, hath run about his yard, leaping in and out of trees and bushes threatening and cursing of him and as well had spirited his money from its hiding place."

"'I do charge the dame with thievery and witchcraft and demand thou tak'st her strait to the gaol from whence she can be tried and burned!'"

"The constable was much confused. Surely Farmer Totwell must be suffering from some strange distemper—Betty Stamp had stopped at his house all the night, having footed into town early in the evening to bring his wife the simples she did yearly mix for her. They did gossip until a late hour touching all the uses that these simples might be put to. And then— it being a passing dark and moonless night—Betty, at his wife's urging, occupied a corner of the kitchen until daylight. That she didst so stay he knew as he hath himself seen her on her way early that morning. 'Twould be better, the constable allowed, for Farmer Totwell to hie himself home to his bed with some of Betty's simples for the curing of the base humor that did afflict him and to stop looking to make trouble for a poor old woman lest he find himself in gaol."

"Farmer Totwell was from that day a sorely changed and chastened man. 'twas even thought his wits had been affected as he was spied on more than one occasion talking to a bush a tree and even his front gate. And 'twas also noted that he did bow and lift his hat most respectfully when Betty Stamp went by, and that this personage did now live much better than ever she had before. And, most especially, she did never lack for fresh vegetables and eggs.

"As for Simon and his raven, they betook themselves to other parts of the country to ply their trade, lest Betty Stamp's voice be recognized when the raven oft repeated "a curse on thee."

Mary and Francie laughed and clapped, their eyes sparkling in their grease and sweat streaked faces. Francis declared that Nicholas was as good a tonic as Mary's herbal teas. At which Nicholas swept his cap from his head and made a low bow. "And surely 'tis true, as I have heard tell, a merry life doth breed a long life."

If there were no more such light-hearted days in the months that followed—all was not gloom either. In the sun bright days of summer the clear cool running waters of Long Creek gave them many a quietly pleasant afternoon. But late in the summer even these small pleasures faded with news from Plymouth that Robert Trelawney had died in prison. And then there was another poor harvest.

The crows for some reason known only to themselves did not pluck out the seed corn they had so carefully observed the planting of. But, when it had ripened, a nimble coon scaled the pole fence and made off with a large share of it. The Martins caught sight of his sharp eyed, black masked face only once. It was the first time they had seen such an animal, and before they could stop gaping and get their musket he was gone. The woodchuck that earlier tunneled under the fence did not fare so well. He did, over several days, consume two rows of young bean plants, but one morning, lulled no doubt by his past successes, he let Francis get too close. And so, in a meal of roasted woodchuck, the Martins—in a manner of speaking—ate some of their beans earlier than they had planned. Mary sighed thinking the woodchuck did but seek to satisfy his hunger e'en as they. 'Twas no easy life for any of God's creatures.

In spite of these losses the harvest was slightly better than the year before, thanks to the extra garden they had been able to plant with Nicholas White's help and to a bountiful crop of large pumpkins. Also, Michael Mitton continued to come regularly—now to fetch Francis to go hunting with him, George Cleeve however was occupied with his attempts to assert his governance of the Province of Lygonia for his patron, Sir Alexander Rigby, against Richard Vines assertion of claims to the same Province for Sir Ferdinando Gorges. Michael brought them news of that contention and Francis found himself torn between his new friend Cleeve, whose honesty and judgment he had much confidence in, and Gorges, his old friend and the respected advisor of his youth. But then he heard from Michael of Vines' precipitous action in arresting Cleeve's partner Richard Tucker when he appeared in Saco bearing a letter from Cleeve with a proposal for submitting their controversy with Vines to the Magistrates of Massachusetts for arbitration. Michael added that Vines had also threatened Thomas Jenner when he protested the arrest of Tucker, this decided Francis in Cleeve's favor.

"We need no such choleric leader in this province to send us following the poor example of our mother country into battle with each other!"

Michael smiled. "Thou dost think my father-in-law to be of a phlegmatically humor?"

"Nay! Surely not—Francis laughed. But in this, at least, he hath shown a most commendable restraint."

"Ay," Michael agreed, "And would that the two Frenchmen to the north did show as much restraint in their land dispute before it spills over on to us."

Francis nodded. This was a matter much talked of by the settlers in the Province of Mayne. The close proximity of these quarreling Frenchmen—not much above two hundred miles away—made them seem hardly less of a threat than the Indians—and to their souls as well as their bodies. Mary had often heard the godly pastors rail at the Frenchmen's idolatrous worship and their venal priests who, in presuming to forgive the sins of their unfortunate believers, did challenge the power of God Himself. She shivered to think of such evil and the eternity of punishment that awaited them.

"Well, mayhap if they keep busy with each other," Francis said, "they will have no time to press that foolish French claim to all New England, as the one called D'Aulney hath made threat to do. Or so 'twas told to me." Francie gasped, "But dost thou not think God would protect us from these Catholic heretics?"

Michael suppressed a smile. "Indeed, as Will Shakespeare hath writ in one of his plays,'tis a consummation devoutly to be wished!'"

Mary could not stifle a quite ungodly delight that made her eyes sparkle and high color rise in her cheeks. She did not notice Michael's admiring glance. Plays—she had seen some strolling players from London perform once when she was small—and her father had told her of many others. They were as fine as dreams and—the damper fell—as much enticement to the devil. She sighed.

"I hope you are wrong Michael. Nature hath already laid a heavy enough load upon us," Francis said with a sigh as deep as his daughter's. "We need no such handsel from the Frenchmen, and if from them, soon no doubt, from their friends the Indians as well."

Michael shrugged. "I know naught of that." But in deference to Francis obvious discouragement he quickly added: "Doubtless their northern territories are vast enough to keep these spleenful Frenchmen busy trading, and, as you have thought, fighting amongst themselves for many years."

Now and again Michael had some gossip for the girls, as on that day. He told them of Johanna Winter's continuing strife with the workers at Richmond's Island, even causing some of them to write to Robert Trelawney to complain. And more recently daughter Sarah's marriage to the church of England minister Robert Jordan.

Francie sniffed. "She hath been treading on his heels these four years past."

"Mind thy tongue," Francis said, frowning slightly.

Michael laughed. "It hath oft been noted that Reverend Jordan is a minister as much of practical affairs as of religion. Mayhap it hath been John Winter's influence by way of Robert Trelawney that hath lured him more than maid Sarah's charms."

"Humph, charms indeed!" Francie mumbled, and Mary put her hand over her smiling mouth, and then with a stab of homesickness, thought how much Francie had come to sound like their mother.

It was also from Michael that they learned of the death of John Winter, who none of them mourned, but which did cause Francis to spin out cautious thoughts about possible trading ventures with a practical Reverend Jordan. But the greatest news of all was word that Charles I had been decisively defeated at the battle of Naseby. The Civil War was over!

Chapter Thirteen

L ate one March morning, only two days after Michael's most recent bountiful visit, the Martins heard a stamping of boots at the door. "That can't be Michael again so soon," Mary exclaimed. "We have not yet sampled the last fowls he brought to us!" But, opening the door, she found not Michael but their pastor, Thomas Jenner standing there in his grey doublet, heavy brown cloak and boots, his earnest face quite red from the weather that had taken a cold turn that day. As Mary helped him take off his cloak and boots Francis, looking somewhat puzzled, wondered what could have brought him to walk the fair distance from his house to theirs on such a cold day. Reverend Jenner sighed.

"I have come to tell you of three unpleasant things which you have need to know. The first will explain to you Francie, why Hannah is not here." Francie looked worried. "She is not sick is she, sir?"

"No, Francie. She is at home helping Esther pack up our clothes and utensils. I have decided we must leave the Province of Maine. But whither to go I do not yet know. I depend on the Lord to direct me. Now I only know that I cannot abide here any longer. Amongst other reasons one, the most important, is my discovery that a Mr. Robinson, unknown to myself has secretly gained the affection of my eldest daughter."

Mary and Francie gasped and looked at each other in astonishment. "Such a saintly face she hath put on," Mary whispered.

"She is taking my friend away." Francie scowled, but a tear ran down her cheek.

Francis's face grew red. "I know had one of my daughters been taken so I would do the same as you are doing. There are too many louts in this wilderness that think doublet and hose make a gentleman."

"What you say is true I fear," Reverend Jenner sighed. "Howbeit 'tis not always safe to trust a gentleman."

Francis smiled. "Having been a trader for many years I know that well enough."

"I do not doubt that you do, Mr. Martin, having heard many good words about your ability and, I should add, your honesty in trading. The last, methinks adding much to the first, especially the approval of our Lord. But mayhap you do not know this gentleman I will mention well enough yet. I speak of the Reverend Robert Jordan, who is now likely to control the trading ventures of his wife's deceased father. Divers of my parishioners have complained of him as being more likely to cheat them than John Winter. And I know that, like John Winter, he continues to claim that what is now his land doth extend to the Presumpscott River, which he insists is really the Casco River named in his patent. I know that is not true since the Indians I have talked to in my efforts to bring them to the godly faith—without success—have all assured me it has always been called the Presumpscott as it is in Mr. Cleve's patent."

Francis shook his head—wondering if he could lose his dream to such as these. Then almost smiled. Knowing himself—he thought not.

"You were right to tell me this and right that I would think the Reverend Jordan to be more worthy of trust than plain John Winter. At least now I will be cautious if I have need to work with him."

"I am glad at least of that," Reverend Jenner said. "But I must no longer put off what I came especially to tell you of, most sad and concerning your good friends. They have great need of your help." He paused, shaking his head and sighing.

"'Tis hard to tell thee of it. Mistress Page—I had such good hopes of her. But Satan's violent temptations, persuading her she was a reprobate, she hath, two days since drowned herself in the river. Her body hath not been found. The current, it is supposed, having carried her out to sea. But her shoes and cloak were found on a mound of snow by the water's edge."

Mary, her eyes wide, stared at Reverend Jenner, slowly shaking her head. "No, she was not a reprobate. So kind and good she was—she cannot have been a reprobate!"

"I do fear it is so." Reverend Jenner spoke with a determined firmness, "though I would it were not, so seeming good she was. But taking of her life did but confirm her own conviction of her sinfulness."

An oath rose in Mary's throat and she clapped her hand over her mouth. She glared at the pious minister. His unctuous voice, his large nose and small eyes becoming suddenly repulsive. A thought pounded through her head; the sinner was not Elizabeth but the godly Reverend Jenner who condemned her. Then a wave of terror struck her and she ran out the door. The cold air stung her face and neck. She stepped on a patch of icy ground and fell. Her heart was pounding. Were the temptations of the devil upon her again? She got to her knees to pray, but the image of Elizabeth's gentle face and the

137

sound of her nervous voice calling to her children filled her mind. And then she moaned as that image was replaced by another—Elizabeth lying face down in the water, her pale brown hair floating about her head, her body rocking slowly back and forth in the icy waves. She felt her father's hands on her shoulders as he wrapped her cloak about her and lifted her to her feet.

"You do no good for yourself or your God thus, and have much frighted Francie and me who count perhaps overmuch on your sound humor to sustain us," he remonstrated gently.

Mary shivered. "I cannot believe she was a sinner."

"Indeed 'tis a hard thing to believe," Francis said soberly. "But there is much that the church would have us believe that is hard, and none of it so hard, methinks, as the way that is taught by the godly people. But you must leave your resolution of this to another time. Reverend Jenner came to us in his boat to fetch us to the Page's house. Thomas, being overcome by his loss, can do little and, with their maid servant recently wed and gone, there is need for someone to look to the house and children for a few days. Come. We have a way to go and the weather is turning bad."

The shallop moved slowly through the dark shallow waves close to shore. Above them the sky was an unrelieved expanse of grey that seemed to hang heavily just above their heads. They passed through occasional brief swirls of white that made it clear what the sky was heavy with and encouraged them to bring their muscles to the aid of the small sails. Mary and her father pulled together on one oar, Francie and Thomas Jenner on the other. This had the added benefit of keeping them a little warmer in the damp freezing air. And, for Mary, as always, the immediacy of physical labor turned her mind away from its preoccupation with the future—here and hereafter—to, this time, a very finite and practical concern for the husband and four young children Elizabeth Page had left behind. A wilderness family, even at its worst, and the Page family had been a good one, is a real partnership—each partner having his or her own sphere to work in and manage. Neither one was more vital than the other and each demanded full time effort. Servants assured a better life, but not one less full. The loss of one partner, then, was a blow on more than one level.

Mary's heart contracted as the Page's house came into view in a clearing along the Saco River. There was a look of barren desolation about it that she had never noticed before. Even when she realized this was the first time she had seen it in the winter—she shivered. Leafed out the trees had formed a sheltering frame around the house. Leafless they appeared to have stepped back leaving the house and its out buildings isolated. They had not reached the house when the door opened and an ample woman, her round face full of worry, stepped out.

"Mistress Warwick," Reverend Jenner greeted her. "As you can see I have brought the Martins as I promised and so am ready to carry you back to your family."

Mistress Warwick looked apologetically at the Martins. "I do be sorry you did have to come so far, but my littlest one hath been taken with a fever. Dear me, I was so frighted you would not get here before the snow got bad—it being near four miles upriver to my house." As she spoke she was hastily tying on her hood and cloak, the latter having obviously had much less to cover once than it did now.

Mary felt a hand slip into hers and looked down to see the sad and frightened eyes of Mary Page looking up at her. The melancholy expression of her face made her look older than her nine years and even more like her mother.

The Martins stayed at the Pages for almost two weeks. At first Thomas Page seemed hardly aware they were there. He seldom spoke and spent most of every day walking around inside the house, from room to room and outside along the edge of the river, through the woods and across the bare white fields. He did not appear to be looking for anyone but walked with a slow pace and an expression of quiet anticipation, as though expecting to meet someone wherever he went. Mary's heart ached when she saw this most eminently rational man thus affected and most of Francis's time those first days was spent following him about, fearful that when his expectations faded he might take the same path his wife had taken. Occasionally, as the days passed, Mary noticed that when his daughter came in his path he paused beside her gently stroking her hair and looking intently into her face. Usually, before he could move on she and the other three children were in his arms holding tightly to him and to each other. They did not ask him any questions, in fact did not speak at all.

Even the usually irrepressible five-year-old Sylvester who followed Mary and Francie about while they did the chores—shouting and chasing chickens and being chased by the goats—was quiet when his father was near. But one afternoon eight-year-old Christopher stopped Mary and looking up at her, an expression of strain and anxiety on his thin face, asked hesitantly, "Please Mistress Mary, why did my mother go away from us?" Mary felt a moment of panic. She understood no better than he.

"I do not know." Her words were spoken more hesitantly than his. She saw his face and body stiffen, and added softly. "Methinks 'tis something only God can know."

"Or perhaps our godly pastor." Thomas Page had apparently come in the room when his son was speaking. From the level tone of his voice it was hard to tell how this comment was meant, but Mary knew that since his wife's death he had refused to speak to the Reverend Jenner or allow him in the house.

Christopher ran to his father and buried his head in his cloak sobbing quietly.

Thomas said nothing more, but from that day he began to improve, to take over the responsibilities of the house and to go about with his children. His son had doubtless awakened him to needs other than his own.

As there became less to do at the Page's Francie started spending much of each day with Hannah Jenner. She was alone in their house most days while her father traveled, despite the cold, carrying the godly message to the scattered settlements around the Saco for whatever time he remained there. At his insistence his daughter Esther was away during the day as well helping at the home of Edward and Francis Robinson who were both sick with the same fever the Warwick's baby and many other settlers in the area were suffering from. Esther had need, her father said, to tread again in the path of righteousness.

Finally Thomas talked of Elizabeth to Francis and Mary. By nature a quiet man he had always taken things as they came. But this he could not, and the pressure of it broke through his reserve. His voice was harsh as he told them of his conviction that the godly faith, in the person of Thomas Jenner, was responsible for her death.

"See what he had convinced her of!" He took a piece of paper from a small leather bag at his waist and handed it to them.

"We found it"—his voice faltered—and he went on with some difficulty. "Pinned to the cloak she left by the river."

The note was in a small neat hand. "My dearest love, I do not wish to leave you and our children thus, to put yet another sin on this my already over-burdened soul. But the fear doth grow ever stronger in me that by reason of your love you wilt refuse to put this reprobate from you and so will share in my sin and doom yourself and mayhap our children as well to an eternity of hell." There was another line, but Mary could read no more. Pity and the same terror that had gripped her when she first heard of Elizabeth's death overcame her again. After a moment Francis broke the silence.

"Reverend Jenner hath said it was Satan's bewitchment did persuade her she was a reprobate."

"I know what he hath said." Thomas clenched his fists. "I know! But what hath Satan to do with such as she? There was no sin in her, I tell you. Only

Thomas Jenner who hath made her think there was." His face was twisted with anger and pain. He turned away from them and shortly after they saw him hard at work at the wood pile where he spent the afternoon.

He spoke no more of his wife—except to briefly ask them to forgive his outburst. His old quiet steadiness seemed to appear more clearly every day as though he had determined to turn his face and his efforts to the living.

Francis learned from Reverend Jenner that the Page's former servant girl and her young husband were but barely surviving in a tiny sod hut about ten miles south of Saco. It was not hard to persuade her to come to work for Thomas Page again and he was quite willing to have the help of her husband as well—which left the Martin's free to return to their own home. Francie had no desire to leave and thus miss what few visits there were left before her friend was gone. And so she sulked, there being nothing else she could do about it.

The day before they were to go, Mary slipped out of the house and went down to the place beside the river where Elizabeth's cloak had been found, drawn by a need to make some kind of farewell to her friend. It had snowed twice in the past week and Mary's were the only footprints in this secluded curve of the river bank. She stood, watching the dark heavily moving water, as she prayed for understanding, or failing that, acceptance of what she could not understand. But, even as she prayed, she could feel that deep resistance, against the way things were, rising once again. A brown oak leaf, that until just then had clung to its native branch, skittered by her feet, swirled upward once and glided into the river where the current caught and carried it, circling erratically, down toward the sea.

Only a week later, Thomas Jenner came once more to bid them a last farewell. He and his son and daughters were leaving the next morning on a ship for England. And he said: "I must once more bring thee bad news. Thomas Page hath died."

Mary stared at him numbly. Besides the usual chores she had been busy the last few days taking care of Francie and her father who had succumbed to the prevailing fever. She was too tired to feel the full impact of this new blow.

"But—what happened?"

"'Tis not known, save that he had not been sick nor was there any sign of a blow about his body when they found him lying dead beside a pile of wood he had been chopping."

"Dost think," Mary's voice shook, "he hath been struck down because he had reviled the godly faith?"

Thomas Jenner shook his head. "Nay." A brief look of gratification crossed his face.

"He was one whom God had lately wrought a good work. And, his soul having turned toward the Lord, he had come to see 'twas not the godly faith had brought his wife to her death, but his own refusal to accept that faith."

Mary caught her breath, thinking of the pain that this conversion must have cost him—and more. It was possible now that he was one of the elect, one of the few that would be saved, and husband and wife would, as Elizabeth had feared, be separated for eternity. Eternity! She felt an oppressive sadness weighing on her tired mind and tears rising that she with difficulty suppressed. And then another painful thought intruded—the children!

"The little ones," her heart ached dully. "What will happen to them? Is there no end to this sadness that is being visited on them—and us?"

"Indeed it doth seem that God is wroth. Most of the families of our river have been visited with the fever." His voice took on a heavily earnest tone. "In the heat of this visitation I began to consider what it might be that did move the Lord so bitterly to afflict us. And, along with other evils, I did come to understand that there was amongst us the sin of contention, as between Mr. Vines and Mr. Cleeve. Mr. Vines even threatening to use armed men against Mr. Cleeve and his partner Richard Tucker."

"But Francie and my father do not contend with anyone—nor surely can the Page's little ones have aught to do with this." Mary sat down and briefly covered her face with her hands to hide the tears of tired irritation, as much as sadness that she could no longer hold back.

"The Page's children—the innocent ones. Who will take care of them?"

Reverend Jenner ventured a small sympathetic smile, "Thou hast a tender heart Mistress Martin. Still thou needst remember that heavy thoughts and sighing do much distemper the body, and the mind as well. But the children—indeed the children. You should know they have not been forgotten. The servant Kate and her husband will stay on to care for them until they be apprenticed to some families. Henry Warwick and his wife—their infant son having died of the fever, do seem inclined to take one of them. For the others, the court will see to them. But I must not bide much longer here, there being others I must see today. So I will go up to the loft and speak briefly to your father and your sister and then be on my way." He put his hand gently on her shoulder. "Methinks thou hast troubled thy soul with overmuch worrying. God will see to't all. Thou hast but to secure thy faith firmly in thy mind and heart."

Mary managed a weak smile. He was not an unkind man. But her spirit sank. How was faith to be made secure? And, if not, how stop worrying?

As it happened Mary had little time to worry about her faith or the Page children in the next few weeks. Before Francie was fully recovered she herself had come down with the fever and Francis, who seemed to be recovering well, was taken with it again. They were more weak and tired than desperately ill. Still, for the next several weeks they seemed able to do little more than keep the goats and chickens fed, a fire going, and a pot of fish simmering over it.

Chapter Fourteen

By the time the pale green of April began to spread like a scarcely visible haze on the trees, and the winter frosts had melted and drained out of the garden Mary and Francie were as healthy and vigorous as they had ever been. Only Francis seemed to keep any ill effects from the fever. There was more of a stoop to his shoulders now, and Mary noticed that he moved as though his legs and feet had grown much heavier.

April's days of slow awakening turned into the violet strewn, bird singing days of May. And the plodding work of the garden that, in the first outdoor days of April had been almost a pleasure, became now harder and harder to concentrate on. Again Mary and Francie tried to make up for their father's slower movements with no better success than before. So it was until one day, toward the end of May, Nicholas White appeared again. He was, as he said, on his way from his land on House Island in Casco Bay to buy some supplies from Robert Jordan at Richmond's Island, despite the high rates of whatever he sold. There was no one else to trade with thereabouts. Again he offered them his help in their planting for a day or two for the pleasure of their good company, which he assured them, a man alone as he had been these several months, was in sore need of, plus a bit of food and a corner to lie in as before. However much he may really have needed their company, they surely welcomed his.

In the next two days the planting moved along in double time, marked often by the laughter that Nicholas White carried with him like some men carry tools or money. He stayed an extra day then sighed and admitted he still had need to finish planting his own garden. But in the morning before he left he sought Mary out at the edge of Long creek where she had gone to get a bucket of water. Her heavy brown hair glistened in the sun as she stood there smiling at him. The hardships of the last few years had only served to add character to her face and heighten a certain wistfulness of expression there.

Nicholas had watched Mary with a growing affection the spring before and again this year, but despite the Martin's obvious poverty, which should have made his hopes seem less unreasonable, he had not been able to bring himself to say anything to her or her father. It was certainly true that men and women of "ordinary degree" and even some of "mean condition," had in this wilderness, an ocean away from England, a feeling of freedom from the old bonds of class. This was something Prudence in her assessment of marriage opportunities for her daughters in New England had not taken into account. Nicholas was no exception, but neither was he a fool like that other suitor, so he knew well enough that his feeling of freedom was not shared by the members of the "better class." If he hadn't, the whippings that the province court meted out as punishment, almost exclusively to the lower classes, would soon have enlightened him. Still he knew that his prospects were very good. He was a fine fisherman and had learned enough about farming and carpentry when he'd worked out his indenture on Richmond's Island that he was easily able to supplement his income. As for his appearance, he was a short muscular man of about thirty with hair as straight and black as an Indian's above a sharp-featured, puckish face that was not unpleasant to look upon. So his own arguments ran, leaning first one way and then another. As it fell out, on this morning of his leave-taking, they had swayed him enough on the hopeful side to bring him to speak to Mary.

Looking fixedly at a scraggly young oak tree just beyond her right shoulder he spoke quickly of his prospects—his land, part ownership of House Island in Casco Bay, his need for a wife, his desire that it should be her—as impossible nay uncivil and foolish or even repugnant as that might seem to her.

Mary felt a quick stab of aggravation. She was Francis Martin's daughter still, even in her threadbare gown. But that feeling quickly gave way to her genuine friendly regard for him, and a concern not to hurt his feelings in refusing him.

"'Twas kindly said." She hesitated, but only for an instant. "And not, methinks at all uncivil or foolish. But my father has still much need of me here, as you have seen."

"'Twould be well with me if your father and your sister came with you to the Island," he quickly replied. The temerity it had taken him so long to rouse was not easily put down.

Mary raised her eyes and gave him a long look that pleaded for his understanding. "You know he would not leave his land," she said gently. And then, noticing that the eagerness had not faded from his face, she sighed. She was not a glib liar. "I believe," she ventured, "in this you have been concerned to help us in our need even as you have helped us with the planting, and I do thank you for it and hope you will accept me as your friend."

Nicholas smiled ruefully. "Well so be it. 'Tis pleasant at the least to have my boldness turned inside out. But you can be sure, Mistress Martin that it was all for mine own sake I did play the fool. But no harm done. And most heartily I accept your friendship and offer you mine in exchange." And, for once, having nothing more to say he brought their mutual awkwardness to an end with a brief farewell.

He was not even out of sight when Michael Mitton stepped out from behind a large spruce tree close by where she stood and impinged on Mary's thoughts. His nostrils flared and his eyes narrowed. He needed only to have snorted and pawed the ground, Mary thought, to have given a perfect imitation of an angry bull. She almost laughed.

Noticing her barely concealed amusement, Michael said stiffly, "You might have taken this good opportunity to teach that knave to recognize his betters, Mistress Martin."

Mary felt her face flush with anger. "How would you have known whether I did this or no except you were skulking like a thief in the bushes spying on us? As to his betters, it doth depend on how you judge "betters." If 'twere done by virtues methinks many now called better would be quick displaced." She stopped abruptly, a new worry had come into her mind. "I pray you say naught of this to my Father. He thinks well of Goodman White, who has so often helped and amused us, but is of a mind with you about the place that any not named gentleman should keep." She had already forgotten her own first reaction to Nicholas' proposal.

Michael raised his eyebrows and smiled. "You have let me feel the sting of your temper once again. 'Tis enough." He bowed in mock surrender. "I will say no more about this—servant—you defend so well, and nothing to your father either, as you would have it."

Mary checked another sharp answer. Her anger had faded and she felt embarrassed by its heat and at having vented it on Michael Mitton who had proved so good a friend—especially since she realized that it had come as much out of her own mixed feelings about Nicholas as from anything Michael had said. As a consequence she tried to be more agreeable than usual toward him. A change well-noted by Michael and attributed by him to his own charms, as past experience with a goodly number of the female sex had given him fair warrant for. Thus are we all, at one time or another, beguiled in our deductions of causes from effects and lead on to who knows what unwarranted actions or metaphysical conclusions.

Michael was on his way back from two days of fishing along the coast as far as Black Point where, the day before, he had heard, as he said, "many pieces shot off, in the manner of a fight," so that he supposed the French or other enemies had been at hand, or Richmond's Island taken at last by Indians or settlers tired of suffering low payments for their goods and over charging for Winter's and now Jordan's. But as it turned out, he laughed, his fears were for naught. It was only a drunken party on Stratton's Island where the guests amused themselves by shooting off their guns after each health was drunk. Their prowess at bottle tipping accounting for the battle like level of the sound.

As for the French, he had been told their feud was at an end. The man called D'Aulney had taken Fort La Tour at last. La Tour had been away so the attackers expected an easy victory. But, to their surprise, his wife had rallied those inside the fort and D'Aulney's men were turned back, not once but several times. At last, however, La Tour's men were forced to surrender. Whereupon the treacherous D'Aulney had executed everyone in the fort except Madame La Tour. She, it was said, had been cruelly forced to witness all the executions and, from the anguish of this had died herself a few days later. Although D'Aulney seemed for the moment satisfied with this present victory such a man as that was hardly to be trusted or expected long to rest content. They had all best be on their guard. Michael and Francis agreed and hoped the strife within the Province would soon be over and one or another of the governments decided upon, so that some defense could be planned against the French or Indians—or both!

Mary lay awake for a long time that night thinking of Madame La Tour. She was full of admiration, pity and a rising excitement. This woman had led the defense of a fort! Mary tried to imagine what she would have done—or would do if the need should arise—if she saw an armed French ship sailing into Casco Bay or a party of Indians creeping out of the woods. She realized, with a sudden dismay, that she was almost wishing for a chance to test her courage. At this point her thoughts were broken off, to be recast by Francie who pushed her body close against her sister's and said, between sobs, "Oh Mary, I do be so frighted. Surely we will all be murdered in our beds by the savages or the French or, mayhap executed! Oh," she moaned, burrowing even closer. "I could not watch them hanging thee or Father!"

Francis lay awake that night too. But it was not a possible raid by D'Aulney or other Frenchmen or Indians that troubled him or even strife between the governments of the Province. These were beyond his influence. It was what Nicholas had said about Robert Jordan continuing Winter's high prices for settlers' supplies and low payments to the settlers and Indians for their furs, pipe staves and other trading goods that had set him to thinking. Now that the Civil War was over, trade should pick up again. Could this perhaps be a last knocking of opportunity that he must not ignore? He felt a touch of his old enthusiasm and a new hope. Having worked for Robert Trelawney in England his abilities were known and, he had reason to believe, respected by the Trelawney family so that he might be recommended as a possible trading partner for someone in Plymouth. But there was little he could do about it from here. Clearly he must make his case in England. And, he smiled, as he thought of what Prudence would have called a good omen. Sitting out in Casco Bay was a ship preparing to leave for England in two days, if the weather held.

The next morning—with only a brief hesitation he put the last of his savings in the pocket of his cloak. And, after a brief visit with the Mittons to make sure of a place for his daughters to stay, he rowed out to the ship and arranged passage to Plymouth. Then, rowing home rather more slowly than he had left, he told Mary and Francie what he was going to do and why. Then he quickly added that he had arranged for them to stay with Elizabeth and Michael who, as it fell out were happy to have some extra help. Their last servant girl had but recently finished her indenture and had at once left to get married—a most regular occurrence here where young working men greatly outnumbered the available females.

"I fain would take thee both with me," he sighed. "But I have not money enough for that."

"You could take me, Father," Francie pleaded, her dark eyes brimming with tears and her face stiff and strained. "Mary doth like it here—she—"

Francis shook his head as he interrupted her. "Francie—there is not enough money—not even for one more. But, if all doth go as methinks it will, your mother and I and your brothers and sisters will return to you in good season, and then, once again all should go much better for us. Even if the trade should go off again we would, with all the family here, soon be fishermen, hunters and farmers enough to live well. Mayhap Grace and her husband would join us."

"But I would not wish to come back here at all," her voice was intense, her eyes fixed on her father's face. "I wouldst go and stay there—mayhap with Grace—until I should have found a husband too. One who would never want to leave England!"

"Say no more!" Francis said sharply to cover his own emotion. "You must do as you may not as you would." He sighed. "As I have already said, there is not enough money."

Mary was as upset as Francie, but it was the dangers of the sea voyage to and from England that caused her distress. She knew nothing about her father's business prospects, except what his optimism, as he spoke about a new trading partner, conveyed to her. So she tried to silence her fears and concentrate on the new possibilities that seemed to be opening up for them.

As it was, so soon was the ship to sail that both girls were too busy getting their father's food and clothes ready for the voyage to have time for either anger or fear. But that night when her father and Francie were asleep Mary crept out by the fire and wrote a letter.

"Most dear Margaret, though you have been always in my thoughts, I have not writ to you this long time since I did know how far gone in your sorrow you must be. But knowing, as well your deep love and care for your children I bethought me you would by now have much righted yourself for their sakes. Are you teaching them to read? I remember how, in the time of the plague, we did ofttimes sit in the garden and read. You helping me with the words I did not know (but now do!) And once again, as it seems I always did, I have need of your help. My father leaves soon on a ship for Plymouth to seek a new trading partner. And, though I fear that no one could do so well by him as John hath done, he must have someone. One like you who would speak to traders there of his experience and skill—which he hath not lost—but cannot properly practice without a trading partner in England. I will send this letter with him and so much love as well for you and my mother and brothers and sisters."

"You and our mother will be glad to hear that Francie and I are to stay with the Mittons. You will remember John's friend Michael who hath married Mr. Cleeve's daughter Elizabeth. They have two small children so I think we can be of help to them. Pray for us, as you can be sure we pray for you Mary."

The scheduled day was a perfect one for the departure. Soon after daybreak, their fathers' clothes and food loaded in the boat, they paddled down Long Creek and along the river Casco to the landing on Casco Bay with no notice this morning of the fish swimming close by their boat and a flight of noisy geese not far overhead. As they stood waiting for the shallop that would take their father out to the ship Mary gave him the letter she had written to Margaret and told him what she had asked her to do for him. The pock marks stood out on his face as he frowned.

"But father she hath said to me so often how John loved you that I knew it would please her to repeat what John hath said."

Francis sighed and smiled at his daughter. "Methinks you have grown wiser than I am."

The girls watched the shallop that carried their father out to the ship, and then the ship itself, gradually becoming a dot on the horizon, as small and alone as his departure made them feel.

Michael had told them he would come with a cart to take them to their new home late that afternoon, which would give them plenty of time to gather their things together. Mary thought ruefully they would need scarce any time at all to gather up what few things they had. The chickens and the one cow that had replaced the goats they could get the next day.

As they rolled up their straw mattress and put their clothes in the small trunk that had served as a seat for five years, Mary realized that talkative Francie had not spoken since they bid their father farewell and she had been so occupied with her own thoughts that she had not noticed. Looking now she was startled to see Francie's set jaw and narrowed eyes. She stared around the room with a look of real hatred on her face which hardly softened when her eyes came to rest on her sister. "You and father have your dream"—on her tongue it sounded like a deformity. "But, what prithee, have I to sustain me in such a place now that Hannah is gone?"

"But you did ask to come with us," Mary said, hesitant before the cold edge in her sister's voice.

"I was then hardly more than a babe," she snapped, the full scorn of her seventeen years in her voice. "But even had I been as old as I be now how could I have known then how strange a way it is thou see the world! Thy dreams and distant futures. Dost thou not see there is no place to live but here and now and it is a misery?"

Mary stood quite still and silent as Francie finished speaking and ran out the door. Her words were unfair but not untrue. Every day words are exchanged—but meanings, do we exchange meanings? There are so many ways of looking at the world. She thought of Margaret, Reverend Jenner and Elizabeth Page; herself and her father; her mother and Francie; the French and the Indians; the King and parliament. She felt suddenly isolated—surrounded by a shell of her own impenetrable thoughts in a world peopled only with other impenetrable shells. She shivered. And the here and now, how substantial was that? This house, was it not the same warm protective place they had left that morning with their father? But now it seemed to have shrunk, to be scarcely more than a hovel. She felt a cold breeze coming through several cracks in the wall and saw threads of smoke rising from holes in the daub chimney. Was this here and now more real than the one she had lived in for the past six years? She knelt briefly, praying once again that she might be satisfied to accept what she could not understand. On the hearth only one or two coals glowed and those but dimly as she closed the door behind her.

Chapter Fifteen

There is something about relative ease that is in itself at first soothing and then exhilarating to those who come into it suddenly from a condition of real privation. So it was for Mary and Francie. It is true that the Mitton's two-story frame house was not so well furnished or provisioned as the home they had left in Plymouth, but it was so many times more opulent than the tiny dwelling they had just come from on Long Creek that it had as stunning an effect on them as their old home would have had.

The house resembled the Page's in its tall square shape, but it was considerably larger. There were two main rooms downstairs—a living room or hall, as it was called, and a kitchen—each one almost as big as the Martin's Long Creek house, and each with a cavernous fireplace. The one in the kitchen was particularly commodious, with an oven in one side and several pot hooks, iron pots and three legged skillets in its wide smoldering mouth. Off the kitchen was a brew room where the beer was made and stored, along with the milk, butter and cheese, and beyond that the store room where the grains and other supplies were kept. At the top of a set of narrow wooden stairs were two bedrooms, one shared by Michael, Elizabeth and the youngest Mitton, an infant daughter, the other occupied by the two older children—a two-year-old boy and a four-year-old daughter now joined by Mary and Francie.

The hall had four small windows, three of them covered with oiled paper and one with the rare luxury of glass brought back for his daughter by George Cleeve from one of his several trips to England. There was a long table and several wooden benches in that room, sturdily, if not very elegantly built by the Mitton's man servant, Amos Gullett, a short, long-nosed, gnome-like man with a fringe of curly black hair around the edge of the Monmouth cap he always wore. He was perpetually smiling, good-natured and willing. His large head atop a small thin body with long spidery limbs, gave him a grotesque appearance, especially since there was scarcely a time when some part of his anatomy was not in motion. And when he spoke, his words seemed to come into his mouth almost faster than he could get them out. He was not the most experienced help, but what he lacked in experience he made up in speed and good will and, above all, in loyalty. He had been begging on the streets of London with a well-scarred back as proof of the effort that had been made to drive him from this "profession," one he would happily have given up if he had known another. George Cleeve had hired him to carry some supplies to a ship and then, impressed by his speed and eagerness, had taken him on to New England as a servant for his newly married daughter. Amos was lifted, as it were, overnight and, as it seemed to him, from Purgatory to Eden and neither hard work nor cold nor the frequent sport made of him by the children and adults alike could dim his enthusiasm. If the children made fun of him they also loved him and Elizabeth found that she could trust him, no matter what else he might be doing, to know where the children were.

Just a few feet behind and to one side of the house was a good-sized barn portioned out just then to four cows, three calves, a bull, eight pigs and a dozen or so laying hens and their rooster. The proceeds of the barn and the large garden, plus the results of Michael's expert fishing and hunting stocked a very ample table, such quantities of food as Mary and Francie had not seen since they left England. There had been plenty of food at Richmond's Island, but Joanna Winter had parceled it out with a very thrifty, or as the men complained, grudging hand.

Although there was much work to be done, it was done in this atmosphere of ease and plenty that soon brought a marked change in the two sisters, body and spirit. Mary lost the appearance of strain and tension that had given her face an almost hard, or as we might say, Puritanical look. Such faces can be seen in the portraits of many early pioneer women, undoubtedly due in their case, as in Mary's, not to the constraint of religious fanaticism but to the constant strain of circumstances that required emergency qualities of courage, self-sacrifice and endurance. Now Mary's face softened and resumed its natural look of dreamy preoccupation which had the double attraction of innocence and mystery.

Francie's sour, frowning aspect and whine vanished and were replaced by her former pert, high-spirited manner and a chirping as gay and frequent as that of a nesting bird. Within a week of their arrival at the Mitton's she had undergone a remarkable change in attitude and outlook. Mary smiled to hear her sister, who had so recently insisted on her hatred of New England, talking to Elizabeth Mitton of marrying one day and having a home as fine as this on her own piece of land, "mayhap not too far from here."

Elizabeth had neither her mother's loquaciousness—or her father's quick temper, but by some fortuitous amalgam of inheritance she ran her household with an unobtrusive efficiency that Mary admired and wished she could have emulated. Everything was well cared for under her quiet control, including her own neat unruffled appearance. She wore her dark brown hair pulled smoothly back from her forehead, and no wayward strand ever fell about her face even on her busiest days. She had large observant blue eyes and a long straight nose above her narrow mouth and rather receding chin. There was little of conventional beauty here. But the better one knew her kindness, quiet intelligence and unexpected sense of humor, the more pleasant her face appeared. That her husband scarcely noticed her, except when he needed something, came to seem a reflection on his taste rather than her appearance.

She had come to New England with her mother and father in 1630 when the Indians were much more frequent and friendly visitors than they had lately become, and the Indian children were her only playmates. Occasionally now an Indian man or woman would greet her by name and would exchange news, half in English, half in the local Abenaki Indian language.

Michael, watching one of these exchanges with a look of uneasy disdain, commented in a fractious tone that his wife was as humorless and silent as the savages she grew up with. Elizabeth answered quietly that the Indians at least were not humorless but full of laughter and talk, when they were with their own kind. Mary, hearing this thought it true as well of Elizabeth herself and remembered how quiet and humorless she had seemed when they first knew her. More than once lately, she had come upon her and the children—and Francie too—dancing around the kitchen. Elizabeth laughed then at Mary's puzzled expression.

"I am not," she said, "of a faith that does not allow this innocent pleasure." At which Mary, to her own surprise, smiled her understanding.

Elizabeth and her mother had acquired considerable knowledge of the native plants and their uses from the Indians in those early days and, in a letter to Plymouth, Mary recounted some of what she and Francie had learned by watching Elizabeth.

"She doth make a bright red dye from the root of a bush they here call Sumac, though 'tis not much like to our English ones, and yellow dye from the flower and the stem of the golden rod. They have here also a most useful berry they call a candle or sometimes a tallow berry that does, as the name says, give out a tallow or candle wax when they are boiled.. The wax rises to the top ready to be skimmed from there and leaving a dark blue water behind that makes another fine dye. And here also is a sunflower that has roots most pleasant to eat when they are roasted in the coals of the fire or boiled. And it seems no matter how many you dig up, there are still more the next year, so well do they grow."

"And of remedies, they have many. For burns she stirs up a plaster of hemlock bark, boiled soft and stamped between two stones until 'tis thin as paper. And with a like preparation of birch bark she did bind up a wound on her daughter's knee. For colds she uses sumac boiled in beer, and for the fluxes, the tender tops of a plant they name sweet fern that they do also boil in beer or possets. I have writ these down for you to have when you come, as we hope, full soon and will do others as I learn them."

Joan Cleeve came often and was most welcome, for her own good nature and for the news and gossip that she brought from her other visitings, as well as word of her husband's struggle to establish Colonel Rigby's government over Sir Ferdinando's New England "cavaliers". That was a major topic of conversation wherever anyone gathered in the province, as the Civil War in England had been. The outcome of which—putting parliament and parliament men like Sir Alexander Rigby in power—brightened the prospects of Cleeve and his patent from Rigby. In fact, Mrs. Cleeve noted, Mr. Richard Vines a patentee and supporter of Sir Ferdinando Gorges and the King's party had taken his family and left for Barbados turning his office of Deputy Governor of Gorges Province over to Henry Josselyn. But, Mrs. Cleeve sighed, the change in leaders brought no fewer threats against Cleeve and his party.

"I pray they do Mr. Cleeve no harm before he can get approval of his patent from Sir Alexander Rigby and the Parliament in England. Howbeit I do doubt that Mr. Henry Josselyn, known to be a most honorable man, would let threats go past words," she sighed.

Along with the other news she brought them that fall was word of the first hanging in this territory north of Massachusetts. This most awesome and debatable power of the law and civilization, long since established in Massachusetts, had taken place some months before in York, a goodly distance from Casco. The news of the end of the Civil War in England and the disagreement over the patents doubtless delayed their discovery of the hanging.

"And most sad, that the first upon the scaffold was a woman, one Katherine Cornish." Mistress Cleeve shook her head with an expression of what one might call righteous pity on her face.

"What hath she done?" Francie asked, her eyes wide.

"She hath killed her husband! His corpse, 'tis said, was found in a shallow cove beside his sunken boat, a long stick driven in his side." Her listeners gasped and she nodded as if to confirm their horror.

Amos Gullett had paused to listen on his way through the kitchen, his feet shifting and his face impatiently grimacing with the strain of holding in the information he had on this subject from his own sources.

"It be said she did cry out her innocence to the scaffold and," his words leaped out, "more—that there be many do wonder at such strength in the wench that she hath drive a stick," he made a fierce stabbing gesture in the air, "near through her man's body." Francie shivered and Mary clenched her fists and frowned at the floor.

"Thy words outrun thy tongue, Amos and, methinks, thy head. Dost think the justices did not search out the truth before they brought her into court? She hath had the test of touch. And those who did stand witness to it say the blood did start up fresh from the corpse where she hath put her finger. Further 'twas said she was a most lewd woman." Mistress Cleeve crossed her arms firmly across her ample bosom as if to give emphasis to this last piece of information.

Amos was almost dancing in his eagerness to release some further words on this happening. He winked suggestively. "If lewdness now be proof of murther, then I warrant murtherers must be full common hereabouts. And there be them do say the justices did 'ave some private knowledge did make them full privy to her lewdness and, withal, there may perchance be one among them more worthy to furnish out the scaffold than she who swingeth there."

"Watch thy words, rogue, when thou dost prate of thy betters!" Mistress Cleeve snapped, glaring at Amos' still smiling face. Admittedly the smile was somewhat more roguish than was proper after such a reprimand. Mistress Cleeve let that pass. Partly, no doubt, because his good-humored face was hard to be angry with for long but also because of what she admitted after he had left the room. There had indeed been much whispering, she said, and some who hinted that this Cornish, being of mean condition and lewd behavior, had been made to take the place of the real murderer. A man, perhaps a gentleman. "Still," she shrugged, "'Tis but talk, and taking all in all the woman is small loss."

Mary gasped, her face flushed with anger.

Mistress Cleeve patted her arm. "Tush girl, I know 'tis pitiful, but no less the truth for that. Thou dost look through dreamer's eyes at life if thou think there be any would go out of their way to protect adulteresses—and that the woman did admit to."

Mary sighed, her anger already fading. A sign she was learning the lesson of submission? Or were her feelings growing dull? A wayward thought entered the debate. How closely were these two related? And she sighed again.

The Mitton house was not infrequently the gathering place for a diverse assortment of Michael's acquaintances. They had in common only their hunting and fishing skills, real or proclaimed, their store of lewd and miraculous tales and their capacity for aqua vitae. Michael showed little concern for social rank in picking his drinking companions, Mary noticed with an ironic smile, remembering his angry scorn of Nicholas White.

There was little use for the women to take to their beds until they were so heavy with sleep that even the shouts of laughter from the other room could not rouse them, and so they sat together in the kitchen talking and nodding as they sewed, plucked fowl or stirred some decoction on the hearth.

A regular member of this convivial group was one John Sears, a scale maker and fisherman but lately come to Casco. He was a large, well-padded man in his early thirties, with long dark hair and deep set eyes that followed Mary around appreciatively and with a dog like steadiness as she set the trenchers of food on the table for the meal that preceded most of the gatherings. She heard he lived alone, and supposing he was, like so many others, looking for a wife to tend his house, she dreaded that he might ask her to fill the job. He was a coarse, ill-natured looking man and might, she reasoned, take offense at her refusal, and so she tried to think of some tactful way to send him off. Howbeit his approach, when it came, was a much different one than she had expected, and her reaction to it swift and in no way tactful.

She was standing alone in the kitchen one late afternoon staring into the fire, her mind far from the task that occupied her hands. They turned a fowl that hung before the fire by a hempen string tied to a peg in the ceiling. Every now and again Mary brushed the fowl with grease from one of the pots on the hearth and gave the string a hard twist, so that it would, in untwisting, twist a little again until it came to rest and all must be begun again. She heard no steps behind her, only suddenly felt an arm around her waist and a large heavy hand on her breast. In one motion she knocked the hand down and twisted away, glaring at the leering face with revulsion.

Sears laughed, but his eyes narrowed as he spoke. "Well, thou art a touchy wench. But, as 'tis said one skirmish doth not decide a battle."

"She is Mister Francis Martin's daughter." It was Elizabeth's calm voice. She had come in as silently as Sears. He shrugged.

"He has left her in my husband's care while he has gone to England."

Sears made a low sweeping bow of mock deference, but said pleasantly enough, "So be it Mistress Martin," and went off to join the men in the other room.

Mary looked down at her apron all bespattered with grease from an encounter with the hanging fowl as she jerked away from Sears. "I be better basted than the bird," she made a feeble effort at a smile.

Elizabeth smiled back reassuringly. "Methinks he will not trouble you more. He would not wish to adventure a court presentment and fine."

The drinking and laughter continued much later than usual, or so it seemed to Mary as she lay drifting in and out of sleep. Michael was telling a story about a mermaid, "marvelous fair" who had risen out of the water one morning like a mist, materializing before his eyes. And, "smiling enticingly the while, hath made trial to overturn my boat." At which another voice she recognized too well made comment. "'Twould seem she had a mind to fish for cod that day."

A loud roar of laughter followed. Mary buried her burning ears under the covers with a renewal of revulsion and anger rather than embarrassment, and with the sound thus muffled was soon solidly asleep.

Elizabeth had been right. John Sears did not bother Mary further or even look in her direction. Like some men, and women too for that matter, he had little sympathy or respect for the feelings of his fellow human beings, but much for their laws and courts. Mary's easy state of mind returned and was even enhanced by the new job she was given.

Amos, having come fresh off the London streets to New England, had no knowledge whatever of farming, but enough native wit to speedily learn, and so well that the animals as well as the planting and harvesting became his responsibility. But this year the unseasonably warm weather made it possible to conserve hay by taking the cattle to graze in a nearby pasture. However the herder, because of the possibility of wolves in the bordering forest, had to spend the day with the cattle. Since Amos' time was still taken with harvesting, Mary, at her own request, was given the job.

The pasture was about a quarter of a mile from the Mitton's house on a point of land overlooking Casco Bay with its numerous islands like phantom green shapes that appeared and disappeared with the vagaries of sun and fog. Mary felt almost guilty. It was surely no work for her to walk about filling her eyes and her thoughts with this expanse, and the beginning of color in the leaf trees while her nose absorbed the smells of the late berry bushes and firs. Amos had assured her that should a wolf appear she had but to fire her musket to drive it off—which much relieved her mind that remembered too well the scrawny starving wolf that would have eaten their pig. She was not sure she could shoot one.

So the pleasant days were passed in as happy a combination of reverie and bible reading as she could remember. If she spent a larger portion of her time in reverie, her dreams, she thought, were now more earthbound and less fanciful. She had in these six years in the Province of Maine come to believe that sin and suffering, the machinations of the devil, were part of the human condition. Still, in this new land, there was, perhaps, a chance to build a society where at least man and his diabolical adversary would be more evenly matched.

In one corner of the field there was a natural rise where she could get a good view of the whole, and here she made herself a comfortable seat of fragrant fir boughs decorated with as many red and gold leaves as she could find. So pleasurable to her senses was this mock throne that she might have thought it sinful if it had not been here that she retired resolutely from her reveries to read her Bible. The cattle, having a surplus of rich grass in this place, found no need to wander. At first Mary, musket in hand, walked about among them periodically checking their numbers. But, after a few days, they had become so familiar to her that she could tell at a glance if one had wandered off from the group.

As she daily watched the changing face of the bay and the sky that hung often low and possessively over it, Mary noticed also the frequent passage of fishing boats to and from the islands, and on one occasion, as one passed close to shore, she spied Nicholas White at the oars. He, catching sight of her also, stopped and pulling his boat on shore, came up the bank for a brief visit. He told her of his impending marriage, causing her to feel a brief irrational twinge at his quick recovery, and expressed his hope for the success of her father's mission to Plymouth, for her sake and her father's. "Though 'twould be no small benefit to the settlers here about to have a fair man to trade withal." He was, as he further said, on his way to finish a house on his island for himself and his soon to be wife. He hesitated, his sharp features softening visibly, then added—"Remember there be someone thou, or thy father or sister, can turn to for help if there be need." She saw that he had not so much recovered as come to accept things as they were, which, she thought ruefully, she had so much difficulty doing.

Other than this one brief visit, Mary's days were all spent alone, save for the numerous foraging birds and small animals that flew, hopped and scurried by her with no more than a casual curious glance in her direction. Though she certainly did not have the soul of a hermit, she was, for that succession of days quite happily alone.

With the first days of November however the inevitable coming of winter became more evident. The wind grew stronger and sharper and Mary found herself spending even more of her time sunk down in her sheltered seat of fir and leaves.

One bright clear day when the air was cool and the sun warm she put aside her bible and, closing her eyes laid back to get the full warmth of the sun on her face. Abruptly the light and warmth disappeared, too swiftly to be caused by a passing cloud, and Mary, startled, opened her eyes to see Michael Mitton standing over her. She sighed and smiled her relief.

"If I had been a wolf you would have been eaten," he said with a mocking smile.

"I was not sleeping," she said guiltily and started to get up, but found that her legs were pinned between Michael's and she could not move. Before the possible meaning of this had penetrated her mind he was kneeling, one hand on her leg the other on her shoulder pushing her down into the leaves. Trying to twist away she only found herself sinking further. She cried out and then pleaded as she felt his hand pushing her skirt above her knees.

"Do not do this—oh I beg you do—" His mouth shut off her words and she felt herself sinking, spiraling down in an abyss of pain, fear and sensual arousal so overpowering that all other thoughts and feelings were shut out, as though a wall had dropped in front of them.

Her return to rational consciousness was preceded by a vague feeling of lassitude and humiliation, slowly replaced, as reason reasserted itself by a wave of hatred for the man who now lay beside her. She sat up and glared at him, her face red with shame and anger. "How could you betray your wife, a good, kind woman you do not deserve?"

"Never fear," Michael said. "I do not neglect her."

Mary scowled. "And how do thus to someone you had promised to protect? Is there no honor then between gentlemen?" His only answer was an amused smile.

"What do you think my father will do if he should hear of this when he returns?"

Michael got up slowly, brushing the bits of crushed leaves from his clothes. "He will not return."

Mary paled. "You lie! As soon as he can get trading goods and money to continue the Trelawney business he will return."

Looking at her tumbled clothes, her hair falling loose from her hood that had slid almost sideways on her head and, most of all, her large frightened eyes, like those he had seen so often down the barrel of his musket, a brief expression of remorse and concern passed over his face. But, as he saw her eyes narrowing in anger, it was replaced by one of cynical condescension.

"Robert Jordan has the Trelawney business now. Your father will get nothing. If one is young, in favor, or of high rank the money flows. But if you are older—as your father is—or out of favor, as he also is, by reason of John Winter's reports of him, which have caused him to fall to the rank of decayed merchant, a drought of money suddenly occurs."

Mary shook her head distractedly. "I do not believe you! Trelawney's sister will speak for him." And then, fixing her eyes on Michael's face, her anger spoke again. "Even were it true you have betrayed the trust your friend has placed in you!"

"Enough!" he snapped, his face now stiff with anger, as her thrust hit too well home. He reacted with as much force and more practiced skill.

"You make too much of nothing. Your virtue! It was made to be lost one way or another." And, he added sarcastically, "you enjoyed your loss as I know and you cannot deny."

"NO!" Mary turned her head and wept. When she turned back again Michael was gone. With his departure her anger and shame turned inward upon herself. She writhed within at the thought of her sinfulness. The act was forced, but she had not fought him hard enough! As she started to get up her hand touched on a familiar shape, her bible. She pulled back as though she had been burned. What hope was there for her salvation now? What hope for a reprobate such as she? "A lewd woman." The words came into her mind like the snap of a whip. And also the frequent insistence of her pastor that if good works were not proof that the performer was saved, evil deeds did give witness that the doer was a reprobate. She sank to her knees and tried to pray. But she could not find the thoughts and words to put together. In her despair she cried out, "I vow it shall not happen again."

For two weeks she easily avoided Michael. His days were given over to shooting ducks in the early morning and fishing the rest of the day. And since the cows had now been brought in from the pasture Mary, working about the house, usually managed quite easily not to work alone. Then— Amos becoming busy cleaning and hanging the fowl and small animals that Michael had brought home—she was given the job of feeding the chickens which meant a daily trip to the barn alone.

With elaborate caution she waited until Michael had left the house to fish or hunt or on some excursion with his friends. He spent, so it seemed, as small a portion of the daylight hours at home as he could and, even when he was there, paid her no attention at all. She began to relax a little and to think that perhaps he had repented his act, or her angry words had destroyed her attraction for him. And then one morning, as she turned to leave the barn, she saw him standing by the door, his arms across his chest, watching her with a look of amused assurance on his face.

"Did you suppose I had forgotten you? Or that you did really wish I had?" He grabbed her and pushed her down on the hay. She struggled briefly, but he took her again.

She now grew steadily more quiet and melancholy, seldom speaking, especially to Elizabeth whose kindness she felt she had betrayed.

However a letter had recently come from Francis recounting the difficulty he had getting any satisfactory answers to his proposals from the executors of Robert Trelawney's estate, and it was to this that Elizabeth and Francie attributed Mary's melancholy. Now it was Francie trying to cheer her sister—reminding her of the unsettled times in England that would surely cause such delays as their father was now experiencing. Mary listened as she stirred a pot or fed the fire or pounded the dry corn kernels with hard and regular motions. Indeed the thought of her father and her mother had increased her anguish. There was the fear Michael had put in her mind that their father would never be coming back to New England with the rest of the family and she and Francie would be left here to fend for themselves just when she had learned how little able she was to manage her own life, much less to help her sister. But even worse was the thought of what her father and mother would suffer. She lay sleepless at night thinking of it. Her own shame she could almost bear—but had she not by her sinning brought the judgment of God down upon them as well? The words of the church were clear. "The soul of the infant—as well as its body—is delivered unto its parents for their nurturing. And it is they who are responsible for its virtuous and godly upbringing." Mary twisted and moaned until Francie muttered angrily in her sleep.

Chapter Sixteen

The first days of December bringing neither snow nor cold that year did encourage visitors. George and Joan Cleeve came one day with news of the court meeting concerning the rival claims of government and, to which the new leader of the Gorges faction, Henry Josselyn and his company, came armed with guns and swords. But, as Mistress Cleeve explained, nodding her head with pride and satisfaction, "They being put to shame by Mister Cleeve and his company standing all unarmed before them did themselves put aside their arms and discourse peaceably. Which hath led to an agreement betwixt them to submit their case to trial before Governor Winthrop at the next court in Boston. And I do not doubt the Royalist claims will soon be dismissed and the government of this province will fall at last on Mister Cleeve where it doth belong."

Her husband only smiled at her firm declaration and shook his head. "'Twould please me to have your confidence, good wife, but I fear that the Governor of Massachusetts and the assistants—though they surely favored Mister Rigby's parliamentary cause in England's Civil War—are still prudent men who do not wish to anger either side, if they can help it, and so, I doubt not will avoid making any decision, if that is possible."

Mary felt somewhat more at ease now. Amos had taken back his chickens and she could stay close to Francie or the children. She also heard with considerable relief that Michael would shortly be off on his yearly trip to hunt deer and trade with the Indians for furs—to be gone until the end of December.

Just to have him gone was pleasant to think about. However there would be as well time to do what she had hardly hoped to do when she learned that George Cleeve would be going to Boston quite soon. She would ask if she might go with him in the hope of getting a job with a family there and so earn money to help her father. Perhaps the Lord had taken pity on her struggle and would give her time to make a true repentance. Then, on the afternoon before Michael was to leave she was walking with young Nathaniel and his sister Dorcas along a snow free path in the woods smiling as she listened to the busy chattering of the children and the not dissimilar sound of a chipmunk sitting on a log beside the path when she felt a hand on her shoulder—Michael! She tried to jerk away, but he had now a tight grip on her arm and pulled her steadily toward the barn.

"Your children," she pleaded. "I am tending your children."

He laughed. "Methinks 'tis more like they have been tending you! See they are sitting under that pine tree with the basket I brought them filling it with pine cones."

"I will scream," she cried frantically.

He shrugged his shoulders. "Only Amos would come. Francie said I must tell you that she and Elizabeth are down by the bay visiting Joan Cleeve so you must not worry if you don't find them at the house." He pushed her along before him through the barn door and down on a pile of hay. She lay limply beneath him, shame and hatred overwhelming her. As he got up he saw the tears that ran steadily down the sides of her face.

"Come, there be no need for tears. I never would call you whore, nor at all think ill of you. I am too fond of you for that."

She said nothing, but stared up at him, all her hatred speaking plainly in her eyes. He whistled softly, then shrugged.

"'Tis all the same to me." He headed for the door, then turned and said scornfully, "Puritans! Thou art no less given to sinning than we, but would deny your joy in it. Thou art naught but unsaintly hypocrites!" She felt the sting of truth in his words and took them upon herself. The godly are not so she thought. Only I—weak-willed and sinful.

With Michael gone Mary still spent little of her time alone. In solitude she could not control her thoughts, used as they were to wander freely. She worked now and talked obsessively to Elizabeth and Francie about herbs and planting and every household method, and with Amos about the care and feeding of the animals.

"Some gentleman will get himself an excellent wife in thee," Mistress Cleeve said to her approvingly and Elizabeth and Francie agreed it was good to see her spirits so much improved.

Then two weeks after Michael left she became sure she was with child. There was now no eluding the dark thoughts that tormented her. A daughter of Francis Martin. She could see the words, bright and sharp as her mother had spoken them. They hung together like a shining flail and she cringed before it.

She had already brought the judgment of God down upon her father and mother and now the scorn of the world would fall upon them as well. Sin she had and she must pay, but why her parents? The heretic questions still rose in her mind. But to what purpose? Neither they nor any other of her frantic despairing thoughts could show her a way to avoid what would surely come. Had she been willing to compound her sin there were, she had heard, potions that could be taken. She did not know what they were nor anyone she trusted to ask. If she were a man she could run away to sea. A painful knot of impotent anger tightened in her chest. If she were a man there would be no need to run away!

One afternoon as she sat sewing in the sun just outside the kitchen door, her mind for the moment numb and almost empty, she overheard Amos and Betsy Smite, Mistress Cleeve's maid servant talking. At first their sentences entered her head only in fragments. "Tamen Dill"—"she who had left the Mittons to get married just before Mistress Mary and Francie came"—"A matter of some haste" —"many a fatherless infant"—Mary became attentive—"doth call a man father who had naught to do with its coming into this world"— laughter. "There be more than one 'gentleman' hereabouts does think it no sin to tumble a serving wench," said Amos.

"And many an ordinary fellow hath got him ground already tilled and planted," Betsy said, laughing louder.

"Ay," agreed Amos. "And neither, I warrant, any the worse for it."

"That's as may be, if they durst adventure an eternity in the devil's company." Betsy warbled out "eternity" with no different quality in her voice than if she gave out a court verdict of ten or twenty lashes.

"By God's blood!" Amos bleated, "If 'tis as the pastor sayeth—and who should know more on't than he—then we be all, or most, of the devil's company already, by reason of the sinful nature we be born with and the sins that do spring up in our path as thick as weeds and as hard withal to be rid of. And Marrie, if eternity be already lost 'tis scarce amiss to look to the present!"

Mary's despair and shame deepened as she recognized the company of sinners she had now joined. But bit-by-bit the foreign logic of the words Amos had spoken became less strange, finally impressing itself as familiar in her mind. If she could not now be saved, so her thoughts went, she might at least, if she found a husband, avoid bringing worldly disgrace upon her family and herself and the child. Until that moment she had given no thought to the child, the most innocent victim of her sinfulness. The story of Louisa and Begette came into her mind. She had not thought of it in all the years they had been in New England. The vivid memory of Begette and her dead infant struck her like a physical blow, from which she recoiled with anguish and guilty despair. But here the harsh unbending spirit of her much tried Puritan resolve served her in an oblique way stiffening her mind against the weakness of anguish and confirming her decision to find herself a husband and at least spare the child a life of scorn and rejection.

That there were many young men in the province almost as anxious for a wife as she was for a husband, she had no doubt. But this helped her little. Most were of the meaner sort and would not think, of themselves, to approach her (the bold young red head had been an exception, but he was married now). Besides, she had not the easy manner with them that the maidservants of their own class had and knew no way to encourage them.

She thought with regret of Nicholas White. What a pleasant and kind husband he would have made. A true friend, if not a lover. But even had he not been about to marry someone else, what kind of a friend would she have been to foist another man's child upon him as his own, not to mention, she thought, with a mixture of scorn and pity for herself, her own degraded person as wife. For despite the easy acceptance of such things she had heard in the voices of Amos and Betsey, and her own admittance of the practical logic of their words, her pride still longed to reject it for herself, while knowing she could not.

The other choice that came to her mind was so repugnant that, after her first revulsion, it perversely presented itself as a fitting punishment to inflict upon herself. The child? Any father, as the world was, had to be better than none. John Sears! Her mind cringed from the name. If the "meaner sort" had been determined by looks and character he was surely a man born to it. But, in her present frame of mind, this thought only seemed to make her resolve more firm.

He did not come to the house now that Michael was away, but that was better for her purpose. She had seen the spot where he tied his boat when she was minding the cows in the fall and knew that her past habit of walking out alone would make it unlikely that anyone would even notice her absence, much less the direction she headed.

For three afternoons she brought an arm load of hay and sat in the small bush-draped cove staring at the empty curve of water—afraid he would come and still more frightened that he would not. It was late on the third afternoon that she finally saw him rowing in, his back toward her. Her whole body shrank from the sight and her feet at the merest suggestion would have lifted her up and away from there. But no such suggestion slipped from the firm grip of her will. She sat motionless as the boat slid onto the sand, almost brushing her skirt. At first he did not see her. The shadowed shore forms had no definition to his sun struck eyes. But she could tell by their slow widening when her shape began to emerge. Looking up at him, she tried to appear both surprised and pleasant, judging her achievement by the succession of expressions that crossed his dark face. There was first surprise, followed by annoyance and then a questioning half smile.

"I doubt you knew whose boat landing this was?" His eyes narrowed.

"I knew," she answered, and watched, her heart sinking, the look of wise amusement that crossed his face.

"Ha! Even gentlewomen get bored then?" He put a heavy fish stained hand on her shoulder. She resisted the impulse that almost brought her hand up to push his away, as she raised her eyes to his and smiled. An answer Edward Trelawney had made to one of Margaret's disparaging remarks about actors—"Self preservation doth make actors of us all at one time or another"—passed through her mind as she said softly—"'tis less bored than lonely I have been with naught but females for company." She swallowed. "Methinks 'tis a longing for mine own home and a husband to attend to doth trouble me."

He gave her a brief look of angry mistrust, as though he suspected her of mocking him in some way. But the vulnerability of her position evidently quickly reassured him. "Ah thou hast then the same need of a husband as I of a wife. 'Twould seem," he paused while his hand slid slowly inside her bodice, "that thou and I mayhap could make a pair Mistress Martin." He began to push her back onto the pile of hay.

Trying to keep the frantic wave of revulsion out of her voice as his foul smelling body descended over her, she said, "Do you not think we should wait until the marriage bed and not risk being presented at court for fornication?"

"The court will know naught of this," he breathed heavily." And 'tis well we know before we join ourselves for life if we do suit one another."

When he had done, he stood over her laughing while she scrambled to her feet and tried to rearrange her gown and tuck her hair back under her hood with a shaking hand. Finally, since he said nothing, she pushed away the equal measures of nausea and timidity that had seized her and said with a weak smile, "Do you not think we mayhap do suit well enough and might set the marriage day full soon?"

"Ha! So you would beg such a one as me, would you, gentlewoman?" She saw with dismay the look of triumphant dislike on his face.

"'Twould seem thou art more whoring wench than gentlewoman. And didst thou really think that even did I not already have me a wife in England would take one of Michael Mitton's leavings to my bed?"

When he had gone Mary threw up in the bushes and then frantically washed herself in the frigid waters of the bay. At first she shivered with a combination of cold and continued revulsion. But gradually a numbness of body and emotion set in and she was freed from the constant bombardment of feeling her mind had been subject to. Reason, in full control, applied its logic to her plight. She was in truth that reprobate Elizabeth Page had supposed herself to be. And, far from any true repentance, she had heaped one sin upon another. Even, her reason spoke on, if there were no vengeful God or punishment hereafter, she would still bring disgrace upon her family here and now and a life of misery to the child she carried. But if that disgrace and misery could, by some act of hers, be avoided would it not be her duty to perform that act though named a sin by the church?

To walk out now into the ocean and let her body and its shame be carried out to sea could not, even if there proved to be damnation afterward, condemn her to a greater depth of hell than must already await her. She stepped mechanically away from the shore, still enclosed in numbness like the mollusk in its shell or the moth in its cocoon. But the abstract casings of the mind are no more impenetrable than their physical counterparts.

A blue jay swooping low overhead squawked, and the sharp defiant sound made her start and turn her eyes on the vanishing streak of blue. The numbness fell away like shattered glass as her senses were assailed on every side—the pungent smell of the sea, the flickering of the bay islands under the late afternoon sun and, on both sides, the full-bodied pines and the bare bone limbs of oak and maple stretching toward the sky. A wave of longing for life and this world washed over her and her body began to shake with cold and fear. She turned and stumbled back to shore where she fell to her knees, burying her hands in the soft sand. A great wave of relief and gratitude engulfed her.

The mental and physical shocks of that day, instead of immobilizing her in a state of desperation and despair, had the effect instead of rousing her out of the morass of self-recrimination that had absorbed her. A degree of numbness remained, but her reason now held sway over her emotions and imagination, that pair to which we owe our greatest creations and most perfect joy as well as our deepest despair and worst destructiveness. She looked now with a detached, even disdainful eye at her former actions and with cool resolve turned her thoughts to the practical concerns of survival. Nor did her once so readable face give any hint of her deliberations to those around her. Francie, in any case, was not given to noticing subtle changes in others. This failure of imagination often made her appear callous and self-centered and frustrated her sister who knew she was neither, or no more than most. Now she was grateful for it.

Her first concern was the obvious necessity of removing herself from that house, and even from the Province of Maine. Clearly she could not stay where the increasing evidence of her condition would only bring distress to Elizabeth Mitton and shame to her sister. The problem of where to go was not hard to resolve. She must do as she had already thought to do—ask George Cleeve if she could go with him to Boston. The prospects there were good, at least for maintaining herself, and that was as far as she allowed her mind to go for the moment. She knew that young women who had completed their indenture frequently left the province of Maine for Massachusetts where, it was said, the demand for servants was high and the pay better than it was here. The high regard the Cleeves had expressed for her almost made her resolve begin to slip, but reason put it quickly back in place. Such regard would doubtless assure that her request would be granted and even that a recommendation to some likely employer would be given if she asked for it. But she would not do that, she reassured herself, and then winced with embarrassment at this piece of hypocrisy. Telling Mr. Cleeve of what she planned to do in Boston, as she must, would of itself bring forth an offer of his help. So be it. She would work hard and, at least in that, justify his recommendation.

The one thing that continued to trouble her about this decision was leaving her now all too beguiling sister in the same house with the man who had seduced her and, as was now plain, others also. John Sears reference to her as one of Michael Mitton's leavings had confirmed her own suspicions. Nor could she take her sister into her own uncertain future, where her chances would be hardly better. She could only try to give her some vague warning and trust her closeness to Elizabeth Mitton for the rest.

Having heard again that George Cleeve was soon to leave for Boston, Mary was relieved when, the day after she had made her decision, he and his wife arrived for another visit. On the pretext of showing him the sturdy calf, dropped only the night before by one of the daughters of the first cow he had brought over from England, Mary took George Cleeve out to the barn and made her request. He looked increasingly disturbed as she spoke.

"Are you then so unhappy here with my daughter that you would abandon this place, where your father would have you stay, for another place you know but little of?" he asked with a slight frown, the first he had ever directed at her.

"Nay—not—never with Mistress Mitton," she stumbled. "She has always shown us naught but kindness and has indeed treated us as though we had been her sisters." She took a deep breath and then went on with the reason for leaving she had rehearsed. "'Tis naught here that prompts my removal, she lied, but rather my—our poverty. We hear but little from our father, and that not good news. There are those," her voice faltered briefly, remembering Michael's scorn, "who think my father too old and wanting in influence to affect the end he seeks. 'Tis time that I looked to my own future and my sister's. Perhaps I might earn money to send to Plymouth or for passage there for my sister and me." Her voice faded as she watched with alarm the growing look of suspicion on her friend's face.

The line between his eyes deepened. "Hath Michael Mitton dared bother thee?" he growled. In a panic, her eyes fell. She could not look at his face.

His voice rumbled out low, like distant thunder. "S'blood, the rogue! Hath he forgotten your father is a gentleman and, more, his friend? The gurly-gutted devil! Whoreson! I would see him whipped in court and banished from the province, if I did not think 'twould be my daughter and her children suffered most." His anger blew out in a quick storm of words and left his face looking sad and tense. "And she will never leave him." He was a man of action yet could not act upon this. He gave a long sigh.

"Yes, I do see—'tis well for you to go from here before he doth do more than bother you—as he hath others," he added sourly.

Mary felt a surge of relief. He thought she was reporting an assault on her virtue, not the overthrowing of it. "And Francie?" she said hesitantly, knowing now where her sister would be most safe.

"You need not fear for her," he scowled. "She can come and stay with us, and Betsy Smite go down to Elizabeth. 'Twould suit our Betsy well enough I know. She hath these past weeks prattled much of how she would wed Amos if she could. I know not if I do him much favor though." A slight smile lifted the corners of his mouth as he looked at Mary. "Come now twill be well. I know many in Boston, good families, who would be glad for one like you to help them—and—I know with money enough to pay you well."

All was worked out with few complaints. Amos, when he was brought to think of it, was as ready to wed Betsy, it seemed, as she him. So there was good enough excuse for sending Francie to take her place. Francie's was the one negative reaction. She had one of her sulking, snappish tempers for several days after she was told of Mary's departure and her own change of residence. She followed Mary around with complaints.

"Why is't that Betsy and Amos must be obliged whilst I am sent off here or there and no one to ask whether I wish it or not? And I do not!" She stamped her foot. Mary did think it was unfair, but could say nothing, which only roused Francie's temper further.

"And why must you bestir yourself of a sudden? Our father will be back." She glared at Mary—challenging her to deny it. "Hath he not said that he would?"

Mary's continued silence provoked her further. Her voice rose "And what think you he would say to you hiring thyself out in Boston like some wench of the streets?"

Mary raised her hand, then let it fall. "'Tis work, as you know well, no different from what we do now, save for the money, which we can use to help our father and mother."

Francie tossed her dark hair defiantly. "That's as may be. But if you would help them why can I not go with you? Can I not work as well as you?"

"You can," Mary admitted with a sigh, "and sometimes better. Still I am older and must decide what seems the best for you. I do not yet know how it will be in Massachusetts. But, be assured, as soon as I can, I will send for thee—for I shall miss thee sorely even with thy tempers." Whereupon Francie burst into tears and in the ensuing flood washed her temper completely away.

Michael was back from his trip, but now it was he who seemed to be taking pains to avoid her. Only once or twice did they meet face-to-face and then she looked at him with a cold detachment which surprised her and watched him lower his eyes and turn away. She wondered what George Cleeve had said to him, and was thankful for it.

On the day of their departure, Elizabeth Mitton came to her while she was putting her few possessions in the small trunk that was more than adequate for them, and gave her a basket of food for their journey.

"I have put some eggs in it and thought 'twould be safer with you than my father." She smiled hesitantly at Mary's sober face. "Thou art brave to set out thus alone in the world. I much admire such courage, though I have none of it." She stared at Mary intently for a moment, as if she would say more, but at last only murmured, "God be with thee."

A faint misty rain blew cold against Mary's face as she stood once again at the railing of a ship leaving now from Richmond's Island as she had come almost seven years ago. She had stood then with her father and Francie excitedly absorbing the details of the approaching land. Now, as she watched them recede, the fields and busy woods of the island were hardly visible in the mist, and only an occasional strident bird call mingled with the shouts of the seaman as they pulled out of sight of the shore.

George Cleeve, standing by Mary's side, looked down at her expressionless face and patted her hand in an awkward gesture of reassurance.

"You must not let this wet mood of nature drown your spirit. Her sun will shine on us again, and just so will your fortune change for the better."

His words drifted by unheard. Only the reassuring tone of his voice had reached her and called forth a grateful smile as Richmond's Island disappeared in the mist.

Chapter Seventeen

*I*f size and architecture were a final measure there would have been little about Boston to warrant the importance it had, for Puritans at least, in old as well as New England. There were, in this year of 1646, no more than forty or fifty houses, scattered on its muddy winding foot paths, and the greater part of these were humble one or two room cottages, some still with wattle and mud walls and thatched roofs. But, of course, for those who looked to this place for inspiration, its importance lay not in these base appearances, but in the vision of a Godly kingdom that its founders had set out to plant, and its modest success and the simple wonder of its continued existence in the face of the devilish machinations, as they saw it, of nature and the savages. To be sure, it was more a village than a kingdom and not altogether Godly despite the many score of weighty sermons that had been delivered, the banishments carried out, the whip, the stocks and the hangman's noose applied. But, withal, its purpose was intact and the effort to achieve it undiminished. Others too found much to admire in this Puritan town, where business as well as religion was pursued with dedication. Prosperity and grace were not thought incompatible. Still their first view of this wilderness outpost could scarcely have much uplifted the many Godly immigrants who strained their eyes across the outstretched water to catch a glimpse of their promised land.

George Cleeve had no thought of that kind of promised land as he stood on the breezy deck beside Mary while their ship, slipping carefully between the scattered islands, sailed into Boston Harbor. His mind was busy forming and reforming his justification of Colonel Rigby's government of that land promised by a less exalted authority than the almighty, but one the Puritans were as deferentially aware of as he. His eyes, meanwhile, enumerated the familiar landmarks. To the north the windmill atop its namesake hill. To the south Fort Hill, and between them the tree-topped Beacon Hill. At the foot of these hills the buildings were scattered out on their winding paths like the seeming wayward outcroppings of plants that are joined by a common root.

Mary observed the prospect before her with indifference, a state of mind she had lately learned to cloak her feelings. But then, as the shallop pulled up beside the dock, her nostrils flared. Her condition seemed to have made her sense of smell more sensitive and it detected an odor in the air, slight still, but not unlike the stench of Plymouth streets. A wave of nausea, that the motion of the sea had not aroused, swept over her and the despair she had pushed out of her mind overwhelmed her again, coming now from another source—that dream of the new world she had carried so long. Was this stench an omen, a portent of what the dreams of men and women must come to? Her knees buckled and she stumbled as she stepped out onto the dock. Cleeve's quick hand caught her arm and righted her.

"You don't have your land legs yet." He smiled, and then, seeing the bleak expressionless stare on her face and, recognizing it from his own experience of despair, said gently—"I think this motley village does not fit your dream of it?"

"There be scarce any trees," she murmured. Her voice was matter-of-fact expressing neither surprise nor regret. "But, if I did have a dream of Boston, I do not remember it. I am little given to idle dreaming of late."

Cleeve clenched his fists and scowled, "The whoreson! You must not let that wretch," he suddenly remembered there was more to her despair—"nor your father's reverses keep you cast down. Dost think I do not know the bitter taste of failure?" Mary saw his body stiffen. "But, by God's blood, that bitterness will not make an end to my plans—or dreams if you will." The sounds, the mingled high and low of voices, the clatter and thud of movement, the sights—men, women and children in groups and singly, assailed his thoughts. He frowned slightly. "Howbeit, with naught beyond the day's business to think on, what are we but beasts scrabbling and begging to stay alive."

As they walked, Cleeve began to speak again, as though conversing with himself and so low that Mary just barely caught his words. "So, dreams must needs confront reality. But I fear me I would as soon abandon the real world as my dreams." He sighed, then added ruefully, "But this world will not take leave of me."

As for Mary, she too found herself weighted down by reality. If there was little of a London or a Plymouth in the aspect of Boston, the level of activity in proportion to the population was surely as great. This was no sleepy little fishing village. Those sights and sounds that had thrust their way into Cleeve's thoughts reflected this. Several trading ships were anchored in the harbor, and at one wharf men clambered about with hammer and saw on the rising skeleton of a ship. On the paths men and women, seldom empty-handed, came and went briskly—some stopping to buy or sell where a ship had docked or at some convenient corner. A sleek hog hastened down one path with a very small boy panting in pursuit behind it. Mary's senses, now used to the less obtrusive presence of nature, were assailed and buffeted by this busyness.

Cleeve directed her attention to the ship. "I warrant yonder ship rises at the bidding of my friend, Major Nehemiah Bourne, a much-admired builder of ships in Boston. He hath but lately returned from England where he had command of a regiment in battle against the King." He paused—looking down at Mary's stiffly quiet figure.

"'Tis to his house we are going." Mary took a deep breath. "There is naught to fear," he quickly reassured her. "Major and Mistress Bourne are godly people, but jolly withal, and Mistress Bourne, as her husband has writ to me does sorely lack for another maid to help her in the keeping of their house—one of the finest in Boston."

The corners of Mary's mouth twitched at this, and Cleeve, much relieved to see even that faint hint of a smile, returned it in good measure, and agreed that being the finest in Boston might not seem overmuch guarantee of excellence. However, as she would soon see the Bourne's house was as finely built as the Bourne ships and comfortable as well. And in truth it did come quickly in view, being but set some way back on the same large lot that included the wharf where the ship was being constructed.

Sadly it reminded her too much of the home she had left behind in Plymouth. Like her childhood home it was a narrow wood-frame house with a second story that jutted out over the first. The leaded windows, too, were much the same as those so often seen in English cities. Inside there was a hall, or parlor, and large kitchen downstairs with a narrow staircase off the entry way that lead up to the three bedrooms. The furnishings, though not elegant, were plentiful and sturdy and included several cupboards and tables, numerous chairs, most of them handsomely carved, as befit the talents of a shipbuilder of the day. There was as well a bright profusion of decorative cushions, intricately embroidered, expressing in this case the talents of the mistress of the house. There was even a looking glass in Mistress Bourne's bedchamber.

Mary tried to mask the sadness that such resemblance as there was brought upon her with grateful words to Cleeve for his kindness in finding her so fine a place, and was rewarded by the look of pleasure—and relief—that crossed his face. Relief because he had, after all, more than her troubles to attend to here in Boston.

Mistress Bourne had met them at the door and insisted on taking them on an immediate tour of the house, apparently seeing no need to conceal her pride in it, though Mary noticed what Hannah Bourne seemed unaware of—a general dustiness and disarray, attesting to a lack of servants, a state of affairs that would never have gone unnoticed or ignored in her mother's house—servants or no! Mistress Bourne had, as many easygoing people seem to have, a high tolerance for disorder. She was quite small, a slight, fluttery, birdlike person and gave Mary the impression of being both indefatigably cheerful and harassed, a rather charming and disarming combination.

Her cheerfulness appeared not only in the present smile she wore, but in the clear laugh lines beside her large grey eyes and wide mouth, and was added to by the red and blue of her waistcoat and gown respectively. The air of harassment was the combined effect of the stray wisps of dark brown hair that had slipped from under her cap, the slightly askew angle of her apron and the two small muddy handprints that decorated her skirt. The latter contributed, it was not hard to guess, by one or both of two young children—a boy of five or six and a girl no more than four who ran and skipped around their mother.

Mary was quickly settled in a back room, off the kitchen, by the talkative Mistress Bourne, who chirped and flitted about her delightedly. "To have an English girl, and one of the Godly faith besides. Surely I have in some way pleased the Lord that he hath sent me such a one as thee," she said, looking Mary up and down with as much satisfaction as if she regarded a well-turned out pudding of her own making. It seems her patience had been much tried by the last domestic help—"the Indian girl," as they always referred to her, who knew no word of English nor aught of their ways. "She must needs be dragged to every task and then shown how it should be done. Mr. Bourne did think I had most surely lost my senses when he spied us going about our work e' the house—she appearing the mistress and I the maid." She laughed heartily. "She could in nowise understand what was wanted, or so she did make it seem, 'til I had finished a task. And so our days were spent with me doing the work and she doing naught save walk about at my heels. No doubt 'twas a mirthful sight. But you canst be sure I did no laughing then. 'Tis true the children liked her and she played well enough with them, when she did list, which was not often, so that I was not much dismayed when she hath disappeared one day. Nor did we seek to find her." She paused for breath. "Though surely we did miss that chance we might have had to turn her heathen ways to the godly path as we had thought to do."

This last was said offhand and as a matter-of-fact and not of troubled guilt.

The Bournes were both, as George Cleeve had said, devoutly of the Godly faith, but relaxed and good-humored in it.

Major Bourne, thin like his wife, but muscular and tall, with laugh lines as marked as hers, was of a quieter nature, given only occasionally to outbursts of enthusiasm over shipbuilding and the parliamentary cause in England. Both husband and wife had been born into the godly faith and had never been troubled by doubts or by thoughts that they might not be saved. They were virtuous, as they believed the bible and their pastor defined virtue, and they had no fear that their good-humored ways would slip over into loose behavior. Sin seemed more repellent than tempting, especially to Mistress Bourne who found it as offensive as ugliness which she also tried to avoid. Major Bourne's mind was simply too much taken up with shipbuilding and politics to give overmuch thought to sin. Being little tempted themselves they were not inclined to suspect temptation or evil doing in others until it was made plain to them, unlike their friend and leader, Governor Winthrop. He was, by his own admission, all too familiar with temptation and so was a severe task master, hoping to keep the frail from succumbing. But his own weakness made him more understanding of those who did succumb than were the Bournes. However, in the matter of punishment for proven sinners, they were in agreement, regarding it as a final chance to save the souls of the fallen. Though Governor Winthrop also saw it as a deterrent to those sorely tempted souls he recognized all about him.

The Bourne household proved an easy one to live in. Even the children were good-humored and their mischief was more often an excess of high spirits than a display of ill temper or unhappiness. At another time Mary could have been quite happy here and some of her doubts about the Puritan faith relieved, but now this happy household seemed to taunt her and make her own sin, and her deceit, the worse. She worked very hard, partly as a scourge, partly as a counter, an atonement for her deceit. But perhaps most of all to keep from thinking what would, what could possibly become of her and of the child. The thought of Begette and her child never completely left her mind.

There was actually less work to be done here than there had been in the Mitton household or in the Martin's house in Maine or Plymouth. The laundry was taken care of by a local laundress, new clothes made up and sent from England, as was the yearly supply of such necessaries as candles and beer. But still, with only two to do the work and Mary taking on the greater part of it, there was enough to keep her mind and body occupied from before dawn to dusk, and to call forth both exclamations of delight and concern from Mistress Bourne.

As she herself had no liking and little patience for household tasks she was the more impressed by Mary's concentration and efficiency and though constantly admonishing her not to work too hard continued to leave more of the cooking and cleaning for her to do, or to find most of it already done by the time she got around to helping. She began happily to concentrate on her needlework. And, in acknowledgement of the gift of time that Mary had given her, embroidered a sumptuous array of summer flowers on a piece of pale blue silk, "Left over from the gown I had made when we were last in England."

"Twill make thee an apron, if thou hast time to stitch it up," which she didn't. But it was so beautiful she hung it like a tapestry on one of the bare walls of her tiny room where the delicate twining stems and the bright red and gold flowers Mistress Bourne had so artfully worked seemed to revive her spirit and, oddly, to strengthen her will when, as frequently happened, that dark wall she had built in her mind against all thoughts but those of the immediate present threatened to crumble. It was an effect quite unlike that of those vast beauties of sea and land which, when she had time to view them, did revive her spirit, but also called forth those thoughts she did not dare to think.

One afternoon, when she had been at the Bourne's better than a month, Governor Winthrop and his lady came to call, bringing with them his son Deane, about her own age Mary judged. He was of a height with his father, and his features taken one by one were much like his father's, but in expression the son's seemed amiable, the father's stern. Doubtless the latter reflected the strain John Winthrop had so long been under as Governor and deputy Governor of the colony of Massachusetts. But later she heard the two talking and smiling with equal good nature about their mutual friend Roger Williams and the excellent land he had bought from the Indians and called Providence. He had been exiled from Massachusetts for some difference of opinion with the Puritans about religion, but this obviously had had no effect on his friendship with the Winthrops.

Deane introduced the friend he had brought with him, John Rolfe, a pleasant-looking young man, just lately come from England. He had dark brown hair and eyes the same that echoed the smile he gave Mary and she found herself hard put not to return.

"He would learn the skill of shipbuilding," Governor Winthrop said. "So we have brought him to the best builder of ships in Massachusetts." Major

Bourne shook his head at the compliment, but was soon off in a corner absorbed in conversation with young Rolfe.

The rest of the company was soon occupied in a discussion of the late Civil War in England. That being thoroughly discussed their talk turned to the civil war in miniature in the Province of Maine. Mary was pleased to hear Governor Winthrop admit that he would, for his part, as would many of the Magistrates in Boston prefer to see George Cleeve and his parliament supporters governing in that neighboring province. But, in justice, as Cleeve had agreed when he came to bid them farewell, neither party had had sufficient documents to prove their case, and so there was a legal draw, as it were, and the jury could not decide.

"Because of which," Cleeve had remarked to Mary and the Bournes, ruefully, "Mistress Cleeve will assign our defeat to my bad temper and some uncontrolled remarks she will be sure I have let fall, and will lament that she, being more politic, had not the pleading of the case instead of me. But I do swear, this time I did behave me most wonderfully reasonable, as Governor Winthrop will attest…"

And so he did that day in the Bourne's parlor, accounting Cleeve most honest and, withal, though much provoked by the failure again of his claim, had remained restrained in word and deed.

"But," he smiled, obviously pleased with the latest news he had brought them, "the Lord hath taken note of his forbearance. I have but two days past received word from England that the Commissioners for Foreign Plantations have determined that Alexander Rigby is the rightful owner of the Province of Lygonia and upon resistance of any of the inhabitants the governor of Massachusetts shall assist the officers appointed by Mr. Rigby. 'Twould seem that Mr. Cleeve's patience and persistence have at last been rewarded."

Mary felt a quick surge of pleasure for her friend that brought a light to her eyes and color to her face. The change was much like that on a darkened landscape when the clouds are suddenly breached by the sun, and brought another smile from John Rolfe.

Later, when Mary was out of the room fetching food and drink for the guests, Mistress Bourne began to extol the virtues of her new maid. And, the doors being open between hall and kitchen, and Mistress Bourne having a high and resonant voice which she made no effort to soften, Mary, to her embarrassment heard the fulsome praise her Mistress lavished upon her, "Modest, hardworking, honest, pious"—she heard herself described and cringed.

"Her grandfather hath been the Mayor of Plymouth," Mistress Bourne announced with a smile of satisfaction—as if this circumstance confirmed her astute opinion of Mary's worth. "And her uncle also hath lately held that office, as Mister Cleeve hath told us. And her father, as we have further heard from Mister Cleeve, is a most goodly gentleman who by reason of some ill fortune and much sickness hath fallen on bad times and now hath neither money to come back to New England nor any to bring his daughters to him there. And 'tis for this cause, methinks, that Mary doth suffer so often from the vapors and, withal, doth work so hard—as if she would of herself restore her father's fortune, or at the very least earn passage for herself and sister to England." There were murmurs of praise and sympathy and Mary cringed again.

Later, as they departed, John Rolf cast approving glances at Mary. Though it is questionable if these glances had much to do with the discourse of virtues they had just been entertained with. Mistress Bourne had in this an observant eye—as women had ever need of if they were to make the most of such opportunities as came along, for themselves and later for their daughters. She chided Mary for having paid no special heed to the Winthrops or their friend.

"A smiling look or a pleasant word would scarce have been amiss. Indeed 'twould have been as respectful, withal, as politic. And where dost think you would be like to meet a better match than this young John Rolfe—eh?" She did not pause for an answer. "Hardly in all of New England, and surely not in that Province of Maine you have but lately come from, where tis, as I have heard, peopled mostly by fishermen and farmers and those not of the better sort."

Mary bristled but said nothing.

"Come, dost suffer from excess of pride or from that shyness that hath before now robbed many a comely wench of a husband she fain would have?" There was no sharpness in her voice. All was said with kind good humor. But good-humored interference is interference still and Mary briefly longed for Elizabeth Mitton's quiet forbearance. She could see no way to avoid answering a question so kindly meant and so amiably spoken or to keep from entangling herself further in the net of hypocrisy and lies she had woven.

"I am not such as he could think to wed," Mary began. "I have no dower to bring to any union." At least this was a true reason, if not her true reason.

"Tush, girl," Mistress Bourne brightly pounced. "You cannot so easily escape as that. You must know that settlements of money, though not unwelcome, are not so much looked for here as in Old England. And surely you must further know that there be scarce enough maids to go around, and other things save money better prized in this godly community. Methinks thy virtues that I have this day recounted to the Winthrops are a most excellent dower to bring to any husband in this or any country!" Mistress Bourne's face and voice overflowed with happy conviction. She had quickly become genuinely fond of Mary and certainly convinced, not just of her goodness, but of the overweening, even self destructive nature of that goodness. And, above all, she truly enjoyed helping people—even those she was not fond of.

As for Mary, she stood in front of her would be benefactor with downcast eyes full of despair, increased by an accurate understanding of the character of this warm-hearted woman. How easy hypocrisy was to sustain and how hard to penetrate. It was too sadly simple to fool someone as kindly disposed as Mistress Bourne. She wondered how full the world was of reprobates like herself that no one detected.

"I cannot marry any one," she murmured dully, "whilst my sister, or any of my family want as now they do."

"Oh my child, my child—what can you with your small wages do to help?" She sighed, seeing how increasingly distressed Mary was becoming. "But come, I had meant to make you merry with this talk not sad, so I will say no more of this. What the lord would have done will be done. I will leave you in peace and would have you only, now and again, think on what I have said."

She was as good as her word. But it was plain to see that this restraint was hard on her concerned and sociable nature. She often shook her head in exasperation when Mary slipped to the back of the house or elsewhere out of view when the Winthrops or others came to call. And then there was the day when they were out walking together and just happened to meet young Deane Winthrop and John Rolfe on the path—or so the young men made it appear. Deane began talking with Mistress Bourne and John Rolfe stopped beside Mary and hesitated as if he would have started a conversation with her. She, however, kept her eyes on the ground as though she had not seen him at all and walked on in silence. Seeing John's look of embarrassed disappointment, as the two young men walked off together, Mistress Bourne briefly broke her silence on the subject to scold Mary, with only a half teasing shake of her finger, for a hard-hearted wench and allowed that mayhap it was better he did not win such.

"Indeed," said Mary. "'Tis true." Mistress Bourne threw up her hands and was silent.

However she dissembled for Mistress Bourne Mary would have been less—or more—than human (and she had given much evidence she was neither) if she had not noticed the good qualities of young Rolfe and thus felt herself for a moment seized by the pangs of loss. A young man, eminently suited by her father's as well as her own standards, had entered her life too late. But with as much dedication as some have been known to give to the pursuit of pleasure Mary sought work and immersed herself in it. And the latter had as numbing an effect as the former is rumored to have.

Work also made the long hot days of summer run by as swiftly as a mountain stream and with a like appearance of sameness, so that she hardly noticed their passage except when the increasingly vigorous movement of life within her brought time and the present chillingly before her mind. But plan she would or could not, and such chilling reminders as her body presented her with were quickly dismissed. To make the present bearable she banished the future and the work she forced herself to keep steadily at every day assured her nights of deep, dreamless sleep, the which she was deeply grateful for.

It was soon after the meeting with Deane and John Rolfe that Mistress Bourne decided to give Mary another job—the weekly trip to the market. This required a walk up the main street or path of the town to the market place, a spot near the common where most of those with something to sell or to buy were in the habit of gathering. Sellers attracted buyers and these included, for one or the other or both of these purposes all of the population of Boston and often the surrounding towns as well. So the market had become a social as well as a business gathering place where the latest local gossip and news from England and the other provinces of New England were exchanged along with money and a great variety of goods and services including, occasionally, indentured servants and slaves.

The crowd made a crazy quilt pattern of colors and shapes. High fashion cloaks, waistcoats and feathered hats interspersed with homespun and plain-colored caps and breeches. All in all, for most, a welcome feast of sound and color as it had always been for Mistress Bourne. So it can only be supposed she had hopes that encounters with others of her kind would cheer Mary, or that chance meetings might eventually wear away her resistance to John Rolfe. But Mary drew the hubbub around her like a cloak and seemed more by herself in the crowd than she was at home. However, on one such day she had just finished purchasing several plump pigeons from a young man with flaming red hair that blew about his face like a devilish halo, when from behind his wide back a vaguely familiar voice broke in upon her.

"Mistress Martin?" She recognized the hesitant voice before Priscilla Bickford's now even more ample figure appeared. Clinging to her skirt was a small replica of the seller of pigeons, disclosing her relationship to that young man. "I be Goodwife Gill now." She spoke with pride, but the red that rose in her round cheeks and her fingers twisting the corner of her apron revealed that the shy inept servant had not been totally routed.

"That be Willum, my husband. 'Tis Mistress Martin, Willum, who hath helped me when I worked on Richmond's Island. Doth remember that told thee of her?" Her husband nodded and briefly ducked his head in Mary's direction, then turned with some relief, it appeared, to serve another customer.

"And this be little Willy." Priscilla beamed with pride as she lifted up the small figure for inspection.

Mary acknowledged this introduction with a smile and thought, with some wonder, how good a wife and mother the awkward Priscilla had become, to judge by the clean and healthy look of her small family. She felt a dull stab of envy that slipped quickly into the full store of guilt she held against herself.

"I thought you did mean to go back to England?"

And so she had thought herself, she replied. "But whilst I was working in Boston for my passage I didst meet my Willum. He had a bit of land near Salem town and need of a wife to help him." The color rose in her cheeks again. Mary forced another smile and congratulated her on her good fortune, thinking of the reversal in their respective fortunes. What advantage now to be a gentlewoman! A sigh escaped her.

"Thou hast come upon bad times," Priscilla wondered softly. Mary noticed the glance at her worn clothes and repressed another sigh. Nodding, she briefly recounted her father's reverses and return to England, and her own, official, reason for being in Boston.

Priscilla clucked sympathetically, and if she felt complaisant managed not to show it. Then apparently she spied someone or something disagreeable, because her plump, pleasant features suddenly stiffened into an angry grimace and she mumbled, not entirely under her breath, "Thou lying, black-arsed whore!"

Mary turned and saw the lumbering figure and sullen face of Bessie Wicken—the woman who was laundress for the Bournes and many other Boston worthies, and also acted frequently as a midwife and dispenser of herbs for minor ills as Mary's mother had done in Plymouth.

Catching the tone if not all the words Priscilla threw at her, Bessie scowled, her eyes first on Priscilla were turned next on Mary, and suddenly brightened as they looked her shrewdly up and down. Then, with no word, she turned her back and directed an obscene curtsy in their direction.

Mary looked embarrassed and puzzled.

"By god's blood." Priscilla, scowled, "she be a villainous witch and I like her not, and no more do divers others she hath put the lie to for her own mean purposes!" Mary continued to look puzzled.

"I heard tell from them as had passage to New England in the same ship as her that she did leave on the run and scarce ahead of the torch that would 'ave burned her for a witch."

Mary shuddered, whether for the fear of witches she had early taken from her mother or the horror of witch burning she had later learned from her father, she did not know.

Priscilla chattered on, her angry conviction lending her voice an unusual assurance. "Once here she hath put on repentance like to an ill-fitting gown, and I warrant a stolen one, though her pastor doth use her as example of how the most fallen and depraved can have hope still for salvation. And she hath bought his good opinion as, methinks, she wouldst buy her salvation by keeping count of her neighbors sins and seeing that her pastor and the court doth know of them. Marrie, I warrant her mouth hath occasioned more whippings and duckings and fines than any other means in New England! 'Tis even said she hath been known to waylay suspected wenches in the woods, and by means of some devilish spell hath made them to swoon upon the ground where she could betimes examine them for signs of fornication." The fear Mary felt now went deeper than any brief dread of witches.

"She hath accused my Willum and me of fornication and might have had another whipping to watch if our Willy had not been nigh on to a month late in coming." She patted his head—her cheeks a shade redder—but, withal, a satisfied smile on her face that bore not a trace of puritan guilt. "And 'twas she then did suffer a fine—for lying!"

The fashions of the day, including a high-waisted bodice and full skirts, often turned under and looped up fully on either side of the apron, made the concealment of a female's "condition" not difficult at all and Mary had worried little about that possibility. But a midwife has a kind of insight, if she chooses to exercise it, that most professionals have in matters that concern their particular calling. Mary remembered now the long look Bessie had given her and an almost constant fear of discovery, that she could not will away, took hold of her. Her trips to the market were earlier and more quickly made and she remained more often at home and out of sight when visitors came. Most particularly she now avoided Bessie Wicken. The laundry was carefully bundled and set by the door for Bessie to find and not delivered to her hands as before. And, by careful watching, Mary contrived to be in another part of the house when it was returned. But the worst part of this watchfulness was that it forced to the front of her mind all that she had pushed from her thoughts and forced her now and again, as she had years before when her mind was full of dreaming, to forget the work at hand, not to finish or to finish very late the jobs she was supposed to do. Any other Mistress would have quickly noticed and upbraided her—even, perhaps become suspicious. But Mistress Bourne's sharp eye for detail in matchmaking did not, as Mary had noticed when she first came there, carry over to housekeeping which she had little interest in. Besides, she was convinced of Mary's excellence in the matter of keeping house and was not given to easily admitting evidence contrary to her settled opinions.

But the Bessie Wickens are not to be avoided. One afternoon she came to the Bourne's house with neither laundry to take or bring. Mary, recognizing her heavy footsteps at the back door, had barely time to slip into her room before Bessie was in the kitchen. As it happened Mistress Bourne was just coming in to the kitchen to speak to Mary on some small matter as Bessie entered.

"Mistress Bourne." Bessie spoke firmly, but dipped her head in brief evidence of humility.

"If you wish to speak about the laundry or some other household business it is Mary Martin you should see." Hannah Bourne said hastily. She tried to avoid contact with Bessie Wicken whenever possible. Unarticulated in her mind, beauty and goodness were one as were ugliness and evil, though she always managed to find other reasons to account for her attraction to or revulsion from certain things or persons.

"No, 'tis you I must speak to, touching this Mary Martin. For in keeping her here thou art harboring sin in thy house."

Mistress Bourne made a choking sound, but before she could speak Bessie almost shouted in her high-pitched voice, "Mary Martin is with child! Thou must see she is presented at court."

Mary sank to her knees in the back room.

"Are you mad, you street wench? Accusing a virtuous maid of such a thing?" Mistress Bourne's small features were drawn tight in unaccustomed anger. "I have heard of your slanderous speeches before now, but have not believed you would dare to go so far!"

"The court will see if I am lying," her voice was firm but much lower.

"Dost think for e'en a minute, you villainous witch, that I would shame Mistress Martin by allowing her to be brought to court? And should you go further with this 'tis thee I will see brought before the magistrates. So you had best watch thy tongue Bessie Wicken lest the court doth pluck it out for bearing false witness against your betters!"

Bessie's mouth snapped open as though she would say more and then as quickly closed. Truth to tell though she was quite sure she was right in her accusation, she was not sure enough—having been convicted of lying once already—to adventure the loss of her tongue—not, as she knew, an idle threat. Had not one man—for malicious and scandalous speeches—been sentenced to be whipped and have his ears cut off. She backed toward the door.

"And thou wilt speak to no one else of this?" Bessie nodded. "No Mistress, no," and curtsied her way out the door.

Mary, her heart pounding in the darkness, went limp with relief and fell against her bed crying softly.

Later that evening she heard Mistress Bourne's still agitated voice telling her husband about Bessie's visit. "Such a one as she is should be whipped and sent back to England!"

Mr. Bourne laughed. "'Tis not likely they would take her, since if I have heard aright, it was just so she did come from England here."

"'Twas an evil practice of those cavaliers," Mistress Bourne knew well from whence all evil in old England flowed, "to send all rogues and lying drabs to plague us here."

"Doubtless, doubtless," Mister Bourne said soothingly. "But no harm has been done. You have seen to it Hannah. Mary Martin's virtuous reputation is protected," he cajoled. "Methinks, my wench, thy biggest fear has been that this rumor might reach the ear of young John Rolfe!" Mary heard a laughing scuffle on the narrow stairs as they went up to bed.

There was no doubt that Bessie would hold her tongue. She had a respect for her betters, and for the magistrates, grown out of long experience. And Mary, with her present fears, had no trouble understanding that. So, in the days following Bessie's visit she experienced a great sense of relief, a sudden release from the pressure of fear. She felt almost gay. That this gaiety—this vast relief—was irrational in view of what soon must be faced Mary's reason noted. But it was a reaction solely of her body to the release of tension and, for the moment, it overpowered her reason with a pervasive feeling of well-being.

Mistress Bourne, solicitously observing her, marked fewer signs of the vapors and more smiles which she put to the salutatory effects of her advice at last being felt, plus, of course, the simple fact of virtue rewarded. Having defended Mary's virtue and position she had further convinced herself of both.

She did not speak to Mary of Bessie's accusation and endeavored to keep that person away from her. "I shall not have that ugly, foul-speaking wench any more about my little ones," she told Mary. "If need be we can ourselves do the laundry." Mary heard this with further relief. Should it be necessary, it was after all, a job she and Francie had been used to doing in Long Creek.

It was only at the weekly meetings that she now even caught sight of her accuser who sat, as required, in the back of the Meetinghouse with the others of the poorer sort and came nowhere near the Bourne's or Mary. But, as the hours passed Mary often shivered, despite the warmth of summer, from a feeling that those piercing eyes were on her and might yet find a way to reveal her sinful condition. There were also the unrelenting sermons of the pastors Wilson and Cotton exhorting her to keep to the path she had already strayed from or face eternal damnation which contributed, in no small way, to the shivering cold that possessed her and struck at her heart when she tried to pray.

Her sense of well-being in any case was short-lived. And as the days of July slipped away toward the month of August when she knew her birthing time would come she had at last to face the problem she had so long put out of her mind. What would she do when the child was no longer hidden in her body? If she had vaguely entertained thoughts in the past that she might miscarry or the child be stillborn, the lateness of the date and the vigorous movements that she felt had banished them. In truth there was, she thought, little to ponder. She had but a single choice. The newborn child must somehow be quickly spirited away to the Meetinghouse or to the home of one of the pastors. She had not hesitated to think of this before from any small pangs of maternal affection. She could discover no love at all for this creature that swelled her belly. Nor could she even think of it as being part of herself. It was Michael Mitton's seed grown large—a foreign object lodged within her, but not of herself. But even had she wanted to keep it she would not even have considered doing so for the same reasons that had brought her to Boston and made her keep her secret all these months—a future together would be a sad one for her family, herself and perhaps most of all for the child—the truly innocent one. The remembrance of Begette holding the dead infant out toward her appeared often and clear in her mind of late.

But this simple necessity had many difficulties that seemed beyond her control. Might not the infant choose to enter the world in midday? In which case her secret would most surely be discovered. Or if this difficulty was averted was there not still the problem of how to spirit a strong-lunged infant silently from the house? Why not give birth outdoors in some wooded spot? But, if she had time and strength enough to get at a distance safe from human detection, might not the smell of the birthing blood attract the wolves? A clear memory of the ragged bony wolf gnawing voraciously on the still living pig flashed before her mind and made her flesh contract with terror.

It was in the midst of these recurring thoughts that Mistress Bourne dropped the announcement of their imminent departure for England. Major

Bourne's latest ship being finished, he could no longer ignore his desire to be part of the new government being formed by the victorious parliament and its supporters.

They were to go on the next ship—expected to leave sometime between the tenth and fifteenth of August—weather permitting.

Mary took a deep grateful breath. She did not calculate her child would be born until the last week of August, and she knew from her mother and others that a first child could be expected to arrive late more often than not.

Mistress Bourne smiled happily at the prospect of a more active social life in England and as well about her new plan for Mary.

"You must come with us, Mary. It would much please me and the children to have you with us on that long journey. And we would surely have as much need for your services there as here—and of course—you could visit with your family in Plymouth."

A brief look of anguish passed across Mary's face.

"I cannot," she said dully, "My sister would then be left here all alone in New England. And I know not if I should ever be able to return or send for her."

"I would we could take you both," Mistress Bourne sighed. "Though even had we the money for so many passengers, 'tis not likely there would be time enough to fetch her here before our ship sets sail. Howbeit, suspecting what your answer might be, I have this day spoken to our neighbor, Widow Tims about thee. She hath had no house servant since her last one finished out her indenture these three months past and was most eager to have thee."

Mary stood by the kitchen fireplace, occasionally stirring the large pot of fish and corn she was tending. Her cheeks were flushed from the heat and Mistress Bourne took this for an expression of pleased acceptance of her plan and proceeded, with increased enthusiasm, to describe the still better part of the arrangement she had made.

"Now you must know the Widow Tims can pay but little, and I would not have spoken to her of you had I not heard her say before now, speaking of the sewing she doth to sustain herself, that she has more than she can do. And of this, when I did make mention of it for you, she hath said you could, in your free time—and surely you will have more of that there than you have here—you could have whatever sewing she hath not time for and keep the wages for it to thyself. You should, in this way, methinks, get more money there than here." Mistress Bourne crossed her arms emphatically across her small bosom and smiled her satisfaction at having contrived this excellent arrangement.

Even though the Widow Tims was well known for her sharp tongue and her frequent use of it Mary was so much relieved at the prospect of having a whole empty house to creep into when her time had come that she had no difficulty in expressing her gratitude. And then, with an apology, Mistress Bourne unknowingly gave her a further cause for gratitude, an excuse for being in the house, by asking her to pack up and take care of whatever of their household effects they left behind.

Mary slept well that night, which was a blessing since on the next day Mistress Bourne set in motion a whirlwind of activity, if not accomplishment. Lists were begun, chests packed then unpacked, Mistress Bourne clucking distractedly. Not being sure when or even if they were coming back to New England she was in a constantly alternating condition of decision and indecision regarding what to take and what to leave. Even the ordinary matter of supplies for the journey was affected by her vacillating state of mind, so that Mary was sent on a dizzying succession of errands—to put in an order, increase it, cancel it, re-order it, not necessarily in that sequence. It would have been hard to say which of the two women was most tired by the end of each day.

After four such days, late in the evening, Mary was wearily putting the kitchen in order before making her way to bed when a hard, sharp pain struck her and made her grab the table for support, partly because of the strength of the pain, but more because of its suddenness and the wave of panic that swept over her. It was just then that Mistress Bourne entered the kitchen and even in the shadowy light cast by the dwindling flames on the hearth it was obvious in the way Mary stood, almost doubled up over the table, that something was wrong.

"Mary! Hast hurt thyself? Art thou ill?" Her voice was filled with quick concern.

Mary pushed herself up straight. The shadows cast on her face by the flickering light from the fire emphasized its pallor. She did manage a stiff smile. "Methinks 'tis something I ate did cause a turmoil in my stomach."

"Oh la!" Mistress Bourne shook her head. "'Tis more like thy stomach doth complain of thy too little feeding of it. I do think I have worked you these past days as though you had been two maids. Come sit down and will fetch thee a dram of Governor Winthrop's receipt for the torments that so much eased little Ned when he had a like torment of the belly."

"You need not trouble. It hath already eased of itself," Mary murmured nervously. She feared any moment the pain might come again and Mistress Bourne discover how different her torments were from little Ned's.

"Tush. 'Tis not likely you are done with it so easily. You must have your dram of physic and then get thee to thy bed," she said firmly. Mary protested no more. But when the remedy was found—by herself—she took it and then let herself be led to her bed.

"Should you not feel better e' the morning you must stay in your bed until you do," Mistress Bourne directed kindly as she left to go up stairs, and none too soon. She was scarce out of the room when the pain struck again. Mary clenched her teeth and buried her head in her pillow.

Hours passed, and again and again the pain wracked her body and stiffened her with fear lest she cry out. Once, briefly, she fainted and came to damp with sweat and terrified at what, uncontrolled, might have passed her lips. But the house remained silent. An occasional snap from the dying embers of the fire or a hiss from the candle by her bed seemed loud against the silence.

The pushing, searing pain grew worse, a force that lifted and then thrust her body down again—over and over—until at last, with an even harder thrust of a pain that seemed to tear her back apart, it was done. She could feel the child between her legs. A slight movement. It was alive. Feeling hardly conscious, she raised herself and looked down on the small bloody figure. It—she—lay on her back, small perfect hands and feet faintly flailing.

Having aided in three births by others she had known what to expect. A low moan rose to her lips. A wave of weakness and nausea swept over her. Her vision blurred and then, like a deluge, the emotions shut off since the day she walked out into the bay, burst forth. Silent tears ran heavily down her face and a rush of fate and love churned inside of her. She touched the tiny head and face, and ran her fingers softly over the warm fragile body then convulsively held it to her breast and gently rocking it softly sang in tuneless words, "Oh my small sweet one do not go from me. I cannot bear to be so all alone." Then shaking her head: "No! No. I must clean and wrap thee in a blanket and take thee to the meetinghouse where the pastor will not let thee die like Begette in a cave."

She reached for a blanket and the small one slipped from her arms onto the bed and there began to cry. Whereupon Mary in a panic lest Mistress Bourne should hear and recognize that sound dropped the blanket on the babe and held it tight until the cry had stopped. But no sooner was the blanket off than the babe began to cry again and Mary crying now softly herself, put the blanket over the babe again. This time when she took the blanket off the babe cried no more and Mary sobbing knew well enough the tiny motionless babe was dead. She fell forward unconscious. How long she remained so she did not know, but when she came to the candle had burned out and she knew dully that night was dwindling and she must rouse herself to clean the room. Her body and mind now numb and empty. She put the lifeless babe, still wrapped in the soiled bedding, in her chest and, making the bed fresh fell on it and slipped immediately into a state of dreamless unconsciousness rather than sleep.

When she woke, some hours later, sunlight was visible through the cracks of the tiny shuttered window in her room and she could hear the scuffling sound of small feet and muted voices from the kitchen as she pulled her clothes on as quickly as she could. Her body now throbbed and ached, her mind was still mercifully numb.

Mistress Bourne, unsuspiciously solicitous and grateful, as she said, that Mary's ailment had not proved to be a fever like to the one that had carried off so many these seven months past, soon forgot all about Mary's brief illness in the fluster of activity of the next few days. Mary's mind too was kept on the departure at hand by Mistress Bourne's constant questions, anxieties and demands. But her aching loins and the painful fullness of her breasts would not let her put completely out of mind what lay silent in her room. Every night she stared at the chest with longing and revulsion and slept fitfully those last days before the Bournes departed.

With only a change of clothes and her bedding bundled together, she moved in with Widow Tims that same day.

Chapter Eighteen

Widow Tims was a short, stocky person with sharp eyes, with nose and chin to match. Her hair, under her tight cap, was brown bleached with gray, her face unlined. She looked somewhere between thirty-five and forty-five. In truth she was fifty, strong and healthy in body but bitter in mind. It was her firm conviction that she had been weighted down with more troubles than she should have had to bear. She was too seriously pious to have blamed the Lord for this yet, unlike most of her fellows in the Godly faith, she could see no sin of hers sufficient to have brought these troubles upon her. She had no difficulty however in assigning blame where she saw it due. If a sinner, so she reasoned, had, by his sins, brought down a hail storm on his head, the innocent standing near him could not fail to be pummeled even as he. So it had been for her.

Her father, by his sin of Popery, shared by her mother, had lost his profitable position in the Civil Service in London and his small country estate as well. He could no longer keep it up and needed the money to live upon, in a most reduced style. The estate was bought by one Andrew Tims, son of a blacksmith, but now a rising merchant. The not unhandsome, blackened girl she was then had caught his fancy, and over her most vehement objections, her parents insisted she marry the large, rough-speaking merchant.

The years brought acceptance if not joy in her marriage. Her husband grew more successful and his money, and her former position, allowed them—mostly her since he was usually busy—an acceptable social position. Then, through the eloquent preaching of John Cotton, he, and then she, were conveyed to the godly faith. His further success seemed to indicate the husband had made the right choice. But then, without warning, he came down with a serious case of plantation fever. They must, he declared, transplant themselves to New England and help in the building of the new godly nation. In vain she pleaded, begged him, to consider that godly folk were needed in England as well, to reform the church and his quite visible success was surely a proof that what he was doing now was most pleasing to the Lord.

He had no ears for any but promoters of New England. Its opportunities for wealth and piety combined seemed to him a utopia indeed. So they took themselves across the waters, but the displeasure of the Lord came quickly down on Andrew Tims in the form of a fever he took on the ship and from which he never properly recovered. Within a year he died, leaving her what she still was, the Widow Tims with a small frame house and an equally small income which she was able to supplement by sewing. She had one ten-year-old indentured servant to attend her cows and chickens and fetch in her wood. And, now, Mary Martin, to help around the house. There was no doubt in her mind, after careful consideration, that she had been brought to her present condition by the sins of others.

Although she was indeed self-centered, irascible, and indiscriminately sharp-tongued—for which last, had her social position been lower she would have faced a fine or a split stick on her tongue—she was not mean-spirited. Her servants were housed and fed well and not overworked. She was also kind to those who had troubles she judged to be similar to her own. That is, not of their own making. Mary she was most kindly disposed toward, having heard from Mistress Bourne of her most excellent work and her troubles. Widow Tims sighed at the seeming close parallel to her own case and happily turned her extra sewing over to the maid, even designedly failing to notice when some of the household chores were neglected for it. Though, in truth, Mary seldom neglected her household work, not out of conscious intent but because she now worked in a mechanical manner. When a task was begun she followed it through, step-by-step, one step leading to another without thought, until it was finished. Her mind did not wander from the job at hand. If it was a bit of sewing that needed to be finished, only then might some household chore briefly be left undone.

She scarcely ever spoke unless spoken to and always gave her full attention to the speaker, which caused the Widow at first to nod with pleased approval. But, after a week or two of their association, she one day suddenly clapped her hands to her head and snapped, "My faith wench, hast thou lost thy tongue? 'Tis like talking to a stone. Dost thou not have but to say of yourself by 'yes' and 'nay'? Having thee about is not much more than being alone. Even my last maid, the lazy wench though she was, at least spiced up the days a bit with her spicy tongue. Surely you can find something to talk of—thy Province of Mayne?—thy home in Plymouth?"

Mary, her mouth seeming always dry, strained to comply. But try as she would, she could come up with little beyond a comment of the effect of the fire or the state of the weather. To which the Widow tartly replied to the effect: "Can I not feel and see these things as well as thee?" But Mary's problem was beyond her control. Her mind, or a portion of it seemed, as an arm or a leg might be, to be in paralysis, her memory, her thoughts, there but bound down, not to be summoned up in the form of coherent language. But her mind and memory were not shielded and impenetrable. Every now and then a chance view across the field of the hues she had left brought a searing pain of longing and revulsion that made her sway weakly with its impact. Briefly it passed in and out of her mind that she must go over there someday and remove, bury, do something with, the contents of her chest. But only the day-to-day tasks occupied her. She could not do what she knew she must do however often the reality of her need flooded her mind.

The widow at last gave up trying to draw Mary out and began to make short visits about town for companionship and conversation, complaining often to her friends about that vaporish girl who had no concern for any but herself, no care for the suffering of those about her. At which point a red spot would appear at the end of her nose and she would look down at her clasped hands and sigh profoundly.

Late one afternoon when the widow was thus occupied Mary was alone in the house, sitting by the fire concentrating on the final alteration of a gown that the widow had promised for the next day when she was interrupted by loud knocking at the door, repeated twice forcibly before Mary could put her sewing down and get to the door. As she opened it her heart sank and only with great effort did she keep her legs from collapsing and her body upright facing Bessie Wicken and a man she recognized as one of the magistrates.

As they stepped through the door the magistrate, an imposing, broad-shouldered man with a dark, pointed beard and a well-fed stomach, wasted no time in stating their business, though he did speak kindly, almost apologetically. "Mistress Martin, I am here by petition of this midwife, Bessie Wicken, to examine thee. This—Wicken doth swear thou has committed the sin of fornication, and that thou ar't now with child or but lately hast delivered one."

Mary saw Bessie watching her with narrowed eyes and cynical half smile that gave her round pocked-marked face the look of a vindictive gnome. She closed her eyes, pushing her back against the wall for support. Bessie, like so much else, had gone from her mind. Only now did the obvious become apparent, Bessie's fear had departed with the Bournes. The only wonder was that she had waited this long.

"Mistress Martin!" Mary felt their hands on her shoulders, pushing her down. Her eyes opened wide and all the color drained from her face. She jerked herself out of their grasp. "Prithee stay! There is no need for an examination." Her voice was low, almost hoarse, but firm. "I—am—as she hath said—guilty of fornication." She paused looking slowly around the room as though she looked, even now, for some way of escape, but she did not. Her look was aimless. She had but paused to search her still reluctant mind for words to put together. "Two months past I was delivered of a child." She paused again, staring now into the fireplace at the implacably devouring flame that drew the great log lying in its midst steadily into itself. It was not as Bessie supposed, seeing where she stared, a sudden dread of hell fire that kept her eyes fixed, but only the strangely mesmerizing motion of the flame.

"Where then be the child?" Bessie directed the question to the Magistrate.

"Where indeed Mistress Martin!" His voice had lost its kindly tone. "Wench! Thou'll answer! What hath become of the child? Speak!" She turned and looked at them. Her eyes squinting from the firelight gave her face a look of puzzlement. "Speak!" the magistrate repeated.

She started, and then said mechanically, "'Twas stillborn—I did give it to the fire."

"Faugh! Methinks thou'rt a damned lying wench!" Bessie's lip curled with triumphant scorn.

The magistrate looked narrowly from Mary to Bessie. It was surely not Mary that looked to be of the devil's camp. He scowled at Bessie. "Sounds! If thou dost hint at murther and hast no proof of it I will see thou dost have close acquaintance with the whipping post!"

Bessie's eyes widened in brief hesitation, but quickly narrowed again. Her instinct, nurtured over many years of survival on the London streets convinced her Mary lied, enough at least to chance a whipping. Two months past Mary was still at the Bourne's and putting the babe to the fire, Bessie reasoned, with the consequent smell of burning flesh, would have been to run too great a risk of detection. She suggested they go to the Bourne's now empty house to seek the missing proof, watching Mary's features closely for some reaction to this. There was none. Her face showed neither fear nor confidence nor anything else. Despair has a blank countenance.

The magistrate was anxious to get home to his own fireside, his supper and a full tankard of beer. He had expected this to be a brief business. A simple and all too common matter of fornication, requiring nothing more than a quickly delivered order for the sinner's presence at the next session of the court. Now this—complication—this, like as not, fruitless search of an empty house. His beard twitched as he glared his aggravation at both women. But he knew his duty and could not but agree to Bessie's suggestion. "E'en so then—but let us be quick about it." He snapped.

And step quickly they did, even Mary, to avoid Bessie's arm that reached out to pull her over the short distance through the fallen leaves to the Bourne's empty house. Inside all the cold of the past month seemed to be caught in the walls and floor, the stones of the fireplace and every molecule of air, and it in turn caught Mary, numbing her arms and legs as she stood stiffly by the door while Bessie, with the magistrate standing over her, scratched through the ashes of the fire.

"No sign o' bones in there." Then at Bessie's direction they went toward Mary's room—and the chest. Mary could see it wavering in the light of the candle the magistrate had lit.

"Gods wounds! And there be y're proof." Bessie's voice was shrill with triumph and relief. "There in that chest 'mongst the bloodied sheets. 'Tis a newborn babe—decayed but all!"

"S'heart! The murthering whore!" The magistrate recoiled from the chest as Bessie held the tiny form aloft like a trophy, her eyes gleaming.

"Marrie! Methinks it doth want naught save the test by touch for certain proof that she hath murthered her own defenseless babe." Her voice dissolved in unctuous tones of outrage. She walked toward Mary, a mocking smile on her face as she cradled the cold stiff infant in her arms as though it were alive.

A hot wave of anguish and longing swept through Mary's body. She moaned and reached out for the infant.

"That's right, that's right," Bessie coaxed. "Touch it!"

Mary's hands fluttered ineffectually in the air as she crumpled unconscious on the floor. She came to with Bessie's foot pushing roughly at her side and the magistrate glaring contemptuously down at her. "Get up thou murthering wench. Dost think we would carry thee to jail?" He jerked at her arm until she rose unsteadily to her feet, whereupon he shoved her toward the door.

"Now that we have put thy hand upon thy poor infant's head and seen the blood start forth—thy guilt is proved. Is't not so, magistrate?"

"Belike, Belike. Thou hast an eye for such things," the magistrate agreed. "Howbeit, she hath guilt enough to want jailing till the court doth sit."

They walked out in the now full darkness that the pine knot the magistrate had lit did but little to relieve. Mary did not feel the cold now. Her face was burning with the same painful longing that burned in her breast to hold the cold dead infant in her arms and quicken it to life, against all reason and possibility. She stumbled several times along the half mile or more to the jail, but scarcely noticed when Bessie or the magistrate jerked her upright, each time with a curse.

The jail was a gloomy, windowless, wooden building with heavy oaken

194

doors and two small rooms for prisoners—each furnished with a pile of hay, an odorous slop bucket and a small fireplace that delivered more smoke than heat. A small hole high in the wall of each room let in a bit of light and ample cold. The jailer had a smaller more comfortable room with a desk, chair and a window.

The Puritans had two purposes in confining sinners thus: one was to protect the rest of the population from bodily injury and the subversive, that is to say devilish influence of the prisoner, and the other was to mortify the flesh and thus, perhaps, redeem the souls of those imprisoned there. For both of these purposes the jail was most admirably designed. It is true that the physical discomforts had, sometimes, the counter effect of distracting the minds of some poor inmates from the contemplation of their sins. As well—that portion of the population that most commonly furnished residents for the jail were used to living under conditions not much worse than these, in Old as well as New England. But for such unfortunate circumstances the courts devised punishments to make sure that none escaped that fleshly mortification that was held to be the first step on the path of true repentance and spiritual redemption.

Mary was one of those on whom the surroundings had little effect. Her early years in New England had somewhat inured her to hardship. However it was her mind, now shaken out of its paralysis that obscured the physical discomforts and delivered its own incessant flagellation. Her memory and imagination set out her life before her, as once it had her dreams, in vivid pictures, convicting and condemning her pride and weakness, lust and lying and sentencing her, well before her trial, to death and to the farthest depth of hell.

She knew the names of sins now better than she had when she was thirteen, but understood no better the nature of "sin." "Thou shalt not kill" did not apply, it seemed to witches, Indians, Quakers, or enemies in war. Nor "Thou shalt not steal" to those who, like John Winter and most of the merchants in Boston, did their stealing with high prices. How could such nice distinctions be so easily made and still a newborn babe be weighted down with sin? Were these the laws of God or only the pronouncements of men? She leaned over the abyss of unbelief and stared into its darkness, which struck her at once as no more dark than its opposite and yet more empty. A vast eternity of nothing, where imagination and memory were not. She could not even think it and so stepped back and faced what she could at least imagine.

The trial, when it came was but a brief and predictable interlude in these deliberations. Mary showed no flicker of emotion at any of it—even the sentence of death by hanging. She had rehearsed it all many times and more vividly in her imagination.

Outside the courthouse Mary was steered through the hostile crowd by her jailer. More Jehovah than Christlike, the gathered "gentlefolk" muttered righteous curses while the others shouted lewd invectives. Mary, her eyes lowered, her face impassive beneath her hood almost ran into the Widow Tims who stepped out of the crowd and confronted her—throwing a bundle at her feet.

"There, take thy tainted things, thou murthering whore!" The widow's sharp nose was pointed at Mary like an accusing finger. "Dost know, thou black-hearted wench, what further trouble thou hast brought down on me who hadst more than a full share to bear already? My neighbors, thinking me privee to thy secret, look mistrustfully on me and, belike thy very presence hath infected me with sin before heaven." Although her pastor had several times assured her that sin unlike the plague could not be thus acquired from another, she was not convinced. After all if the sin of Adam and Eve could reach out over a thousand years or more to taint her why not this—in her very house?

Two magistrates led the still protesting widow away and bade Mary pick up her bundle and move on. They were almost up to the door of the jail when Mary felt a hesitant hand on her arm. She raised her eyes and saw Priscilla's plump face—red and tear-stained.

"Oh, Mistress," her eyes filled up again. "I will pray for thee." Her voice shook with distress and disbelief, "I know thou 'art not wicked."

At this the magistrates stared sternly at her and her red-haired husband, who, looking even more distressed than his wife, began to tug frantically at her sleeve. When this had no effect he put both arms around her ample waist and pulled her into the dwindling crowd whose reforming spirit, once more aroused, directed a few parting curses at Priscilla as well as Mary.

Both before and after her trial Mary was visited regularly by the good pastor of Boston, John Wilson, in determined combat with the devil in her soul. Nor was he at all displeased with his progress, as he informed his colleagues and the Governor. Though quiet, speaking only with brief answers to his questions, she did always nod her head when asked if she repented and prayed when told to pray. Nor did she rail at her condition, but rather sat, her eyes cast down in meek acceptance of the judgment of the court, and of God's will, whatever it might be. So John Wilson spoke of her hopefully.

If she did not share his hope it was because, though her repentance was sincere, as far as it went, she did not now see sin in all that John Wilson saw it, and did sometimes see it where he did not. If she accepted the judgment of the court it was not with the Christian meekness of spirit that John Wilson saw, but out of a despairing rejection of life. The court was completing for her the suicide she had failed at.

But occasionally still—at night when the darkness entombed her—she could feel in that darkness itself the palpable presence of death, heavy and slowly smothering her, and she would sit shivering and gasping most of the night, her young body revolting still at what her mind now welcomed. It was with a great effort of will that she kept herself from screaming aloud against her fate and crying out for mercy. But as the darkness gave way a little to the light that came through even the small hole in the wall at dawn so did her panic. And her calm rejection of life was uppermost again as was her reason that assured her there was no mercy to cry out for.

On the last day but one, before still another affirmation of and exception to the seventh commandant was scheduled, Mary had a new visitor. Hearing the great iron key clank in the wide outside door and then a smaller in her own door, she stood up, automatically brushing at the hay on her dusty gown ineffectually. She expected to see one or the other of her only two visitors so far—the pastor or her jailer. Instead, with a gasp she shrank back into a corner as she recognized Deane Winthrop blinking in the dim light of the cell.

His eyes quickly adjusting to the light, it was his turn to gasp and restrain the groan that rose in his throat as he looked at Mary's pale haggard face. He had not come to the trial nor been part of the crowd that assembled outside the court house, reproaching himself for having earlier encouraged John Rolfe's admiration for her, admiration that had now turned to disgust at this depraved and fallen woman. He was there that day only at the request of his brother Adam's friend George Cleeve, from whom a letter had come that morning. The letter itself had made him doubt somewhat his recent opinion of her. And now he saw in her face not the signs of cynical depravity but only deep and constant suffering. He looked away to hide the wave of distress that swept over him. But then, remembering why he had come, he mastered his emotions and faced her.

"My brother has lately received a letter from his friend George Cleeve and has asked me to tell you of it." He spoke softly and with nervous hesitation, but his words were clear enough in that small space.

"Mister Cleeve has sent word of your sister that he thinks you would like to hear." Mary leaned forward. "He says," Deane pulled the letter from a pocket in his waistcoat, and, holding it up to what light there was from the hole in the wall read, "Upon our telling Francie of her sister's fate, thinking it better to tell her of it ourselves lest she hear it distorted from some gossip, she did run forth from the house her face full of rage. And before we could do aught to stop her, did hunt down Michael Mitton and taking up a large stick did accost him with it, beating him several times about the head before his servant, discovering them, grabbed the stick and her. She would have Mary know of this, because she did worry about leaving her sister here."

"It seems she knows better how to take care of herself than her sister does," Mary said with a faint smile, grotesquely incongruous on that gaunt sad face.

"She should know, also," Deane read on, "that I do plan to take ship for England in a few months and, if Francie would return then, I will take her with me and see her safely to her mother and father in Plymouth."

Mary gave a sigh of relief and said in a low voice, "I would have you tell your brother to thank Mister Cleeve for me for this and many other kindnesses. He is a good man."

Deane stood awkwardly by her side, trying to give voice to his growing compassion, "May the Lord in his mercy deal more kindly with thee than we have done," he murmured. "And if there is aught else I can do for you—?" She shook her head.

As he opened the door to leave he turned once more to look at Mary's straight still figure a question rose suddenly from the residue of doubts.

"Thy babe—?" It hung on the air—a final agonized accusation.

A moan rose in her throat, but did not pass her lips. She stood staring silently at him until he turned and stumbled through the door and it closed behind him. Then there came into her eyes a look of dull pleading and she whispered, "Have I not given her back to Him you did but now hopefully commend me to?"

The End

Afterwords
[The Author's]

A few months after the execution of Mary Martin, Governor Winthrop received a letter from George Cleeve asking for advice about the authority of Mr. Rigby's government in the prosecution of capital offenses. He mentions some cases; including "some adulteries committed and yet unpunished—as that of Mr. Michael Mitton and John Sears, committed with Mary Martin, whereof you have had from me and others some knowledge; and now seeing you have a copy of our constitution and are better able to judge of them than myself or any of us, and seeing you are appointed to be Commissioners by the High Court of Parliament, for our aid, I hold it my duty to apply to you for your grave council and direction wherein myself or our assistants are defective. My humble desire therefore is that you would direct us by your wisdom and council to act and proceed in a way of justice, according to God, and also justifiable before men and to favor me so much as to dispatch your directions herein before our court, for which favors I shall be a petitioner to the throne of grace for you all and rest

Your obliged servant to command to my power, George Cleeve"

[There is no record of the Commissioners "directions" or that either man was ever brought to court for what was, in those days, a capital crime.]

Editor's Afterwords

The author, in her last draft, included, as afterwords, only the letter from George Cleeve to Gov. Winthrop. I have decided to add a relevant excerpt from Gov. Winthrop's journal, which the author had attached to an earlier draft and a brief biographical passage on George Cleeve, the father-in-law of Michael Mitton and sometimes called "the father of Portland (Maine)."

Governor Winthrop's Journal: 1637

There fell out at this time a very sad occasion. A merchant of Plymouth in England (whose father had been mayor there) called ——— Martin being fallen into decay came to Casco Bay, and after some time, having occasion to return to England he left behind him two daughters, (very proper maidens of modest behavior) but took not that course for their safe bestowing in his absence, as the care and wisdom of a father should have done, so as the oldest of them, called Mary, twenty-two years of age, being in [the] house with one Mr. Mitton, of Casco, within one quarter of a year, he was taken with her and solicited her chastity, obtained his desire, and having several time committed sin with her, in the space of three months, she then removed to Boston, and put herself in service to Mrs. Bourne; and finding herself with child, and not able to bear the shame of it, she concealed it, and though divers did suspect it and some told her mistress their fears, yet her behavior was so modest, and so faithful she was to her service, her mistress would not give ear to any such report, but blamed such as told her of it. But her time had come, she was delivered of a woman child in the back room by herself on the 13 December in the night, and the child was born alive, but she kneeled upon its head to it, till she thought it had been dead, and having laid it by, the child being strong, recovered and cried again. Then she took it again and used violence to it until it was quite dead. Then she put it into her chest and having cleansed the room she went to bed and rose the next day about noon, and went about her business, and so continued unit the nineteenth day, that her master and mistress went on shipboard to go for England. They being gone she removed to another house, a midwife in the town, having formerly suspected her, and now coming to her again, found she had been delivered of a child, which, on examination, she confessed, but said it was still-born and so she had put it into the fire. But, search being made, it was found in her chest, and when she was brought before the jury, they caused her to touch the face of it, whereupon blood came fresh into it. Whereupon she confessed the whole truth and a surgeon being called to search the body of the child, found a fracture in the skull. Before she was condemned, she confessed she had prostituted her body also to another, one Sears. She behaved herself very pertinently complaining much of the hardness of her heart. She confessed that the first and second time she committed fornication, she prayed for pardon, and promised to commit it no more; and the third time she prayed God, that if she did fall into it again, he would make her an example and therein she justified God, as she did in the rest. Yet all the comfort God would, was only trust (as she said) in his mercy through Christ. After she had turned off and had hung a space, she spake, and asked what they did mean to do. Then some stepped up and turned the knot of the rope backward and she soon died.

George Cleeve

George Cleeve's dates are approximate but bridge the span from about 1586 to 1666 when the last official record is known. Born about 1586 in Stogursey, Somersetshire, England, he immigrated to New England in 1620. He lived first in Spurwink and then moved to what is now greater Portland, Maine, in 1633. In 1637 Cleeve and associate Richard Tucker were granted 1,500 acres at Machegonne, and area which now includes downtown Portland.

Under Massachusetts governance he was Commissioner of Falmouth (now Portland) from 1638 and representative in the General Court, 1663 - 1664.

He married Joan Price in 1618. His daughter Elizabeth married Michael Mitton in 1637 to which the Wikipedia entry adds "from whom there were many descendants" —which has a certain irony in the present context.

CPSIA information can be obtained at www.ICGtesting.com
Printed in the USA
BVOW04s0237240913

331928BV00001B/3/P